SINNERS

AND

THE SEA

{ THE UNTOLD STORY *of* NOAH'S WIFE }

REBECCA KANNER

HOWARD BOOKS
A Division of Simon & Schuster, Inc.

NEW YORK NASHVILLE LONDON TORONTO SYDNEY NEW DELHI

Howard Books
A Division of Simon & Schuster, Inc.
1230 Avenue of the Americas
New York, NY 10020

First Howard Books hardcover edition April 2013

HOWARD and colophon are trademarks of Simon & Schuster, Inc.

For information about special discounts for bulk purchases, please contact Simon & Schuster Special Sales at 1-866-506-1949 or business@simonandschuster.com.

The Simon & Schuster Speakers Bureau can bring authors to your live event. For more information or to book an event, contact the Simon & Schuster Speakers Bureau at 1-866-248-3049 or visit our website at www.simonspeakers.com.

Designed by Jaime Putorti

Manufactured in the United States of America

10 9 8 7 6 5 4 3 2 1

Library of Congress Cataloging-in-Publication Data

Kanner, Rebecca.
  Sinners and the sea / by Rebecca Kanner.
     p. cm.
  ISBN 978-1-4516-9523-6
1. Noah (Biblical figure)—Fiction. 2. Noah's ark—Fiction. 3. Deluge—Fiction. I. Title.
  PS3611.A5495S56 2013
  813'.6—dc23
                              2012026293
ISBN 978-1-4516-9523-6
ISBN 978-1-4516-9524-3 (ebook)

For my father,
and for all of my teachers,
in and outside the classroom.

CONTENTS

CONTENTS

❦ BOOK TWO ❧

{ BOOK ONE }

CHAPTER 1

A MARKED AND NAMELESS GIRL

They say it is the mark of a demon. When I was a child, none took their chances by coming close to me, and certainly no one touched me. It looks as if a large man dipped his palm in wine and pressed it to my forehead above my left eye.

After I was born, the midwife seized the afterbirth and rubbed it over the mark. Then the afterbirth was buried, so that when it decayed, the mark would disappear too. But the mark grew darker. By my second year it had gone from red to purple.

My father tried every known remedy. He anointed it daily with olive oil, rubbed it with a sheep's hoof, even offered the gods the smallest finger on his left hand to take it away. But the gods did not accept his finger. They dulled the heat of the fire he set to send it up to them so that it only smoked and did not burn.

He had not named me for fear it would be too easy then for

people to talk and spread lies, and he was glad of this when the gods would not hear his plea.

There was not another tent within fifty cubits of my father's. So as not to catch my affliction through their gazes, when people hurried past to catch an errant sheep or child, they looked at me out of the corner of one eye or not at all. Once a man four tents away chased his goat to only a few cubits from my father's land, then stopped suddenly when he saw me at the cookfire and ran back in the direction he had come.

The goat was never seen again. It was thought that I had changed it into a newborn, the one who was left outside the midwife's tent one night. Rocks were tied to the newborn's hands and feet, and he was taken to the Nile.

After this, pregnant women sometimes went to stay with tribesmen in other villages so they would not accidentally see me and have their own child marked in some way. I thought perhaps they also feared that looking at me was a death sentence. My father had told me that my own mother had choked to death a year after I was born. Pregnant women, being the most superstitious of all people, likely thought it was me who sealed her throat around the goat meat.

While I could not tell you what the people of my father's village looked like up close, the traders were different. They did not fear the mark so greatly. They ventured from the cities along the Nile to haggle with my father for his olives. They brought fruit, nuts, honey, spices, incense, and every kind of grain. They brought flattery, promises, lies, and wine to make my father believe them. He pretended to entertain thoughts of buying large quantities of grain to store in case of a famine, and wool and salted meat in case all the sheep died of the plague that had first fed upon people very young and old, even upon men and women who had been strong only half a moon before their deaths. What he really wanted from them was stories, thinking one might instruct him in how I could be saved.

The traders squatted around our cookfire and let me serve them. But if I accidentally brushed against one as I went around filling their bowls with goat stew and lentils, the man would jump up, curse, and sometimes run to wash himself where I had touched him. One trader even burned his tunic. So I was careful, because I loved to listen to their tales of other places, imagining one of them might be a place where I would not be thought so strange and dangerous.

The traders only spoke of one town with fear: Sorum, Town of Women. It was also known as the Town of Exiles. Though some traders would not venture there, many were their stories of Sorum. It was a town of whores and exiles, people whose foreheads were branded with the X of the banished. Unlike the protective mark that the God of Adam had put upon Cain, the marks on these people were not meant to save them from harm. An X upon your forehead meant that you had committed a crime in one of the cities along the Nile and were no longer welcome. I took a great interest in the stories of Sorum.

An old trader called Arrat the Storyteller told us most of what we knew of Sorum. Whenever he coughed and spat, it meant he wanted to speak. One night the other traders were so raucous, he had to do this over and over again until everyone went silent. Then he rubbed his hand along his beard, rocked forward to his toes, and said, "Sorum. Town of Women."

One trader narrowed his eyes, another pressed his lips tightly together, and a third pulled his tunic closer around him.

"Now, it is that a woman who is a cross between a girl and a boar guards the entrance. Not to keep men out but, rather, to lure them in. She is uglier than a rotting corpse and smells even worse, yet a man who looks upon her cannot stop his feet from taking him to suckle at her breasts. He will give her all his goods, even the sandals off his own feet. After they have joined together just once, he will pine for her demon's nectar his whole life. He will bring her fruits and nuts he steals off other men's trees, oxen and mules he kills other men for. And finally, whatever is left of his soul.

"After she has laid waste to it but before he has fully crossed to the other side, she eats his organs and sucks the marrow from his bones. She does not stop, even though his limbs twitch and he screams for death to take him.

"Then she fashions the bones into necklaces and belts and gives them to the women of the town. Some wear so many bones, they stumble under their weight as though they were overfull with wine. The boar woman herself is decorated so completely with the bones of the men she has eaten that her whole body, except her teats and sex, is covered. Even with this heaviness upon her, she can run faster than a man. And worse, she is stronger than the biggest mule. No one dares cross her.

"No one except a crazed man who rides an ass through town, ancient and unseeing. He is as old as the world itself. So old his beard trails along the ground and gets caught beneath his donkey's hooves. He yells at the women to repent. He wants to make Sorum upright for his god, the God of Adam."

This brought laughter.

"His time would be better spent trying to turn a goat into a dove."

"Or grow an olive grove from a whore—"

"Quiet!" my father commanded, knocking the man's bowl from his hands. He stood to his full height and gestured toward where I squatted behind the circle of traders, eating my stew after having served theirs.

My father rarely went into a rage, though he had much to be unhappy about. He had a large olive grove and no heir, along with a daughter who could neither inherit the grove nor entice a match. I had heard a man scream at my father only a few days before: "Not even for every olive upon the earth!" The man stomped the ground so hard walking away that he left perfect sandal marks. He was enraged that my father would think him a match for me.

I hurried to pick up the trader's bowl. "I am sorry," the trader said, not to me but to my father.

My father said, "Do not think on it any longer." But he did not buy any of the man's honey, which surprised me, because eating honey makes a girl more pleasing in nature and shape.

Gods, see how he has lost hope. Please, I beg of you. Help rid me of this mark.

This was my daily plea, the same one I had been whispering each morning upon waking and each night before sleep since first seeing the mark in a pot of water ten years before. But I knew that if the gods had not answered my plea already, they probably never would. I was already nineteen, seven long years past when most girls were taken as wives.

. . .

Then came Mechem the Magical. All the traders had quick tongues but none quicker than his. To a man who labored to breathe, he would sell some wind that he carried in a sack upon his back. He would sell grains of curing sand to the mother of a child with a pus-filled wound. To the sick, he sold the healing droppings of a healthy doe, to the barren, the miracle placenta of a ewe that had birthed three lambs instead of two.

And finally, to my father, for half the olives in his grove, he sold the urine of a great beast. One even more powerful than a demon. The beast had tusks sharp enough to spear spirits, hooves heavy enough to crush them, a trunk long enough to slap them a whole league, and ears big enough to hear them as clearly as a fly buzzing on the beast's own flank. Mechem promised that, after applying the potion to my forehead, the mark would take only a few days to fade.

"Because of the potion's great power," he told my father, "administering it is dangerous. Though I might lose what is left of my life, I will do it for only half the olives that remain."

My father and Mechem argued back and forth outside the tent, until my father conceded three quarters of his harvest. He lifted the door flap, and he and Mechem came in. Mechem held a small amphora in one hand.

"Our troubles are over," my father told me. His eyes were full of hope and fear. I knew the fear. He was afraid that the potion would not be able to overcome the mark. He looked expectantly at Mechem.

But Mechem seemed to be waiting. He frowned at my father.

"You will not even know I am here, unless you should need something," my father assured him.

"The potion will not work with so much flesh vying to be purified."

"Mine is not in need of purification," my father said, then quickly looked to make sure his words had not wounded me. "I can stand behind these pots of lentils so the potion is not confused as to which skin to set upon."

"No, you must leave. I cannot waste what little I have. Unless you possess another olive grove with which to pay me."

My father's jaw tightened. He narrowed his eyes at the trader.

"Three men died getting this potion," Mechem said.

My father came to stand only a few hands' width from the trader. He was a whole head taller than the little man. "I trust you will do as you have promised," he said. Then he slipped out the door flap, and I was alone with Mechem.

Mechem looked directly at me. "I do not flinch from demons," he said. Was this the man the gods had sent to answer my plea that the mark be taken from me? His eyes were glassy and wide-set, like a goat's. His fingers curled and uncurled as he came to stand beside where I squatted at my loom. He leaned down and whispered, "My own seed will master the demon." The smell of the wine he had drunk with my father lingered in a cloud between us. I did not have to wonder what he meant.

9

"But my honor . . ."

"I have two potions, woman. One to remove the mark and one to restore your virtue when I am done." He pulled another tiny amphora from a pouch tied to his belt and held it in front of my face.

I leaned away from him. "My father is already making me a match," I lied. "I cannot be tainted."

"Your father, who did not bother to name you, is now making a match for you?"

"He did not give me a name so that people could not speak of me and spread lies."

He set the potions down and grabbed my shoulder. His nails dug into my skin. "Silly woman. If you do not have a name, people will give you one: Angels' Bane, Demon's Daughter, Demon's *Whore*—"

I shook his hand off my shoulder and stood. He pushed up against me, knocking over my loom. "I will take these names out of their mouths when I take the mark from you. You will be a miracle, a woman who overcame a demon. You will have new names: Demon Slayer, Woman of the Gods—"

"I do not care what they call me," I said, stepping back.

He did not advance. He smiled and said, "You do not know how to lie, woman."

"I am not as skilled in it as some."

His nostrils twitched, revealing the stiff black hairs inside. I knew I had erred in angering him. Even though he was a small man, he was still a man, and I was just a woman who no one wanted to take for a wife.

"Please," I said, "apply the potion only to the mark. All I have is that I am untouched."

He reached out a finger and pressed his nail against my mark. "But you *are* touched, for all to see."

"No one but my father and now you looks closely."

"People look with their tongues and ears more than their eyes. These very traders whose bowls you fill with your father's meat and lentils, whose cups you fill with his wine, they do not profit only from their goods. Just as your father has them here so he can hear their tales, so too does he give them one."

"One is not so many."

"But it is such a good one, it overshadows all the others."

"It is nothing that could compare to the story of the boar woman."

"The demon-woman tale Arrat weaves is riveting. He says your mark changes from red to black and that, after gazing upon it, smoke sometimes comes from his own eyes." Mechem pretended sadness. "He does not have to clear his throat twice when he goes back along the river. The people there want to know what is in a village so near to their own, a distance a demon could hop in one breath. Do you never worry that men of the nearby villages will come for you?"

"Why would they do so?"

"Who wants to live with a demon so close when there are crops, herds, children, wives, and other property to look after?"

"You are not a good liar either. You go too far." But I wasn't certain he exaggerated.

"I do not lie about this."

My heart beat not only because he wanted to come too close to me but because it suddenly seemed that all the peoples of the world were talking about me in hushed tones.

"Let me help you. Another man has to show the demon he is no match, that he does not own you. It is other men's fear of you that keeps the demon's mark upon your brow." His fingers circled a lock of hair that had come loose from my scarf, and gently ran down the length of it. "Besides, it is a shame to have this mark upon you when you would be such a sweet sight without it."

He leaned in close again, so that his nose nearly touched mine, and his breath against my lips caused me to stumble backward. The lock of my hair that he still held stretched taut between us.

"The demon is too strong for a man to survive lying with me," I said, trying to lie more convincingly this time. "He lifts me from my sleeping blanket in the blackest part of night. Things I touch wither and die. If I even look too long at a bird, she will crumple and fall from the sky."

"I am not a bird."

"The demon has infected me with his poison so any man who tries to know me will never know me or any other woman again."

Mechem took hold of my shoulders. He shoved me to the ground.

I could not roll away quickly enough to keep him from falling upon me. The wine on his breath covered a worse odor from his mouth, that of rot, as when a mouse drowns in a pot of nuts or lentils and is not discovered right away. He looked down the length of my body and grasped my breast through my tunic. I struggled to push him off, but my efforts had no effect on him.

He reached his hand lower still and pressed it to my tunic where my legs met. I bit him with all the strength of my fear. I tasted his dry, salty flesh and felt the wiry hair of his eyebrow against my lips. He recoiled, then thrust his hand against my neck. Though the bitter taste of his blood was upon my tongue, I was surprised by the deep gash upon his brow.

His cheeks flared red. "Let me tell you two things, woman. It was not a demon that gave you the mark. It was your own evil mother, and you will do as I say and tell no one, or I will let it be known in this village and all the surrounding ones that the demon has taken every last drop of your soul and uses your body for a vessel. I will show them my forehead, and they will not doubt me."

"Do not speak false of the dead."

"Your mother is dead now?" he asked. "Did she finally drink herself yellow and die?"

"She died a year after she bore me."

He laughed, and his hand loosened on my neck. "And I am the handsomest man in the world! She fled before being branded with the mark of the exile for birthing you."

"No, I do not believe you." But I did. I finally understood why my father looked like he had just been hit with a rock whenever I asked about her.

"Even your own mother did not want you," he said sadly. "Though I am no beauty, and years past the peak of my virility, I am not without an appetite for a woman's softness. I will do what no other man would dare to and bring you into full womanhood." He yanked my tunic up over my thighs.

Sunlight streamed into the tent as the door flap was lifted behind Mechem. Before Mechem could turn around to defend himself, my father knocked him off of me unto the ground.

"Fool!" Mechem cried. "I could bring you to ruin with the slightest movement of my tongue. People would flock from leagues in all directions to tear apart your tent, burn your olive grove to the ground, and kill your worthless demon spawn. Now leave us or I will be gone, taking my potion and my tale."

"We have already agreed upon the price for your potion. I will apply it to my child myself. If the mark disappears within the next four days, then you will have half my harvest."

"You will have neither my potion nor my silence," Mechem said. He picked up the amphora with the urine of the great beast and was moving to where he had left the other potion, the one that would restore my virtue after he had taken it, when my father wrapped an arm around him and tried to yank the amphora from his fingers.

"The demon is unleashed!" Mechem yelled loudly toward the door flap. As there were no tents near ours, I doubted anyone heard him. Still, he began screaming as though he were a man dying a horrible death.

My father put a hand over Mechem's mouth, trying to muffle the old man's screams. He forced the trader to the ground and slammed his head down with the full force of his weight. There was a great thud, and the screaming stopped.

My father stared down at Mechem. "Wake up," he demanded.

The trader did not acknowledge my father, and his head and limbs moved lifelessly when my father shook him.

My father looked incredulously at the dead man for a few shallow breaths. Then he dropped his head into his hands. "We are doomed," he said.

CHAPTER 2

A TRADE

At last my father lifted his head from his hands. He grasped the little amphora, pulled it from Mechem's fingers, and came to crouch in front of me. His hands shook as he poured the potion into his palm. I could not remember him ever touching the mark.

"It will soon be gone," he said.

And I will finally be like everyone else, I told myself. But I did not really believe it. If the trader was not powerful enough to keep from being killed, neither was he powerful enough to remove a mark a demon had placed upon me.

After applying the potion to my brow, my father kept looking at me. I knew from his frown that it was not fading.

· · ·

He waited until dark to carry the old man's body out of the tent. He did not tell me where he was going; he said only to crouch behind our pots of lentils and keep a meat knife in each hand. Even as I clutched the handles of the knives hard enough that my arms shook, what I thought of, above all else, was my mother.

"A good woman" was how my father had described her once I was old enough to ask about her. But the only way I had heard of a mother giving her child a mark was to have an evil thought and then touch her own skin. Arrat the Storyteller had said that wherever the woman touched herself was where the mark would be on her child.

What could this thought possibly have been? Did she lust for a man other than my father? Then came a thought even worse than this: *Is the man who was going to trade half his harvest to rid me of the mark my actual father, or a man too kind and too full of pity to put another man's child out to die?* I pushed this thought aside, but I could not push aside another, which was that my father would have been free except for me. With a grove bigger than any in our village, he could easily have had many wives. Twice he had paid families so that he might take one of their daughters for a wife. Both times the girls had run away.

Mother, why did you not press wool to my face until my heart stopped beating? If you cared for my father, you would have had no choice but to do so.

A couple of times I pointed one of the knives toward my own throat. But I could not do what my mother had not bothered to. My father's kindness was too great. I could not throw away the life he had spent his own protecting.

. . .

J ust after the sun's rays hit the eastern side of the tent, I heard footsteps. Someone raised the door flap, and there was screaming.

"It is only me, child," my father said, and I realized that the screaming was my own. "There is nothing to worry about. All is settled."

We had withstood the gossip my mark provoked, and the scandal caused by my residing in the same tent as my father so long after my first blood. We would, it seemed, also survive Mechem's disappearance.

But five days later, Mechem's body floated to the bank of the Nile on the shore closest us. Neither the crocodiles nor the river would have him.

"It is the first time anyone has seen him since he entered your tent," Arrat told my father.

They were outside but not far enough away that I did not hear them. "That means little," my father said. "Mechem has swindled half the world and me less than most."

"Even the smallest bit of dust means something to your neighbors."

. . .

Two days after Mechem's body washed ashore, the potion had not done anything besides cause my skin to itch so terribly that I could not stop scratching. When a tiny drop of blood rolled down into my eye, my father gasped and stepped away from me.

I held my hand up, palm facing him, so he could see the red under my nails and know the blood had not gushed from the mark of its own will.

That night, as soon as the sun set, Arrat the Storyteller came to stand outside the tent. "Eben. I have news for you."

My father lifted the door flap to go out to meet the trader, but Arrat said, "No. This news I must give you where none may hear." My father stepped back, and Arrat hurried in as though being chased. He cast a sideways glance at me, and I quickly looked back down at my sweeping.

There was little idle talk before Arrat whispered, though not quietly enough to keep me from overhearing, "Some say it was your daughter who killed Mechem, and others say the demon did it, because he did not want his mark taken from her forehead."

"Surely there are more explanations than these, which are really only one," my father said.

"None that I have heard," Arrat replied.

"You must know it was I who killed him. He tried to take my daughter's virtue."

"That would be a good story but for the one already being passed from one mouth to the next. You cannot compete with a demon, Eben."

"And what have you come to offer?" my father asked sharply. Whatever trust he'd had in men had disappeared with Mechem.

"To take the woman to a foreign land."

"To do what?"

"To not be killed by a mob of demon chasers. To not be drowned or burned or worse."

"To be a slave."

"To be alive."

"Leave my tent before I kill you too."

"You will regret this," Arrat said.

"It is my lot to be full of regret. The gods must think I am able to bear up under the burden. It is a testament to their faith in me."

"Though you are too stubborn for your own good, I will do what I can to help you."

"The quieter you are, the greater good you will do me."

At that, Arrat spat upon the ground, threw open the door flap, and left my father's tent.

"You have angered him, Father."

My father let his shoulders and head fall, and with them his show of bravery. "He wanted to sell you."

Did not some part of him wish he could let Arrat rid him of me? "I am sorry to have made your life so difficult."

"My life is not difficult, and what small trouble there is isn't of your making. It is everyone else. They need to fashion explanations for everything. Often the explanation is more terrible than the thing it is supposed to explain."

I gathered together what courage I could and asked in a voice barely more than a whisper, "Do not you too believe I am marked by a demon?"

"You may be marked, but after marking you, the demon must have fled, because there is not a drop of evil in you."

I doubted this. How could I bring my father so close to ruin if I were free of evil? And I was not comforted at the thought that the demon had left me. My mother had left me too. No one wanted to be near me.

Except my poor father, who was too kind for his own interests. "Father, you should send me away and save yourself."

"No, we will find a way. All will be well. But for now hold on to the knives."

.   .   .

The villagers were civil at first. A man came to see my father on the eighth night after Mechem disappeared.

My father put on his sandals and stepped out to speak with him. Before the door flap fell closed behind him, I caught a glimpse of the man's large frowning face.

"You know why I am here," the man said gruffly.

"You are here engaging in an abomination of nonsense."

"None think it nonsense but you, and you are not a reason-able man." The gruffness fell away, and he said more softly, "We have been brethren all our years, Eben." I did not recognize the man's voice, I had never seen his face, and yet I did not doubt that what he said was true. I knew little of my father's life away from the tent.

"I do not wish you ill," the man continued. "No one thinks that you have anything to do with the demon. We know it was your wife who invited it in with her wickedness." His voice dropped, "But now that the demon is here, it is *you* who is feeding it, allowing it to grow stronger in the creature your wife gave birth to. None of us is safe while you harbor it."

"You with your silly tales! You are like an old woman."

"We will take the demon woman if you refuse to deliver her."

My father's calm crumbled. "She is no woman, only a motherless child."

"You endanger us all. But most of all yourself. The demon woman is beyond salvation."

"And you are beyond any privilege due you to stand upon my land now that you have insulted my honorable daughter. Go from this place and never return." My father came abruptly back into the tent. He stayed near to the door flap until he was sure the man had gone.

. . .

Men camped outside the tent and kept a fire burning at all times.

"How many are there, Father?"

"Not but a few, my child."

I did not press him, though at least ten voices tussled back and forth across the flames.

"You gather not more than thirty cubits from a girl you call a demon. How afraid can you truly be?" my father yelled out to them.

"We worry for you, Eben," someone shouted back. "You would make just as good a vessel for the demon as the woman you keep."

"Perhaps the spirit moves his tongue even now," another man said. "Eben himself would not dare yell at his brethren as boldly as this one who has taken his form does."

After this my father could say nothing that was not looked upon as evidence of my demon taking root in him. If not for my father's grove, the villagers probably would have burned everything to the ground. Despite what Mechem had said, they could not risk the harvest.

One of the men spoke of storming the tent and dragging me to the pit where they would burn me. But the man let himself be talked out of it. Seizing me was too dangerous, the villagers agreed. The gods must be called upon to help them defeat the demon.

My father's tent filled with the sickening smell of burning goats and gazelles and perhaps other flesh as well that my father did not tell me of. What he said was, "You see? They are in awe of you. They do not dare come any closer."

But they did dare to throw torches at the tent. My father had grains of the desert in sacks along the perimeter. When torches hit the goatskin walls, he rushed forth with a mat to beat out the fire, then emptied the sacks of sand on it. "If there were a demon here, fire would not scare it," he screamed. The villagers probably did not hear him over the crackling of the flames.

On the ninth night, Arrat came once again.

"You are not welcome here," my father told him.

"I bring news of the miracle I have worked to save your daughter's life."

At this my father moved to lift the door flap, but Arrat would not come in. "They watch now and might think me touched by the demon if I enter. I will stay out here in their sight."

"Speak, then, before I lose patience."

"I have brought word to a moral and upright man of how you killed a trader for practicing magic. This pleases him, because his god is a jealous one and commands all men and all other gods to abstain from these rites. The man has long been in search of a righteous wife."

I sneaked closer to Arrat's voice. I could see that my father had raised an eyebrow. He made no reply to Arrat, who continued, "I will bring about a match between your sweet daughter and this good man I speak of."

"How many wives does he have already?"

"None."

"He is a widower?"

"No. He has been waiting hundreds of years for a righteous wife."

"*Hundreds of years?* You play me for a fool, Arrat. Have you dug a man up from the ground and brought me his bones that I might give my daughter to them?"

"I meant only that though he possesses many years, he has not found a righteous girl to bear him righteous sons. Until I told him of your precious daughter."

"How will we get my daughter to his tent through the mob camped all around us?"

My breath caught in my chest at the thought of journeying through the villagers who were calling for my death. It would be a miracle to escape with my life.

"We need not leave this place," Arrat said. "I will guide him to you."

My father started. "Will he come with a caravan?"

"No, he travels alone."

"He will need strong men of some kind to take my daughter safely from this village. Has he no kin?"

There was silence. Then, as if Arrat had not heard my father's question, he said, "If we promise the villagers she is to go far away and never return, they will likely allow her to leave unmolested."

Never return. I could not imagine never seeing my father again. But at least, whether I made it through the mob or they killed me, I would burden him no longer.

"You had best be right." There was a threatening tone in my father's voice that I had not heard before.

Arrat faltered for a breath before getting out, "They will. I—I will make certain of this."

"But what of the people in the village she goes to? Will they not see the stain upon her brow and spread word of it as quickly as a hawk swoops down to snatch up a mouse?"

"The man is well respected. If he tells the people your daughter is his good wife, they will welcome her with friendship and gifts of honey and the finest cloth. They will give her olive oil for her hair, kohl for her eyes, and rosewater to wash with so that she brings her husband to her. The midwife will supply unctions so his seed takes root. You will be grandfather to many healthy boys."

"What is the name of this well-respected man, and where is his camp?"

"His name is Noah, and he lives five days journey west of here."

"Have you spoken of him before?"

"Perhaps, though not at any great length. You would not remember."

"I will try, in any case. Say again what you have told me of him so it might bring him forth in my mind's eyes."

"He is very upright. He is a man of God."

"Which god?"

"The God of Adam."

Before my father could ask anything further, Arrat said, "As for payment, I know you to be a fair man, Eben. I have saved your daughter's life and, more important, her virtue. I ask not a lot."

"You know me to be more than fair, but I cannot afford anything more than fair now. If this man takes my daughter unharmed from this village, I will give you a quarter of my olives."

"Is your daughter's life worth so little to you? I do you this favor at great risk to myself."

"A quarter of my olives is more than any sensible man would scorn, but I will let you rob me of *half* my harvest for my daughter's safety. You will see to it that she goes unscathed through the mob, or I will burn my grove to the ground myself to keep you from it."

"Your daughter will be safe," the trader said nervously.

When my father was sure Arrat was gone, he muttered, "The trader cannot be trusted. Yet we must trust him." He turned to me. "Pack a sack you can carry across your back. A man comes to take you for a wife."

. . .

My father did not sleep that night. While the mob shouted back and forth over their fire, he stood near the door flap with his feet apart and chin thrust forward, daring fate to try to bring us down now. He seemed very strong to me, strengthened as a man would be in the last length of a journey, knowing he could soon set down his burden.

CHAPTER 3

THE POWER OF THE MARK I

The next morning I was awakened by a booming voice. "Part so that I may pass through your wicked mass into the tent of the only righteous man among you!"

"A man who harbors a demon is no more righteous than the demon itself," said the gruff-voiced man who had first spoken to my father.

"The God of Adam and those He entrusts with His power of sight are the only ones who can see demons. Any of you who claim to see a demon speaks false."

I noticed my father had not lit a lamp. Perhaps he thought that the light would have revealed my mark too harshly. I tried to peer with him out the tiny eyehole in the door flap, but he gently pushed me away. I stood in the near-dark, listening to the commotion as best I could, my heart hammering in my chest.

"Who are you, old man? Can you expel the demon?"

"I am a man of God."

"Let him through. He will do our work for us." This was Arrat's voice.

"Do you promise to take her far from here, and never allow her to return?" someone asked.

"I make no promises to any but the God of Adam."

"Well, if your God of Adam wanted to know if you were taking this woman forever from this place, what would be your answer?"

"I answer to none but Him."

Arrat's voice came again through the crowd. "Does this stranger look like a young man setting out to make a new camp? Does he look like he has come to be a bondsman? Let him take her, and we will never see her again."

A man with an unusually high voice said, "If he means to bring her forth from the tent, we will set upon her then."

"You will do nothing besides tremble in the sight of the One God or feel His wrath."

My father turned to me. "That is the voice of your husband. He has peacefully made his way through the neighbors and slowly draws near."

I did not know how to greet this news. I did not want to dwell where the mob might rush upon me with daggers and flames, yet neither did I want to try to pass through them without an army.

"Hide behind the pots of lentils," my father instructed. He peered back through the eyehole, so enraptured by the old man who came for me that he no longer seemed to hear the voices tangling around us.

"Who among us is strong enough to tackle the demon?" asked a voice that quivered with old age.

"What choice do we have, with our sons, women, and herds defenseless in the surrounding plots?" the gruff-voiced man replied. "How long do you mean for us to stand out here, doing nothing while the demon grows stronger?"

"By what means does the demon grow stronger?" another man asked skeptically. Perhaps the man was one whom Arrat had swayed with promises of olives or other goods.

I moved close behind my father again, trying to peer out the eyehole with him. I wanted to see the man who would be my husband, if my mark did not first send him rushing back in the direction from which he had come.

"The strength of the soul taken from Mechem. It is hers now, to do whatever evil she can think of. She must be burned."

I shrank from the door flap. I did not think I had the courage for whatever was to come.

"Let us see how the God-man fares," the quivering voice interjected, "before we hazard our own souls."

"He will be sucked dry of all the life that still remains in his faded flesh," someone else said. "The demon nightly turns the woman into one beast and then the next—a goat, an ox. Many of us have seen a lizard the size of a woman, running up the inside of the tent wall, feet sticky with blood, very likely the blood of a child. Perhaps the blood of the child who went missing only two moons ago."

"Do you see these abominations before or after you've filled your fifth cup of wine?" the skeptical man asked.

Noah must have stopped and dismounted, because a man cried

out, "Let us watch for the shadows in the tent, so we might know whether the old man will come out again."

"And if he does, whether his soul is still with him," someone added.

They went silent, but their silence was not a comfort to me. I was sure they had cast their gazes upon the tent so that they might find some evidence of evil.

My father quickly stepped back from the door flap and looked at me, his brow lined with worry. He must have wondered what Arrat had told Noah. Did the trader conceal the size and darkness of my mark? My years? Most men would be angry to find a woman so long past her first blood.

This time I obeyed when my father motioned me back behind our clay pots of lentils and dried fruits. He opened the door flap and said, "Welcome!"

Noah wasted no time with idle talk. "I have come for your righteous and pure daughter."

"Besides the wine stain upon her forehead, she is a true beauty, the finest for leagues in all direc—"

"I care not about the surface of things so much as what is beneath them," Noah said. "Arrat has told me that yours is a righteous family who worships the God of Adam. You have proven your devotion to Him by killing the magician who sought to practice secret arts in your tent."

"We worship the God of Adam with each breath," my father lied. "My daughter is obedient to all of His laws."

Noah snorted his approval. He made this sound again when my father presented him with olives, nuts, apricots, bread, cheese, dried goat meat, and water to take on the journey. My father thought it best to give these things to the old man before calling me to come out from behind our stores.

"And before you leave, for your mule—"

"Donkey," Noah corrected. He said this without shame.

My father raced to cover his presumptuousness. "One beast is as the next," he said quickly.

"No. God created them all, one unlike the other, so that each may serve us in a different way."

"Of course you speak true," my father said. "You are righteous and wise beyond your years." Noah neither spoke nor snorted, so my father continued. "For your donkey, as much hay as you would like."

"Thank you," Noah said. "My donkey is much diminished from our travel."

I remained hidden while Noah and my father went outside to gather the rations.

"Have you slain the demon yet?" someone cried out.

"Where is the blood?" asked another man.

"The demon is too great for his god," the gruff-voiced man said.

Soon so many voices rang out that no one would have been able to hear Noah if he had replied. It sounded as though at least twenty men were gathered. One old man could not possibly protect me from them.

If I am to journey soon to the afterlife, let me go with dignity. I will bite out my tongue to keep from crying and screaming, for I will not dishonor my father with a shameful death.

When Noah and my father returned to the tent, there was no shortage of silence between them.

"Well!" my father finally said. It was time for him to call me out from my hiding place.

"The girl?" Noah said impatiently.

"Yes," my father said. "Yes." But he could not bring himself to summon me.

I could not bear to burden him a moment longer. I rose and stepped around our clay pots to reveal myself.

The wrinkled old man—my new husband—peered at me from under his bushy eyebrows. He did not wince. *He must be nearsighted,* I thought. *The stain upon my brow does not steal his gaze from my eyes.*

My father looked at me with great anxiety. "My dutiful, devoted daughter!"

Noah snorted. There was an awkward silence in the space where my father normally would have invited a guest to a meal. The shouts of the mob must have persuaded him it was best for Noah and me to try to journey forth before we lost our chance.

It did not seem that Noah would have accepted a meal, in any case. Seeing that my father was going to say nothing more, he told him, "The girl and I must go at once, unless we can try to make a son here."

My father sucked in his breath. Noah did not take back his question but instead let it grow bolder in the silence. *Perhaps he is deaf to the cries of the mob,* I thought. If so, I envied him. I could not keep their cries from my ears:

"See now what strange light emanates from the goatskin."

"A dark stain spreads along the edge of the tent!"

"Perhaps it is the blood of Mechem!"

At last my father said, "My humble hut is unworthy of you. Forgive me that I have no lodging fine enough to accommodate a man of so great a stature in the eyes of God."

Noah seemed to take this at face value. "Come, girl," he said to me.

My legs trembled, and I did not trust them to hold me.

He must have known that I did not follow. Before stepping from the tent, he turned back. His voice did not boom so greatly now. "Child," he said, "I know what it is like to be called to an impossible task. But you must bear up righteously beneath your burden and put one foot in front of the other, over and over again, until you cannot any longer."

What task did he speak of? Escaping the mob with my life?

Without waiting for a response from me, he turned and left the tent.

I took a deep breath and then stepped into the daylight. The mob went silent.

As though I were dawdling, Noah said, "I have a flock to tend." I assumed the flock Noah had to tend was made up of goats. I wondered how many animals he had and whether he was wealthy. If he were, why did he ride only a donkey instead of a mule? He continued, "And I do not grow any younger."

Once we were fully in the light of day, I thought he might not be getting much older either. I had never seen a man of so many years. His beard was so long and scraggly that I imagined he had been tugging on it for most of his life. His skin was so wrinkled and thin, I wondered how it managed to hold his flesh and blood inside it.

If one or both of us somehow did not die, I would spend my future with this strange and ancient man. While this might be more desirable than death, I did not anticipate it with any eagerness.

This became all the more true when I saw the donkey on which I would travel across the desert. He was sitting on the ground amid a swarm of flies, chewing his tongue.

"The beast does not want the demon on his back," someone cried out. Others joined their voices to his.

Noah poked at the ass's belly with a stick, but the donkey did not seem to notice this any more than Noah appeared to notice the mob. I willed the animal to rise and take us away as quickly as possible. As if in answer, the ass laid his head upon the ground.

If this is one of the creatures the God of Adam has made to serve us, I think I will worship other gods.

"It is as I told you—we will never be rid of the demon unless we set fire to the vessel in which it resides," the gruff-voiced man said.

I hoped to hear Arrat say something, but my hope was in vain. Perhaps he had given up swaying the mob and was only watching, thinking of the tale he would tell in the surrounding villages. I did not dare glance up to look for him.

Finally the ass brayed and rose from the ground, though not very far. I did not need to examine his teeth to know he was not young. He was too mangy to be a colt, yet he was the shortest ass I had ever seen.

"Strong, sturdy legs," my father said with forced heartiness. He helped me sit sidesaddle on the animal, so that I was facing away from where Noah was securing his gifts in one of the saddlebags. The mob would have been able to see me had my father not stood in their way. He reached for my hand, and his eyes fastened upon mine. "Daughter," he said quietly, "it will go well with you to make a show of devotion to the God your husband worships."

"Yes, Father."

"And always know"—his hand tightened upon mine—"it is not because you are unworthy that I have kept you hidden and have not given you a name. It is the people of this village who are unworthy of the sight of you and a name by which to speak of you."

I feared I might weep with the mob's eyes upon me. "You have always done the best for me and kept me safe," I said. "But Father, can you now bestow a name upon me?"

He looked surprised. Had he never even considered a name for me?

Noah interrupted. "Girl, swing your leg around."

I did as I was told, blood surging into my cheeks. The God of Adam must not have valued modesty as much as my father told me He did. Noah did not look at me or touch me other than to pull on my leg to check that I was well balanced on the riding blanket. It was my first contact with my new husband. I noticed his fingers were longer than any I had seen, and his nails had not been cut in many moons. His roughness did not bode well for the son-making to come.

He climbed on in front of me, as agile and quick as a much

younger man, and took the reins. He was shorter on the donkey than he had been standing up. On top of his head, occupying the greater part of my sight, was a shock of white hair as stiff as a patch of weeds.

I turned my face to the side and wrapped my arms around his waist. There was so much grime and dust on his tunic that it seemed to be made of a material I had never touched before. I glanced down at the hem and saw that it was even filthier than the rest of the garment, and badly frayed.

As my father wished us well, his voice trembled so slightly that only I, who had spent every day of my nineteen years with him, could have discerned it. His hand shook when he gave the donkey a slap on the flank to send us on our way. The smack had as much effect on the animal as poking him with a stick. After delivering a few more slaps to the donkey's flank, my father turned and started back to his tent without bestowing a name upon me.

I watched him, and it seemed to me I was seeing him clearly for the first time. He was stooped, with thinning hair around a bald spot made dark by the sun. His hair had turned to gray. One hip was lower than the other, and he had a slight limp. Where his tunic ended I could see how skinny his calves were. My heart grew full for him. I was both relieved and more deeply saddened when he disappeared inside the tent.

Noah and I continued to sit on the donkey without saying anything while the villagers crept closer. When they were not more than ten cubits away, the donkey began walking. He walked toward them. I squeezed him tightly between my legs and was ready to hold on to my new husband with all my strength if the villagers tried to pull me off. There were no fewer than thirty of them. They moved to form a wall that was two, sometimes three, people deep.

I had been planning to press my cheek against my husband's back and close my eyes. I did neither. Though these men had lived near me my whole life, they had stayed far enough away that I did not recognize their faces. There were men with bulbous noses, long noses, hooked noses, noses with wiry hairs poking out. Men with sun-scorched faces, lips ripped into white flakes by years of taking in the wind that blew from the desert. Numerous wide, scared eyes burned red by sun and sand—or perhaps by the sight of me.

Noah and I moved slower upon the ass than we would have on our feet. Our slowness seemed to make the mob uncertain. The men in front of us stepped aside.

Even so, I half expected hands to grab me and pull me from the donkey. A couple of men lunged forward and reached for me. Noah kicked the first one in the leg, sending him backward. I hardened my gaze upon the second one, and he gasped and fell to the ground.

For the first time, just as I was going away forever, I was wielding my gaze like a sharpened blade, pointing it at their throats.

"See the evil that pours from the creature's eyes!" one man said, trying to incite someone braver than himself to grab me.

A man standing near me with a dagger said, "Let her go. We must turn now to purifying the tent."

Though I did not know if my voice would be steady, the crowd's fear gave me the courage to lean toward the man and whisper so that only he and the men beside him could hear: "If anyone touches Eben, his tent, or his grove, I will impregnate all of your wives with demon children and give the children the same mark that burns upon my brow."

The man stumbled back, tongue twisting around words he could not summon the breath to speak.

Most of those who had dared gaze at me quickly looked away. But a few could not help staring, eyes straining wider with fear, mouths hanging open, *watching watching watching* as if I might do something truly horrifying and amazing.

Which I did, by leaving the only person I loved, the only person who loved me.

As the village faded behind us until I could not make out a single tent, I knew that it was not me, nor even Arrat, my father, or Noah who had sent me on this journey. It was my mark and whatever power had placed it upon me.

CHAPTER 4

A JOURNEY DEEP
INTO THE DESERT

I hoped for a normal life like those of the wives in my father's village. Cleaning, cooking, bearing children, gathering with the other wives to talk of . . . I did not know what they talked of, as I had never been near their gatherings. *I will know soon enough*, I told myself. *If I keep my mark hidden, I can be as happy as any woman.*

The farther we traveled from the Nile, the more brutal the landscape became. There were no oxen pulling plows, no rivers to drink from, and few trees to provide shade from the sun or block the harsh, sand-filled winds. The land had not received a single raindrop in many moons. Dust swarmed up from the donkey's hooves, even at the slow pace that seemed to be all the old animal was capable of.

I wondered why anyone would live so far from the Nile, but I knew I would appear bold if I asked. My father had already endured nineteen years of suspicion, which was nineteen years more than most men could have withstood. I would not give

Noah any reason to return me to the newly free man. I did not speak unless spoken to.

Noah moved his own tongue only to make demands: "Girl, get me apricots from the saddlebag." "Girl, pick the burrs from the animal's tail." (Noah had never bothered to name the donkey over the hundred years he'd had him, and this did not give me much hope of receiving my own name from him.) "Girl, mend this tear in my tunic."

I always responded, "Yes, my lord."

Noah often snorted his approval, but he never looked at me. I was not sure whether this was because I was of little importance to him or because, as he had told my father, he didn't care about the surfaces of things.

Though his eyes did not take to me, his hands were not the least bit inhibited. As the journey wore on, my hindquarters became ever more raw from the constant plodding of the donkey and from the things Noah did to me at night. The riding blanket was thin folded over on the donkey, and it was even thinner when Noah spread it on the ground and told me to lie down. The first night he got on top of me was as close to torture as I had ever come, and I hoped it would end as quickly as possible. Yet when it was over, I almost missed it. All the next day I felt the soreness and both dreaded and looked forward to the night.

We did not sleep much; Noah had a great hunger for sons. Also, he did not want to be away from his flock for long.

It was on the third day of our journey that we came upon the first field of bodies. Many of the men whose faces I could discern had been branded with the X of the banished. And so I feared that we were near the town of Sorum, Land of Exiles, and wondered why Noah would live within even a few leagues of such a place.

None of the dead men Noah and I had come upon—marked or unmarked—wore sandals, and no weapons lay upon the ground besides part of a copper sword and a couple of broken spears. Gripping one of the spears was a hand with no body. Where some of the men's mouths lay open, I saw no teeth.

"Thieves have robbed the dead," Noah said. There were vultures sifting through the remains, but they were not the thieves Noah spoke of.

How I wished that he had come for me on a mule instead of an old donkey, so we could trot through the mess of bodies instead of slowly plodding through as if it did not smell of rotting meat, dried blood, and dung.

Out of the corner of my eye, I saw a small movement and had the terrible thought that perhaps evil spirits were playing among the dead. When I turned my head to look closer, I realized that the movement I had seen was only the wiggling of countless little worms. They were eating the remaining flesh on what must have been a very large man, considering how many worms were able to make a meal of him.

I spoke my first words to my new husband other than "yes" and "my lord." "My lord, why have they not been buried or burned? Whose land is this?"

"The devil's."

The donkey stopped. I looked around Noah's shoulder to see

why. Not ten cubits ahead were four spears with bloodied heads spiked upon them. Three had X's on their foreheads, and one looked as if he were smiling. Another spear had not been planted deep enough in the earth, and it lay on the ground in front of us with the head a couple of cubits away.

"Each generation is more wicked than the one before," Noah said.

As if to prove Noah's words, a boy no more than ten years old stepped out from behind the spears. He had one intensely green eye and one black and red eye socket.

"I will have your mule," the boy said. He had a spear in his hand, likely one that had held a head not long before. When he spoke, I saw that he had no front teeth, and his canines had been sanded into sharp points.

Noah said, "This is no mule. It is the donkey that the Lord has given me."

"I will eat it anyway," the boy said, "and you too, if you do not dismount and run away as fast as your skinny legs can carry you." Then he looked at me. His insolent expression did not move a hair's width in any direction. He did not fear my mark. *Surely he is mad*, I thought.

"Let us go on foot, my lord husband," I whispered, "and let the boy have this slow stubborn animal." It was the first time I had called him husband, and I hoped this would make him consider my wishes more carefully.

Noah ignored me. "The God of Adam will have what is left of your life if you continue your wicked ways," he told the boy.

The boy laughed and sounded like a boy when he did. An evil boy but a boy nonetheless. He leered at me and said, "Not before I have your wife." There was something dark on the points of his canines, and I feared it was something of human origin. "Or is she your granddaughter?"

"She is my good and righteous wife. Young, so she will bear many sons."

This caused the boy to laugh harder. I thought at first that he was laughing because I was not young. Most women had already had and lost more sons than I probably would have a chance to in the few years left me to bear. But then the boy said, "From your limp old twig?"

Noah tensed at the insult.

Please put away your pride, I silently begged my husband, *and give this boy your donkey.*

"Besides," the boy said, "this woman is demon-marked, and the demon will dwell in anything that slithers forth from her belly."

I tried to gaze at him as steadily as I had at the men in my father's village. But he lunged closer, and I flinched. His laughter brought blood to my cheeks.

Satisfied, he turned to consider Noah. "You are the oldest man I have ever seen." Now his voice seemed to hold as much awe as enmity. I hoped Noah would say something such as, "Yes, my child, I have lived many years. If you will let us pass, I will bestow a blessing of long life upon you."

"I am older by more than four hundred years than anyone you have seen or will see again," Noah replied.

Four hundred years? Certainly he exaggerates.

His words sounded like the same threat he had already issued, that the God of Adam would not leave the boy on earth much longer. Surely the boy would show us no mercy now.

Noah hit his heels against the donkey, and to my surprise, the animal began to plod forward, though even more slowly than before. When the donkey tried to steer a path around the boy and the speared heads, Noah yanked the rope attached to the animal's muzzle so that he was forced to go straight.

The boy began laughing again, but this time there was a cry in his laugh. Not a sad cry but the cry of a boy gleefully summoning the worst of his spirit. He pointed the spear at us. I could see that the end came to a sharp, bloody point. "Tell your God of Adam that Jank sent you."

I had not come across any weapons in the saddlebags when I'd opened them to pull out the provisions my father had given Noah. But I checked anyway. My hands shook as I sifted through some bread, dried fruit, and goat meat. Unlike all other men, Noah carried no weapon.

Yet he did not try to steer us around the boy. We continued straight toward him. I pulled my head back from where I peeked around Noah's shoulder. My husband's ancient form was not a very good shelter, but it was all that I had.

Jank's laugh turned to a wild scream as he ran at us. The spear hit Noah in the chest, and he was knocked back against me.

"Husband!" I cried. I did not yet love him, but surely I would not survive without him in this land of barbarians.

Noah's voice came as loud and clear as before, so I knew he had not been penetrated by the spear. "The God of Adam is watching you, boy, with a spear much larger than yours."

Now Jank's cry was angry. He drew his spear back and again stabbed at Noah's chest. Noah fell against me once more. He did not move his hands up to defend himself. The spear glanced off his chest, careening to one side with enough force that Jank stumbled after it.

"You will tire before I do," Noah told Jank.

The boy came back and jabbed harder, but still the spear did not enter Noah's flesh.

Jank began to cry big, body-twitching tears of frustration and disbelief. I would not have been surprised if he had screamed for his mother. He stomped his foot, pulled the spear back, and came at us once more. The spear glanced off Noah's shoulder, so that the boy fell against the donkey. There the boy bit Noah's bare leg. Still Noah did nothing to defend himself. When the boy brought up a knife from his belt, I moved to block his attack, and his blade opened my palm.

I screamed so loudly that all the gods must have heard me.

Noah kicked the boy with no great force, and the boy flew backward, landing heavily upon his hindquarters. As the boy rose to his feet, he looked at Noah with a wide, incredulous eye. "I will warn all the world of your wife's demon mark. I will see her burned alive."

He turned and ran across the flat, sun-scorched earth so quickly that he sent up a cloud of dust. It seemed to pursue him as he got smaller and smaller and eventually disappeared into it. I hoped this was the last we had seen of him, but somehow I knew it was not.

Bright, bitter-smelling blood flowed from my hand. "There must be an unbloodied swath of lambskin on one of these bodies," I said, trying to keep the pain from my voice.

"No," Noah said. "We will not steal, even from the dead. God will give us all we need if we fear Him righteously."

Noah dismounted. He tore a swath from the hem of his tunic and wrapped it around my hand. The agony in my flesh dulled slightly. I noticed there were only light markings where the boy had bitten Noah and no blood. Though Noah was not looking at me, he must have known I was staring. "God will allow me to be beaten, perhaps bruised, but He will not let me die."

I was shocked to see that what he said was true. I had never believed that the gods fully watched over anyone, for despite the many animals sacrificed in their names, they were rarely satisfied. My father's own little finger had not been enough to summon them to his cause. Yet before me stood a man who went unscathed by a sharp spear. *But me?* I wondered.

Noah put his hand on my stomach. "Nor will He let my son die."

My belly felt no different than it had a few days before. How could I know if I were with child? My mother had not stayed with us long enough to tell me. Though, after all the laboring Noah had done trying to make a son, I supposed that perhaps I was already carrying a child or even two. But whether or not I was with child, I would do nothing to dissuade him of his belief that I was. I put my hand upon my belly as if I were holding whatever was inside.

Noah looked at it and then directly up into my eyes. "Nor you, my wife," he said. I held my breath, waiting for him to flinch at such a plain view of the stain. Instead, he nearly smiled. Then he climbed back up onto the donkey, inadvertently kicking my leg and not troubling himself to apologize.

Not more than half a league later, I worked up the courage to ask, "My lord, why have you chosen the desert as your home?"

"God is in the desert."

I waited for him to say more, but he was silent.

We traveled until the sun went down. "My lord, let us not stop for long," I said. Surely the God of Adam could not watch over us every second, and I would hate for a band of barbarians to come upon us when He blinked.

And so we only stopped for a short while. If Noah thought I was already carrying a son, you would not have known it. I wondered how many of his numerous years he had gone without a woman.

After our son-making, as we lay in the moonlight, he turned to me. Again he did not flinch at the sight of the mark. "The God of Adam has not made you unfair to look upon." He quickly added, "Not that I care about such things."

Perhaps his sight was not good. But maybe it was. I could not help feeling compassion for this man who found me desirable despite the mark upon me. A man who had outlived all those he might have cared for once, only to find each new generation more wicked than the one that came before it. Why would he allow himself to care for anyone again? Yet for at least a moment that day, he had put aside any bitterness in order to tear off a piece from his own cloak to bandage the wound of a marked woman. I had not really expected any man to care for me, and I had begun to understand that this one would outlive me, in which case would it not be easier for him if he never loved me?

"My lord, will you bestow a name upon me?"

"I already have. Come now, *wife*, onward to Sorum. My flock awaits."

CHAPTER 5

SORUM

. . . all flesh had corrupted its ways on earth.

GENESIS 6:12

As we came within a league's journey from what would be my new home, my heart lurched around in my chest like the heart of a prisoner who had just been sentenced to death. My mark had made me unmarriageable in my father's village and perhaps in any place except the one where we were going—Sorum, the very last town in the world that I would have chosen to live in. Had my father known where Noah would take me? If he had, he must have thought sending me away was the only way for me to escape death, or surely he would not have agreed to it.

Still, I felt like I had been exiled. I was not going to have what I wanted most—an ordinary life.

This was all the more evident as the fields of bodies grew more plentiful. In the light of the full moon, I could see that little else decorated the barren land. No vegetation sprouted from the earth, other than some forlorn-looking scrub brush.

"The God of Adam has withheld tears of joy from the crops of the sinners and taken the succor from their fruit," Noah said. He seemed to sense that I did not know what he meant. "There is a drought," he said.

There was also no shortage of heads on sticks. I soon lost count. Where there were heads on the ground, I assumed someone had taken a spear and left the remains. Over a distant hill, though not as distant as I would have liked, I heard copper swords clashing. Worse than these sounds were the battle cries. I had never heard joy and anguish combined so terrifyingly into one voice. These cries were more savage than any animal's.

I could no longer remain silent. "My lord, do men battle for land?"

"They are sellswords. They battle much for very little."

This was no comfort to me. I tried to keep my voice steady. "For Sorum?"

"Girl, did you not hear me say there is a drought? No one battles for Sorum."

"How do you survive, my lord?"

"The God of Adam provides."

Again I wondered if I would be included in the blessings Noah's God bestowed upon him. Had I somehow found favor with the God of Adam, despite the mark upon my brow? Perhaps He would make me welcome in Noah's town. I doubted the women of Sorum could be as vile as Arrat said they were. "How are the women and children of your town?" I asked. "Are they more righteous than their men?"

"They are mostly prostitutes," Noah said.

We rode on for a few more cubits before I asked, "And the children, my lord?" My voice trembled.

"I was speaking of them too."

This cannot be, I thought. My husband must have gone a bit mad at some point during his many years. But how mad? And was his god also mad?

As the sun rose, we came within sight of the tents. I pulled my head scarf over my brow. While the scarf would have done me no good in my father's village, where everyone knew of the mark as soon as the midwife left my father's side to wag her tongue, in my new town I vowed that no one should see it.

A woman caught sight of us and then disappeared amongst a cluster of tents. Soon a horde of neighbors gathered to greet us. "My flock is up so soon after the sun. Perhaps they have not yet retired to their sleeping blankets," Noah said with irritation.

Instead of walking to either side of the crowd already gathered, people pushed one another to get to the front. Even from a hundred cubits away, I could see two women pulling each other's hair and hear them screaming things that would have made me blush had I not been so frightened that my blood had come to a standstill in my veins.

The horde was made up of women and children in tunics cinched at the waist with ropes. I was surprised that a few of their tunics had very large neckholes—so large that I could see where their breasts began to divide from their chests.

When we were about fifty cubits away, a woman who had a bald patch on one side of her head yelled, "Make way for the world's oldest virgin!"

Noah did not speak; nor did his body tense, as it had at Jank's remark about his "limp old twig." He leaned slightly forward, as if eager to be among the people gathered before us. I was holding on to him and could not help but lean with him.

Many of the women and girls were quite pretty, but few were without injury. One girl had a leg made of wood. As everyone fought to get a better look at us, a child easily kicked the girl's leg out from under her, sending her sideways into the hard-baked dirt.

"What have you got on the back of your donkey?" someone cried. This caused the others to stop what they were doing and stare at me. I cowered behind my new husband, afraid that somehow they could see through my scarf. But they hurled only common insults at me.

"I have never seen anything like it," said a tangle-haired girl with a black eye. "It looks as though the old man impregnated his donkey some years ago and only now brings the product of this coupling out into the light of day."

Another girl built upon the black-eyed girl's insult: "Even the part that is not donkey is dreadful." She was pregnant, had only one hand, and wore a necklace of human teeth. "We should be glad Noah would not rut any of the rest of us."

"I would still let the old bone collection mount me!" a woman with an X branded upon her forehead yelled. She looked older than the rest. She lifted her tunic above her waist and thrust at us a few times, until laughter overcame her balance.

"God watches you, Javan," Noah said, "and next time He has to throw you to the ground, He will do it with more force."

Some small children, most of whom were naked, ran up to us and pawed at the saddlebags. "I'm hungry!" yelled one little boy whose nose bled. He was nearly as thin as my leg.

"My lord," I said, "perhaps—"

Before I was able to ask if we could spare any of our rations, Noah said, "Because you sin, you starve." Then he turned his head, and I knew he was looking out over the horde. "But you do not have to starve or suffer at each other's hands any longer. There is a way."

"We have heard this already! Have you thought of nothing new the whole time you have been away?"

"*There is a way*," Noah repeated, his voice suddenly so loud that the raucousness of the crowd died down. "God has called upon me to lead you to righteousness. Put down the dagger you threaten your neighbor with, give back the cloth you have stolen from him, and you will not starve another day."

Javan stood up again. "Do I look like I am starving?" This time she lifted her tunic not only above her waist but all the way over her large stomach and sagging breasts. When she let go of it, it fell to rest on the upper swell of her belly.

The girl with the black eye yanked it down over Javan's hips. "You are cruel to make us look upon any more of you than we see already," the girl said. This seemed to delight Javan, who grabbed the girl by the hair and pulled the girl's face between her drooping breasts.

While the other children begged for food and untied our sandals, one tiny girl with a flat face and narrow eyes that slanted upward at the corners reached into my sandal to tickle the bottom of my foot. She smiled up at me. It was the first kind smile I had seen in Sorum. I was surprised to find myself smiling back at her.

"You want my simpleton?" Javan yelled. "I will sell her to you for half an apricot."

Despite the unruliness of the crowd, they made a narrow path for us as we neared.

"If your God were powerful, He would not have given you such an old wife," cried a woman with a belt made of bones. I wondered if the bones of her belt were human. She had stepped back with the others, but she was not more than a cubit to our left, and her eyes were level with mine.

The one-handed girl's eyes were also level with mine. Jank's threat rang in my ears: *I will see her burned alive*. I did not like how the girl narrowed her gaze upon my brow. She kept her position beside us by slashing in front of her with a dagger.

I pulled my head scarf so low that I could see it and tied it tightly enough that it dug into my skin. When I blinked, my eyelashes brushed the bottom of the linen. The girl watched.

"If the God of Adam has to show you His power, it will already be too late for you," Noah said.

"Too late for us to *what?*" The woman whose belt was made of bones grabbed Noah's tunic. "What exactly is it we want to do but haven't?"

The tangle-headed girl with the black eye stood ahead to our left. She was breathing heavily from her brief imprisonment between Javan's breasts. "I, in fact," she panted, "have done everyone I wanted to and more."

Now the one-handed girl lowered her head, trying to peer beneath my head scarf.

"Repent of your wicked ways, or soon it will be too late for you to find favor in the eyes of the Lord."

"Will His favor feel as good between my legs as my neighbor's husband?" Javan asked. Then she turned somber and stepped into our path. "Will His favor undo my daughter's simpleness?"

Noah said, "Your daughter is your punishment for lying with a man who is not your husband."

I no longer saw the smiling little girl. I did not dare turn my head to look for her lest I upset my scarf. Was it really her mother's sin that had made her slow? It seemed more likely to me that Javan had lain with a man after conceiving, and his thrusts—not the evil in her heart—had damaged the girl. In that case, I might also have a slow child. Noah had not let up in our son-making. If our child were slow, would Noah think *I* had lain with another man?

I closed my eyes for a couple of homesick breaths. I had tried not to think of my father, but all his kindnesses came back to me, and each one hurt like a fresh wound. Instead of preparing his morning meal of porridge and barley cakes, I was holding tightly to an old man whose God punished a girl for the sins of her mother. An old man who wore a tunic so layered with dirt that I felt I might lose my grip at any step and be snatched away by one of the numerous vile women who surrounded me.

"The simpleton could be my dead husband's," Javan said indignantly, as though Noah had offended her. Then she became jovial again. "Or at least *somebody's* husband's."

"Wicked woman," Noah said, "the God of Adam will have a hard and heavy hand when he deals with you."

"That is how I most enjoy it," Javan said.

We were journeying upon the tent-lined road so slowly that I feared we might not make it to Noah's land before someone—likely the one-handed girl—suspected there was something beneath my head scarf that had caused me to pull it so low. Another woman shoved Javan out of the way and took her place in front of us. It was the woman with a bald patch on the side of her head. Up close I could see that she was unusually beautiful. She had thick black hair, except where the handful-sized patch was missing, and big almond-colored eyes ringed with kohl. "After seeing your new wife, I know you will want to lie also with a *young* woman sometimes," she said.

Javan grabbed the girl by the hair. "I will halve your whore price by taking the rest of your mane," she said merrily, throwing the girl in front of the donkey. The girl rolled out of the way in plenty of time to avoid the slow animal's hooves.

The one-handed girl gave up trying to see what lay beneath my scarf and demanded, "Are you branded, woman? What is your crime?"

"Perhaps," said the unusually beautiful woman, "she hides an X from her righteous old husband."

The little boy whose nose bled jumped up and yanked upon my scarf. I brought my hands hard against my head and held fast.

"Look!" the one-handed girl cried. "She has a mark upon her brow. *Demon woman!*"

I tried to hide behind Noah. *I will be an exile among exiles, or perhaps they will burn me alive.*

"You would be better off blind than seeing demons everywhere you look," Javan said, taking a step toward the girl. Color had rushed to Javan's cheeks. "Your sight is even worse than your skill as a thief. Careful your loose tongue does not cost you the hand that remains."

Was this crude woman my ally? Her words had called people's attention to her, and I had been able to pull my scarf lower without—I hoped—too much notice.

Noah did not let Javan have the last word. He turned his head toward the one-handed girl. "You will bring God's fist down upon your back with talk of a demon." To the whole crowd, he yelled, "You are all wicked, and the wicked do not know the difference between demons and angels. My good wife will earn her way to the Lord and His blessings through righteousness."

The women's laughter was a relief to me. They would not have laughed if they believed a demon woman were in their midst.

"While she is busy being righteous," the black-eyed girl said, "I will take in your withered old branch for a handful of the fruit on your trees."

I assumed the girl was taunting him when she spoke of the fruit on his trees. I had not seen a fruit-bearing tree in the last half day's journey.

One giggling girl rushed forward to lift my tunic with a hand that looked as though it had not met with water or a clean animal skin in many rotations of the sun around the earth. She lowered her head to peer in. I kicked her in the eye, and her giggling turned to screams. She called me things I had never heard before.

We continued to make our way slowly westward through the rows of tents, and the women and children continued to follow along beside us. They grabbed at our tunics and legs with dirty hands and said vile things. I wondered if this was how Noah's tunic had become frayed.

The donkey must have been used to the commotion, because he did not seem bothered enough by the mob to quicken his pace. I felt sick to my stomach, and not just because I worried that my honor would be taken from me. It was clear from the smell that the population of Noah's town could not be troubled to wander any distance from the tents when they had to relieve themselves.

A man and woman peeked from one of the tents. "Look," the man said, "the fool has found someone other than himself to talk to. Now he can stop pretending he is talking to a god." They laughed and went back inside the tent.

I looked behind us for the tiny girl who had tickled my foot, but I did not see her. Her mother, Javan, was still beside us. The X upon her forehead was not fresh; all the color had faded from it, so that it was not red or brownish like some of the ones I had seen on dead men in the battlefields.

Hands yanked at my tunic, some attempting to lift it and some to pull it off. I was certain I would be naked by the time we reached Noah's tent. I did not like to think of what might happen then.

The horde began to slow their pace and to go quiet. All except Javan, who yelled, "Welcome to the sweet teat of Sorum!"

"You are almost home," Noah said. I had not yet heard him talk to his donkey, so he must have been speaking to me.

The neighbors slowed until none was beside us any longer. I looked back and saw that they had come to a complete stop. I could not think of what, besides one of the giants made from a son of God coupling with a daughter of man, could have caused this.

CHAPTER 6

GIANTS

When men began to increase on earth and daughters were
born to them, the divine beings saw how beautiful the daugh-
ters of men were and took wives from among those that
pleased them . . . It was then, and later too, that the Nephilim
appeared on earth—when the divine beings cohabited with the
daughters of men, who bore them offspring. They were the
heroes of old, the men of renown.

GENESIS 6:1–4

I had never seen one of the Nephilim, but when I was a child, my father had tried to keep me from wandering from our tent when he was overseeing his grove by warning me that there were creatures that had fallen from heaven. "They are angry at humans, and also," he said, "hungry."

"Why are they angry with people," I asked, "when it was the sons of God who came down and defiled the daughters of man?"

"And so they are angry at these daughters of man for their father's seductions."

"But without these seductions, they would not exist."

"They do not understand this, and much else. They think girls are wicked. They will eat you and worse if you stray from the tent."

"But if they look at the ugliness upon my brow, they will see I could not seduce a mortal man, much less a son of God."

"They are so big that, to them, we all look like flies. They are not blessed with their fathers' perfect sight."

My heart swelled like an infected wound. I knew my father was exaggerating to scare me and keep me safe. These Nephilim could not possibly be angry at mortal girls when, without these girls, they would not be alive.

I tried not to smile or sing that day, for fear my father would know what I was thinking, which was that someday I might be able to win the favor of one of these massive creatures who could not make out the dark stain upon my brow.

. . .

In my father's village, there had been only one girl who was not filled with fear at the sight of me. She did not want to be any less than ten cubits away from me, but that was closer than most people let me get, and her eyes did not shun me. I sensed that the other children did not want to be around this girl any more than they wanted to be around me. Otherwise, why would she have allowed me near her?

Not half a moon after learning of the Nephilim's poor sight, I sneaked out to the girl's tent to borrow a cup of lentils. Like me, she had no mother, and her father was off plucking olives for my own father. I placed my cup on the ground, called to her, asking her to fill it with lentils, and backed away so she could pick it up. As she did, she told me a man had recently come to speak with her father about taking her as a wife. "Has any man come to talk to *your* father about taking *you* as a wife?"

Surely she knew no man would have me. I was both angry and ashamed. I surprised myself by saying, "Yes."

The look of disappointment on her face was very satisfying, and I wished to deepen it. "Well, not really a man," I said.

She smiled. "I did not think so."

"No, not a man. One of the Nephilim."

She laughed. "Why would a grandson of God, who could have any girl he wanted, take a marked one for a wife?"

"They do not see well," I told her. "They choose their wives not by how they look but by the strength of their spirits and their ability to bear sons."

She looked skeptical, but the disappointment did not fade from her face, so my work was done. "Thank you for the lentils," I said. "I hope your husband is a big and powerful man. Or at least as big and powerful as a mere man can be."

I secretly followed my father the next day as he made his way to the trade route with a sack of olives he intended to barter for some incense. That is when I saw the man, the donkey, and the girl. The man was neither large nor powerful. Well, he was not *tall* and powerful. He was so fat, and his donkey so old, that he did not ride it.

The girl rode the ass, staring down at the animal's neck as though she might wring it and bring the slow journey to a halt. Then she cast her gaze around her to see who witnessed her humiliation, and her eyes landed on me. She straightened her back and held her head high. Perhaps it occurred to her that this only made her husband look even shorter, because she immediately dropped her head again.

I had no right to pity her. Unlike me she had a husband to serve. But I was sorry for her nonetheless and said a little prayer for her to the gods of happiness, wealth, and fertility.

If I ever did manage to win the favor of one of the Nephilim, no one would have to pray for me. I would get to ride away on one of his shoulders, holding a lock of his legendary purple-tinged black hair, while my neighbors stared up at me in awe.

Despite my secret wanderings after receiving my father's good news about the Nephilim's poor sight, I had never seen one. And so it was with great anticipation that I peeked my head around Noah's shoulder.

CHAPTER 7

MY HUSBAND'S TENT

To my disappointment, I saw only trees.

Someday soon I hope to see one of the Nephilim and have him look upon me and find me ordinary and unmarked, no different than any other woman. Gods, is this so much to ask?

"You see how God provides for the righteous," Noah said.

My disappointment faded, though not completely. "Are those *your* trees, my lord?"

"They are mine, but their gifts shall be ours."

And what gifts! There were bunches of dates hanging heavily from beneath a palm's long leaves. Nuts from another palm decorated the dirt. Leaf-shaped pieces of shade lay sweetly upon the ground. Yet somehow the horde of women and children's voices continued to grow quieter, and when I looked back, I saw that they did not follow, but instead grew smaller and smaller as we traveled away from them.

"My lord, how do you keep the neighbors from raiding your bounty?"

"Any man who tries to steal from me risks his life. If he takes one of my sheep or goats, it will bite him and cause him to stumble so that he falls and breaks his neck. If he steals from my well, he will tumble in and drown. The God of Adam also watches over my trees. He riddles their leaves with thorns so that only I can reach between them for the fruit. You will sometimes hear people thudding to the ground, and these are the wicked who try to steal our fruits. The Lord sends poisoned juices down the bark when thieves come near." These were as many words in a row as Noah had spoken to me, and I hoped they were true.

The ass huffed in indignation as he was forced to step on the nuts that lay in his path. But he continued until he reached the deepest shade of the palm trees, where, abruptly, he came to a halt.

"We are home, child," Noah said.

In the morning shade of the palm trees was a small tent. Noah's tent.

I waited for his command. "We are home," he repeated. "Get down." I dismounted as quickly as I could, considering the raw state of my hindquarters. Noah dropped the reins and climbed down in front of me.

The trunks of the trees were too large to tie a donkey to without a long rope. Noah did not seem concerned. He took the riding blanket and saddlebags off the animal. The donkey sat down, and I could not blame him.

I, however, would not sit down again for as long as possible. Before journeying across the desert on Noah's donkey, I had spent most of my life standing, squatting, or lying on my side. My hind-quarters were so thoroughly chafed that I would have to sleep on my stomach for many nights. If I could manage to sleep in a town so full of barbarians.

A herd of goats and another of sheep grazed on the first patch of grass I had seen all day. I had never observed goats so close to a sleeping tent, but perhaps Noah had no choice. If the women wanted to tear off my tunic, then they might also risk being bitten and stumbling upon their heads in order to tear the wool off Noah's sheep and roast the meat beneath.

Noah gestured at the herd. "You will gather their milk and wool," he said.

I did not want to be outside the tent long enough to do either. I would have to find a way to get out of these duties.

"Come," Noah said. I followed him past a loom and sacks of lentils into the tent. It was dark because of the morning shade of the palms. Noah banged two pieces of flint together and produced a spark much sooner than was natural. He lit a lamp.

Upon the dirt lay several jars of clay, a pot, and a large spoon. A knife lay on a piece of goat hide beside them. These were the sum of Noah's possessions.

After taking in my new home, I squatted to look at the bottom of my tunic. It was dirty and ripped where the horde had grabbed at it.

"It is best," Noah said.

I wanted to know why it was best that my tunic was ripped, but I feared that if I asked him, he might think I was vain, or worse, that I was questioning his wisdom. I reasoned that it was better for my tunic to be undesirable so the people would not become aggressive about stealing it from me.

"My lord, our neighbors . . ." I said. "I have never met such as them."

His eyebrows moved toward each other. I should not have spoken ill of his flock. "At least they do not adorn themselves with finery," he said.

I would have preferred they be decorated with jewels instead of human teeth, but I kept my thoughts to myself: something that I would learn one is more prone to at the beginning of a marriage than at the end.

Noah snorted as I took the riding blanket from him and spread it on the floor in the corner of the tent. As I waited on hands and knees for him, I prayed to his God and others. I asked that they protect the son in my belly, if there were one.

CHAPTER 8

NOAH

. . . Noah was a righteous man; he was blameless in his age . . .

GENESIS 6:9

As in my last days in my father's village, I left the tent only to bring up water from the well and to relieve myself. I drank little of the date juice I made for Noah, so I sometimes managed not to leave the tent for a whole cycle of the sun around the earth.

Not a day or night passed without the sound of swords clashing, or screaming orgies of wine and flesh. These sounds were often accompanied by the conversations Noah carried on with the God of Adam as he paced inside the tent. I could sometimes make out a sentence or two of his mumbling. Usually he was hopeful:

"They are not lost to us. Your words stick in their ears, and eventually, they will hear them."

"Little by little, my Lord, the wicked come closer to belief. They are on the very verge of fearing You."

"It will not be long now."

He often paused, and I suppose that was when he was listening for the God of Adam. I do not know if He responded.

Noah was able to walk only a few steps before changing direction. This was because I had asked him if I might stay within the walls of the tent in order to protect my virtue.

"God watches over your virtue," he had replied. But he sounded slightly anxious as he said it, so I continued to stand before him with my head bowed. The silence argued better for me than I could have argued for myself. "But He can watch over it more closely if you are here in the tent," he said. Thus, everything I needed to perform my chores had been brought inside. Surely, when the neighbors saw Noah carrying in all of our food stores and the loom, they thought he was even more mad than they had suspected.

A couple of times I even prepared meat in the tent. Flies or worms—not so unlike those that had crawled on the corpses we had seen on our journey from my father's tent—congregated on the unusable pieces of meat, which I threw out of the door flap, and in the little pools of blood on the ground of the tent. These creatures were preferable to the ones outside; they did not hurl insults at me or wrench my tunic over my knees to peer at my woman's parts.

Inside the tent, I also wove clothes and blankets for the people of the town, who were constantly in need of new ones. When Noah had told me that making clothes would be my primary chore—despite that we would not profit from it—he had explained, "I am leading this lost and unruly flock back to the righteousness of the Lord. Immodesty is an abomination in His eyes."

On days when Noah lost patience with the sinners, immodesty was one of the many things he complained to God about as he ranted around the loom, through the rows of clay pots full of lentils, over our sleeping blankets, and beneath the nets full of fruit and nuts that hung off lines strung up from one end of the tent to the other. Fornication was another. He did not omit any details when he talked to God about the flock he was trying to bring Him: "Among all the children as much as ten years of age—both male and female—I am certain there are no virgins. Even some of the younger children are no longer pure."

I could not keep myself from interrupting him. "What about Javan's daughter, my lord, the one who is simple? Surely she is a virgin."

Noah kept pacing as if he had not heard me. When enough time had elapsed that I had given up on receiving an answer, he said, "Unlikely."

During his silence, I had thought about it myself, and I doubted a man had known the child. She had not seemed wanton or harmed by men. She appeared to possess the boldness of an innocent, one who does not yet know the evils of which men are capable.

So as not to seem as though I were questioning Noah, I said, "This saddens me, my lord. At least the God of Adam has left her heart innocent."

"She is not innocent. She is just too depraved to know the seriousness of her misdeeds in the eyes of the Lord."

I said nothing. After a few more paces, he continued, "She is Javan's daughter; wickedness has been sown into the very center of her soul."

I knew that was the child's true crime in Noah's eyes. He seemed to have a place in his heart for all the sinners but Javan. "Yes, my lord," I said quickly, hoping to end the conversation. He snorted.

When Noah was not talking to or about God, he seemed to be at an utter loss for words. Perhaps this was why, when he was not tending the herd or sleeping, he spent most of his time in the road yelling about wickedness.

One day I put down the lentils I was sorting and watched out the tent flap as he moved slowly down the road on the back of the ass, shouting at the people of the town to repent. "It is not yet too late to atone and find favor in the eyes of the One True God!"

"This One True God must have a lot of time on His hands, to listen to the ravings of a lunatic," a man coming out of one of the tents shouted back at him. "Why do you wear His ear out, along with ours, all night and day?"

"If you did not blather on so much," another man added, "maybe more than one god could bear to listen to you."

Often at night I lifted the flap of the tent window and saw these men in the light of the fires they roasted goats over. Their clothes were tattered, despite the new ones I was always making. A few times I saw a man close enough to decipher the scarring on his face. The more I looked from the window at night, the clearer it became that all the men were marked not only by an X upon their forehead but also by the sword, spear, or club of another man. Broken, bloodied noses, busted lips, small craters where eyes had been—these were the features of the men's faces. A couple of the men even had holes in their cheeks through which, at a shorter distance and in a little more light, I might have seen teeth or a tongue. Unwieldy gashes jaggedly separated one part of a man's face from another. Infections ate at their skin, and pus bubbled from their wounds.

Time had not managed to mark Noah's face as deeply as battle had marked these men's. Noah's skin was thin and wrinkled, yet his features were easily recognizable. I was afraid for Noah and his unscarred face. What if the God of Adam broke from His vigil over him? I thought that surely someday a mercenary would take the opportunity to make his mark upon this unscarred surface, there being so few such surfaces in the town.

As I worried for Noah, I could not keep a startling realization from making itself known to me: I had somehow come to care for the strange, self-righteous man to whom my father had given me.

CHAPTER 9

HERAI

One day when Noah had climbed onto his donkey and ridden ever so slowly into town, I heard a strange sound. It was a child's voice, fearful but without intonation or inflection. Other voices grew louder until I did not know whether the child had gone silent or was being drowned out.

"I will have this virgin half-wit to earn back the money Javan stole from me when I lay with her."

"And I as well!" another man said.

Javan's voice was full of rage yet steady. "Leave my simpleton alone, or I will unman you with a dull knife." I had no doubt she would follow through if the men raped her daughter, but by then it might be too late to save the girl's good nature.

Why had Noah not provided me with any weapon other than the wrath of his God? I did not know how to call this God to my aid. Besides, if what Noah said was true and God had crippled the girl's development for her mother's sins, why would He help her now?

I secured my head scarf, lifted the door flap and peeked at the road. A man stood with his back to me, staggering under the effect of too much wine, with the girl held high over his head. A smaller man was jumping up and down, trying to grab at her. "Me first!" he cried. They were less than thirty cubits away. Javan was pounding her fists on the first man's chest, but the man was too large and too drunk to care.

I emptied lentils from a large clay pot and brought it to the door flap of the tent. Knowing that people usually hear their name above all other sounds, I called, "Javan!" She peeked her head around the torso of the man who held her daughter in the air.

Though her daughter may have been slow, Javan herself was as quick as a man chased by fire. I flung the pot along the ground, and she ran to pick it up. The men were still playing keep-away with the child when Javan came up behind the smaller one and slammed the pot across the back of his head. He cried out and went down. The larger man turned around in time to be hit in the neck. He dropped the girl to the ground and reached for Javan. But the strength was draining out of him, along with the blood that flowed from his neck.

I would have given each of the men a few more wallops to the head, but Javan was confident of the quick work she had made of them. She grabbed her daughter by the hair and pulled her to her feet. "Dreadful simpleton!" she yelled. "Where is the knife I gave you? I should have let these diseased cocks have you. Will I have to waste the rest of my life trying to make up for your slowness?"

Without thinking, I ran to defend the child, then stopped abruptly. Javan had just injured or killed two men. Why would she not do the same to me?

"Javan," I said, "I have some milk for the child."

Javan looked at me without any gratitude for the pot I had given her or how I had risked drawing attention to myself to do so. "And for me?" she said.

There seemed to be no other choice. "For you as well," I said.

She let go of her daughter's hair and followed me back toward the tent. The girl trailed behind her a few cubits. "Come, child," I called. She looked at me without smiling. *I hope it is not too late for her*, I thought. *She is the only source of joy in this town.* I stopped outside the tent. "Wait here."

"You keep milk in the tent? Do you also keep mule piss inside?"

I did not answer. I skimmed the cream off some goats' milk and put it in a small bowl for the child. Then I poured most of what remained of the milk into another bowl for Javan. When I came out of the tent, Javan was standing on a pile of dried donkey dung, likely for the fraction of a cubit it added to her height.

I gave Javan her milk first, so that her hands would be full and her attention would be on her own bowl. Then I held the cream out to the child. *Hurry, child*, I thought, *drink before your mother notices your cream.* She smiled at me and clapped her hands together before taking it. My heart lightened for the second time in the two moons since I had left my father's tent. The girl had not been harmed by the drunken men who now lay in the road. Perhaps it was her slowness that kept her from becoming as hardened and mean as everyone else.

When I raised my gaze from the child's face, I saw that Javan was eyeing me thoroughly from head to toe. Then she rested her gaze on my stomach. "Is there a brat in your belly yet?"

"I do not know."

She smiled. "But he thinks there is." She did not so much ask me as tell me.

I waited for her to finish the milk so I could take her bowl and wish her well, but she left a couple of drops to prevent me from doing this. I kept my hands at my sides and tried not to frown too deeply. I was hoping Javan would not prevent me from looking after her daughter sometimes.

"What is your name?" I asked the girl.

She just smiled.

"She comes to 'simpleton,'" Javan said.

"But what did you call her when she was born?"

"It does not matter now."

"It does matter," I said sharply.

"So then what is *your* name? Or do you want to go on being called demon woman?"

"I do not have a name."

Javan raised an eyebrow. Had she heard the anger in my voice and the shame beneath it? "Well, do you at least have more milk, perhaps some goat meat?" she asked.

"No wonder there is so much of you."

She laughed. "Yes, there is plenty to make a man comfortable."

Before I could think better of it, I said, "Do you do nothing besides copulate all day and night?"

"Yes. I just killed two men."

I had somehow forgotten this, and she must have enjoyed the shock on my face. I suddenly wondered what she had done to earn the X upon her forehead.

"With a pot you gave me," she added.

I got more milk and dried goat meat for both her and the child. "Now tell me the child's name," I said.

"She is Herai." The girl did not react as her mother said this; she just kept smiling up at me. "She likes you," Javan said. "Perhaps due to her slowness. I myself prefer whoring to mothering. Men's appetites can be sated, but children's grow just as quickly as their bodies do. You will know soon enough."

If I have to feed an appetite larger than Noah's, I do not think there will be much left of me.

Javan seemed to enjoy talking, and I did not know anybody else, so I asked her, "How does the town sustain itself? I see no crops."

"Do not be simple, woman."

I would not be checked. "And why do the men fight among themselves while they are here in Sorum, where surely they are not being rewarded?"

"The men are hired as soldiers by any tribe with enough meat and wine to pay them. When no tribe needs them, the weapons, teeth, and bones of other mercenaries are reward enough for battle. They are gamblers, of a sort. Besides, they know nothing else." Though she had not answered my first question, she waited for some sort of response from me. When there was none, she asked, "What is it you do when Noah is too far away to rut you?"

I should not have spoken so carelessly of Noah. But I had not gotten to talk with anyone besides him in two moons, and he did not actually talk *with* me. He talked *at* me. "I make clothes that Noah gives away, and blankets he takes from my loom before I have had a chance to knot the last yarns. I never see them again, not even when I look at the people he has given them to."

"The men prefer to wear the clothes of the dead. Who would be foolish enough to wear new clothes and risk having his life taken so that his clothes could be cut off of him?"

"Then what do the men do with the clothes Noah gives them?"

"Give them away in exchange for the very things Noah is always telling them not to do. The best whores have whole stacks of tunics. Sometimes the whores present them to traders for food and wine."

"And what do they do with them otherwise?"

"Trade them for children that they can prostitute, which is what you could do, should Noah ever tire of you. You like children."

I had seen many traders when I dwelled in my father's tent, and they were all men. Some of them had seemed greedy enough that I could imagine them trading in children. "Men might do such a thing, but not women," I said. "You lie."

"I just killed two men. I do not have the energy to lie."

Indeed, she did not seem like a woman who would bother to lie. She did not have the decency.

"Families come from surrounding towns," she said, "or sometimes from far away, to trade their children."

My husband's town was hardly better than Arrat's tales of it. My knees buckled. Sorum was no more than a large brothel for mercenaries.

"Perhaps you should give each piece of clothing some flaw," Javan taunted. "Make the tunics too short, or with an odd tear here or there, or spill some grape juice on them. Better yet, soak them in blood. Then the traders will not want your clothes, and our men will not be afraid to wear them."

I could not speak. Javan was no doubt overjoyed at the effect her words were having on me. She kicked my knee to make sure I was listening, then went on: "Though pulling the clothes off the dead is great sport. No matter how you damage the clothes you make, still they will not be as lucky to the men as the ones they pull off each other in battle."

She kicked me again. She did not kick hard, but I would not have cared if she had. "The men must fight the bodies of the dead for clothes and teeth even as the battle wages around them, because afterward nothing will be left. Not one single tooth. And this is honorable because it is more dangerous than fighting the living— another man can see you pillaging a dead man and kill you while you are distracted."

She is mad, as are all the rest who have not fled this place. A small, sweet hand touched my hair and played lightly with it. *Except Herai. Thank you, God of Adam, and all other gods, for this one joy.*

Javan continued, "They never fix their clothes, because why spend time mending something that will tear again? A man can only mount so many whores, and then what else is there to do besides drink and fight? You see? You see, *simple woman?*" Suddenly she clapped her hands together and cried, "Ah!" as though she had been struck with an idea. "You could make necklaces of teeth! These are stolen so often, there is always a need for more."

I did not open my mouth or move my eyes to Javan's face. I reached for the little hand in my hair and squeezed it weakly between my palms.

"Well, if you have no more milk or goat meat . . ." Javan said.

It was a relief when she started walking away, and a heartbreak when Herai drew her hand from mine and ran after her.

Before they had gotten ten cubits away, Javan turned back to me. "Do not fear a mob, demon woman. Your secret is safe with me." She touched her finger to her brow and continued away.

CHAPTER 10

SONS AND DEMONS

It was clear I would never be part of a gathering of women like the ones I imagined in my father's village. But even in the worst of places, people long for company. Especially in the worst of places. I hoped Herai might come back for milk. After a couple of moons, I grew tired of waiting and decided I would have to go into town to find her. I could not work up the courage though.

One day it was unusually quiet. I heard no people screaming or fighting, only the occasional bleating of one of Noah's goats. The quiet called up a loneliness so deep within me that I knew there was no son in my belly. I was empty. I felt the loss of my father as deeply as if it had only been yesterday that I'd watched him weakly slap Noah's donkey and limp back to his tent. *I must see the girl today, before my solitude drives me to madness.*

I wore a swaddling cloth under my tunic and left my sandals inside the door of our tent. The sandals were only thin straps of leather, but still I feared I could lose my feet for them in town.

With my head scarf secured over my brow, my heart beating hard in my chest, and stones piling up in my belly, I went to find Herai. I saw no one until I had ventured at least a hundred cubits. Men and women were gathered with their backs to me around a tent. The tent hung from old wooden supports that leaned toward each other beneath its weight.

Vultures circled above. I heard babies crying, and over their crying, a woman shouted, "We must kill them."

"No, only two of them."

"But which two?"

"They are all spawn of the demon that split a man's seed into three parts. Each of them must die," said the unusually beautiful girl with a head of very long hair except for one patch that was only a few moons long.

"A demon does not waste time with a woman once a man has left her," Javan said.

"Then what is it that happened to your daughter? What was it that made her slow if not a demon?"

Javan was silent. I had not thought it was possible to silence her, and I was surprised to find that her silence did not please me. A few breaths later, she again tried to save the babies. "The girl has lain with three men, and they each planted a son in her."

"Then why has no one else had three at once?"

Again Javan made no reply. I tried to think of something to defend her argument, though I was not sure I had the courage to risk the wrath of the mob. People were starting to raise their voices and shift around. I was glad when another woman cried out, "If we kill the demon's babies, will not the demon kill us?"

No one listened to her. Shoulders collided, and elbows stabbed at the ribs of the bodies around them. Shoving broke out. Through the gaps that appeared in the mob, I saw the girl with only one hand lying on a blanket stained with afterbirth. Babies' cries rang out from either side of her. The arc of the mob tightened.

I called upon Noah's God: *God of Adam, these babies need your protection.*

It would have taken two hands to hold one baby, and the girl was trying to hold on to all three with only one. They were quickly ripped away from her. Each baby was taken by a different woman, separating the mob into three parts. One part came rushing toward me.

I felt something sharp against my head and then warmth. The warmth quickly ran down my neck. I looked down at the rock that had hit me, and then I was slammed to the ground. A foot stepped partway on my head, and another crushed my thumb and forefinger.

I will see her burned alive echoed in my head. I did not know why I bothered to pray to Noah's God, but I did: *God of Adam, please help me from this place without allowing anyone to see my mark.* I held my scarf to my brow, stood up, and started stumbling home. A few times someone knocked into me hard enough that I should have fallen, but I did not. Perhaps Noah's God had heard my plea. Perhaps he was my God too.

. . .

That night Noah raged through the town. "The fury of the One True God grows. It is *His* place to do as He will with the lives of children. Who are you to usurp Him as ruler of all the world?"

I had no way of knowing what had happened to the babies. *Perhaps that is best,* I told myself. Now that I suspected the God of Adam was as powerful as Noah said He was, I would not be able to help being angry at Him if He had let them die. I laid the side of my head that did not ache on my sleeping blanket and hoped I would not wake up for a long time.

I dreamed that the sea fell from the sky and beat upon the earth with fists of rain. The rain piled higher, until it was as tall as a man. People screamed as huge hands made of water pulled them under. No one was spared—children, women, people who had lost a hand or foot, slow people, blind people—all of them were strangled by the sea. But I did not drown. *Where am I?* I wondered.

I was awakened by babies crying. I did not know why these cries woke me when looters ran loose through the town, whooping and screaming. I heard clay pots being smashed and the crack and whoosh of wooden tent poles breaking and dropping their goatskins. Yet it was the babies who woke me.

In the light of the full moon, I saw the figure who held the babies standing in the entryway to the tent, the door flap over her shoulder.

"Sons for Noah," Javan said between hard-fought gulps of air.

In her meaty, bleeding arms were three babies. Without checking to make sure my scarf was pulled low over my brow, I ran to her and took them one by one. I laid them gently on my sleeping blanket. The first labored for breath more quietly but less successfully than Javan. He seemed to be choking on something, and his eyes were wide with panic. The eyes of the other two were still.

I labored over them for what remained of the night, while Javan stood guard in the doorway with her sword. I took the baby who was still trying to breathe and placed him on his stomach so that he might stop choking. The back of his head was flattened and bloody. I pressed my garment to it, but the blood soaked through the fabric. Javan helped me cut a small swath of goatskin from the tent and I pressed it to the child's head.

When the looters no longer ran through the town, Javan joined me over the three little bodies. By dawn they were cold and their eyes shiny.

"We have done what we could," Javan said. Her voice was garbled, but I could still hear the anger.

As we had labored, blood had dripped from her face onto the babies and the sleeping blanket. Now that there was nothing more we could do for the babies, I looked at her. Her face was so badly battered that she was recognizable only by the X upon her forehead and her large sagging breasts, which hung loose from what was left of her tunic. Her lips had swollen around a gash that ran the length of her face, just to one side of her newly crooked nose.

I quickly rose and went to the other side of the tent for water to wash her wounds. She stood too. Her eye—the one that was not swollen to the size of a fist—was as blank as the babies' eyes.

"I am sorry," I said. I was sorry for the babies and, I must admit, for myself, but even more for her. She had risked her life to take the babies from the other women, and she must have believed they might live. Only someone desperately hopeful would have believed this.

She did not wait for me to wash and bandage her face. She left the babies on my sleeping blanket and walked out of the tent. I didn't know, as I watched her leave, that five people would die by her hand before the sun rose again.

. . .

Noah did not return that morning. I lay with my head upon the ground where my sleeping blanket had been, and I spoke to Noah's God. *Why did You not send these sons one at a time, so that they might live? And what was most strange to me: Why did You protect me from the mob and not them?*

"Where is your sleeping blanket?" Noah asked when he returned.

"It is wrapped around three boys whom your God let die." I did not address him as my lord. I thought he might strike me, but I didn't care.

"He will not let their deaths go unavenged."

"What good is that?"

"You are a child, so your vision is small. When you cry one tear, you see the whole world through it. I have lived for hundreds of years. In those years, thousands of children have been born and thousands have died. They have been born to good and born to evil. There is more evil now than good, but God will find a way to make us righteous again. He will do it on His time and not that of an ungrateful child."

I did not bow my head, and I did not speak.

"You see that ours is one of the few tents left standing," he said.

I remained silent.

"Wife, you should know"—he leaned his face down so that his fury-filled eyes were level with mine—"He counts those who lack gratitude among the wicked."

. . .

The goats sniffed at the ground where I'd buried the boys. Noah saw this and went to bury them deeper. When the ground was flattened again into a thick blanket of dirt, I went and knelt over them. I asked the God of Adam and all the other gods I knew of to watch over the children in death better than they had in life.

. . .

My anger at Noah and his God did not keep me from him that night. I had to make up for the three babies who had died right where we laid. I could not rest until I did, and neither could Noah.

At dawn he lay panting beside me, muscles shaking from the night's exertions. "Child," he said when I reached for him again, "you will make a widow of yourself." But he did not keep me from climbing on top of him once more.

CHAPTER 11

JAVAN'S MARCH

It is not easy to be legendary as a murderer in a town where blood-shed is commonplace. But Javan became renowned.

The legend begins with her lurching into the daylight, dripping blood. The three boys who came out of their mother all at the same time had just died. Javan was blind in one eye and weeping from the other. "I'll kill you," she yelled to no one in particular, or maybe to everyone. "But first I will tear your tongues from your mouths and your arms from your shoulders. I will bury you to your necks, pour honey on your heads, and let the ants have their fill. I will tie mice to your hair and call hawks down from the sky!"

Javan was not so much walking as falling forward and roughly catching herself with each step. More monster than woman. The first people she came upon were our closest neighbors, a woman with a daughter and two sons. The wooden poles and stakes of their tent had been snapped in halves, thirds, and quarters, and so the family was eyeing Noah's trees. When they saw Javan, they scattered.

The daughter wasn't looking where she was going—she was looking back at Javan—and she stumbled on a man who lay drunk or dead in the street, one of her feet tangling in what remained of the man's tunic. Even as the girl fell forward, she stared back at Javan in horrified awe.

"If I let you live," Javan told the girl, "you will work for me."

Without waiting for a reply, which surely the girl couldn't have provided anyway, Javan picked up the dead man's sword and continued down the road.

Next she came upon one of the few tents that had survived the night's looting. Inside she found a man and woman. "You have taken half my sight, and I will take all of yours," she told the man. His screams could be heard for a hundred cubits in all directions.

The second to die was a girl who was trying to comfort the one-handed girl where she lay upon the ground, crying in the burned remains of the tent they had shared. Javan sneaked up on them, which must have been hard to do in the silence she brought with her. When the people of the town saw Javan, they became as silent as they had been for a few shocked breaths the day before, when the three boys were born at the same time.

"It is better this way," the girl who was about to die was telling the one-handed girl. "The demons that lived within your womb are gone, and there is nothing for anyone to remember them by."

"Is this why you helped tear them from her arms?" Javan asked as she stepped into view.

The girl spoke swiftly, because she knew how quickly Javan could kill her. Also how slowly. "I was afraid they would be torn in half if the women fought over them, so I gave them to the most nimble and good mothers from among the crowd." She turned to the one-handed girl. "Is it not true?"

"It was you who called the mob around us in the first place with your talk of a demon," the one-handed girl replied. "You are the murderer."

"As am I," Javan said, and drove a broken tent post through the guilty girl's chest. As blood flowed out from where the post entered her flesh, Javan turned to the one-handed girl.

"What three men did you lie with nine moons ago?" she asked.

The girl spoke the names of three men. It is uncertain whether they were ones she truly had lain with, or ones who did *not* lie with her and therefore didn't give her food, wine, and clothing. Men of no worth to her.

In the chaos of the demon frenzy, most of the men had looted what they could and left with it, so that no one else could steal what they had stolen first. But Javan knew that when night fell again, they would be back. She waited, and not idly. She did not sheath her sword.

"You!" she demanded. She had come upon three girls using cloths to rub dirt from their skin before the men returned that evening. One was also rubbing blood off her arm. It was the unusually beautiful girl with long hair except for a patch that was only a few moons long—the one who had said each of the boys must die. This was the girl to whom Javan was speaking.

The girl looked up. She did not seem affected by the appearance of Javan's mangled face and angry eyes—one wide open with the sight in it and one swollen to the size of a woman's fist.

"Yes?" the girl said.

"I've come to kill you."

"Good."

Javan said, "Because you meant to—"

"I do not care why."

"Then I will kill you in such a manner that you do."

Javan threatened to cut off the other girls' ears if they didn't run away. They could not afford to be badly disfigured, so they rushed from harm's way and left their friend in Javan's hands.

Javan knocked the beautiful girl to the ground and fell on top of her so she couldn't get up. But the girl did not even try. As Javan held the sharpness of her sword to the girl's cheek, she couldn't help looking into the girl's kohl-ringed eyes. Insolent, exquisite eyes. Because the girl did not struggle, Javan did not have to fight with her, which gave her time to continue staring. The girl was too lovely for a seller of women to kill.

"You do not care if you die, so you should not care too much about having to lie drunk on your back while I collect the money," she told the girl.

Without waiting for a reply, she moved on.

The men were of some value to Javan, though less than her women and girls, because the men mostly passed through and sometimes never came back. But that night, when the men returned, Javan asked around, and she did so with her sword. A few of the boys in her service asked around too, and they were not as self-possessed as she was. If we were to add in the people who died while Javan's boys looked for the three men Javan would kill, the death toll would be twice as high. And so this is what the townspeople did when they talked about how many men Javan killed. I heard one girl tell another, "Javan left Noah's tent and did not rest until her work was done, except to run the blades of her long sword and small scythe along a whetstone until they were so sharp, people bled from just the sight of them."

Knowing what I know now, of water hungry for sinners, I would rather say the blood on Javan's hands that day was piled only five lives high and not ten.

One of Javan's boys told her that the first of the three men she sought was in a flesh tent, and asked if he should kill him.

"No, leave him for me."

"He is as large as a donkey," the boy said. "He will not easily be killed."

"The bigger he is, the more breath he needs."

Javan, the boy, and two other boys hurried to the tent. The man was not the only one inside. Laughter, talk, and moaning came from all corners. "Show me where he is," Javan ordered the first boy.

He walked around to the back of the tent, and Javan followed. They soon heard the snoring of a man on his back.

The boys held the tent up as Javan went around to pull the stakes up and hack at the wooden poles that were all that was left to support it. The laughter inside stopped, along with the sounds of pleasure and exertion.

"Now," Javan said, and they brought the tent down over the man, who had stopped snoring and was trying to roll away. Javan used a club on the man's legs and torso.

"Whath duth you want?" the man cried through the goatskin pressing down on him. The other people had stumbled from the tent and were rushing away.

"Only your life," Javan said.

"I have things muth more valuable than thath," the man said. "I haf the bones of a great cat and a collection of human skullths."

"So do I," Javan said.

"You haf not seen my face," the man said. "Ith dishonorable to kill a man without first seeing hith face."

"You did not take the time to see your own child's face. Do you think yours is so much better?"

"None of those demonths were mine, but if they were, you would be wisth not to crosth me."

"It's not my aim to be wise," Javan said. And she smothered the man with the full weight of her body on the goatskin over his face.

The next man was at the bonfire, passing around a jug of wine. Javan sent one of her girls in to offer the man a good price on her comforts. The girl brought him to lie on his back in a ditch lined with sheep's wool. By this time Javan was tired of talking and she simply rolled a boulder onto the man's head.

The third roamed aimlessly, but Javan knew she would catch up with him. It was said she had eyes in her heart and a vengeance the strength of a hundred men in her hands. Even without these advantages, she would have found him. One of her boys saw him on the road leading out of town, struggling beneath the weight of the wine he had drunk and a limp little body slung over his shoulder.

Javan came alongside him. "You should be running," she said.

He looked at her. "I have paid a good price for your whores. Why should I flee from you?"

"Because I'm going to kill you. Show a little respect for my abilities."

He did. "The small young bones will make the best necklaces for your girls," he said, dropping the body. Then he started running. But Javan had slipped a rope through his belt, and she yanked the man toward herself and a dagger she held level with his back. As he died, he asked her, "Why do you care so much about little demons and so little for yourself?"

"I do not know," she said.

.   .   .

As legend of Javan's march grew, so did the stories of how she had come to be exiled.

"She took the intestines of one enemy and stuffed them into another."

"She killed thirty men and ate their hearts."

"She put so many heads on stakes that there were no trees left for a league in all directions."

Javan's march angered Noah more than all of the other transgressions of the townspeople combined.

I was saddened to see my husband distraught, yet I felt much safer after Javan's rampage. There was finally some sense of order, however cruel.

One night when Noah was complaining to the God of Adam about her, I interrupted. "Perhaps, my good husband, she is doing the best she can, just as you are."

He was kneeling on his sleeping blanket, mouth moving, eyes closed. He opened them. It looked as though there were little fires crackling inside him. "Doing her best to what?" he asked. He did not usually ask questions; likening his struggle to Javan's had roused him to anger. He waited for my response.

I came as close to a good answer as possible: "To avenge those who are too weak to avenge themselves. Is not this what the God of Adam does?"

He sat for a few breaths with the fires crackling madly in his eyes. Then he said, "I have already told you, only He can mete out justice."

"What is He doing now?"

Noah did not answer this question. Instead, he said, "The God of Adam doesn't need the help of a woman."

I was not so certain.

CHAPTER 12

NOAH'S SONS

Noah begot three sons: Shem, Ham, and Japheth.

GENESIS 6:10

My belly filled with three sons to make up for the ones Javan and I lost. Because I feared they would have stains upon their brows, I hid my belly beneath a huge tunic whenever I left the tent to relieve myself or go to the well. Only Javan was with me when I gave birth.

Shem was the first, the one who gave me a new name: Mother. But he did not want to do it. He held fast to my womb. It was not until eleven moons had passed that water suddenly gushed down my legs. Even then, as I squatted and had to bite my lip to keep from crying out, Shem clung to me.

Finally, Javan reached in and grabbed him. "The next one will be easier," she said. Which made me wonder how many children she had birthed and lost, or would have had I any strength left with which to wonder.

When Javan had bathed him and placed him at my breast, I closed my eyes, too afraid to look at his brow.

"He has a face like his father's, except hundreds of years younger and without the madness in his eyes."

I opened one eye just enough to peek at his brow. When I saw that it was smooth and unmarked, I cried with happiness.

He always wanted to be held and would cry whenever I set him down. I feared his cries might anger his father, so I held him even as I cleaned and cooked. I rarely squatted at my loom.

My womb was not as tight after Shem, and Japheth entered the world quickly, screaming with rage. I pulled him from Javan's arms and took a blanket to his brow. He too was unmarked.

We were deafened by his screaming as Javan bathed him. When she returned him to my arms, I hurried to silence him with my breast. Already he had a tooth poking up from the bottom of his mouth. I did not reveal this to anyone, not even Javan. I would not chance my son being thought a demon. As soon as he grew others, he bloodied my milk, and Shem would bunch his lips when I brought him to my breast. So I gave one breast always to Shem and the other always to Japheth.

Ham was born laughing. I could see this not by his mouth but by his eyes, which were crinkled with happiness. His cries did not pound as hard upon my ears as his brothers' did.

I was grateful that God sent the boys unmarked one by one, so that the people of Sorum could not argue that they were demon seed. Though if the townspeople had spent any time with them, they would have realized that they still had a case. The boys' cries shook the dates from the palms and caused the goats to bleat in sympathy or perhaps agony. The boys had the spirit of a large celebration or a small mob. It felt as though there were at least ten of them.

After Ham was born, if Noah and I accidentally made eye contact as we lay on our sleeping blankets, children screaming around us, we quickly rolled away from each other. *Three is enough,* I thought. *God has repaid His debt, the world is right again.* Or at least right enough to go on living.

And truth be told, in spite of my exhaustion, the boys delighted me. I felt pure joy as I looked at each son and saw his unmarked brow. *God has wiped my stain from future generations. It will die with me and leave no trace.*

I even loved my boys' endless games. Ham would tip over a pot of lentils, and when I went to gather these up, Japheth would hit his hand into his date juice so that it splashed Shem, who would roll back and forth on the ground making farting noises out of his mouth until I picked him up and pressed him to my leaking nipple. He was four, too old to be suckling, but there was nothing he loved more. This would not change much when he became a man, though the breasts he pressed himself against would not usually leak milk.

Though I missed my father, and regretted that he would not get to see my boys, my first years as a mother were full of joy. I never tired of tickling my sons' bellies. We slept little and laughed often. At least the boys and I laughed often. Even when Shem was four, Japheth was three, and Ham was two, Noah would come home from tending the goats or riding through town and stand in the entryway to the tent with his shadow cast long before him, onto the overturned pots, lentils, millet, fruits, nuts, and wool scattered over the ground. He waited for the children to be quiet.

But it was not in their nature to be quiet.

One afternoon Noah gave up on waiting for silence. I had been holding Japheth, which caused Shem to scream and cry until I put Japheth on the ground and picked Shem up. Then Japheth started to cry, but his cries were not as piercing as Shem's, so I left him where he was. "The God of Adam has given you much to be grateful for," Noah told us, flinging his arms out to the sides. Ham was taken with the shadow's movements and reached for the darkness one of Noah's long hands cast upon the ground. "Let us pause and give thanks to Him." He bowed his head.

Japheth watched Noah, his tears drying and cries going silent. Already I could see he was going to be astonishingly handsome. He had big yellow-flecked brown eyes with which he watched Noah. He was the only one who ever took an interest in Noah's sermons. His brothers continued the activities of their day—rolling around, throwing things, cooing, and suckling.

I watched all of them with insatiable eyes. Outside were the cries of men in pain and sinners in love. Women yelled, children shrieked, and fires raged. My nipples were raw, my loom lay bare. Yet I was never so happy in all my life.

CHAPTER 43

HAM

Though I tried to stop them, my sons got older. They did not like being confined to the tent. They wouldn't play Knock Over the Pot or Splash the Juice with me no matter how many times I turned my back to give them the opportunity. Their lack of interest in dirtying the tent space must have been a relief for Noah; his sight was growing weaker, and sometimes he walked with his staff swinging across the ground in front of him. I stopped cooking in the tent because I was afraid he might stumble into a pot of hot stew. Poor Noah. It seemed to me that I alone got to enjoy seeing our sons' first smiles and watching them learn to walk.

But I worried. Once I had sons, I had sons to lose. If Jank ever made good on his long-ago threat to warn the world of my mark, a fire might be built not only for me but also for them. I kept my head scarf on at every position of the sun. At night I tried not to toss upon my sleeping blanket for fear the scarf would come loose.

Whenever my sons pulled on it, I hurried to make sure it had not moved enough from my brow that they could see the stain. Perhaps they saw it anyway but did not know it was worthy of their attention until one day when Ham returned from sneaking off to town.

He came to stare at me. I was making stew, and at first I thought he was only hungry. "You should not have sneaked into town if you wanted supper tonight," I told him. I did not like for my boys to stray far from the tent.

"Is the mark upon your brow really from a demon's paw?"

Twelve whole years had passed since I first rode into town and the little boy yanked upon my scarf. And still the one-handed girl's long-ago shout of "demon woman" had not yet gone silent among my neighbors?

I let go of the spoon I was stirring our stew with, grabbed Ham by the shoulders, and squeezed. "*Never* speak of it. Not even when you are alone." I could not help imagining his little eight-year-old body being carried away by a mob screaming of demons. "Neither should you even *think* of it."

"But Mother, where is the demon now? I want a mark too."

"Who told you the mark was from a demon?"

"I will tell you if you tell me where the demon is now."

I pushed him into the tent and called Shem and Japheth to follow. When they were all squatting upon the ground looking up at me, I untied the scarf and let it fall to the ground. Their eyes fastened upon the stain.

"For this the world has shunned me. All but my father, Noah, and Javan. I almost lost my life because of it, and I might still."

"Cannot the demon who put it there defend you?" Ham asked.

He would get himself in trouble, and his brothers too. I remembered the three boys who had come from their mother all at once. I saw the crushed skull, the glassy eyes, the blood. I shook my head to expel these visions, but they would not be moved. Instead, the dead babies took on the faces of my sons.

"Cannot the demon who put it th—"

"Boy," I yelled at Ham, "there is no demon but you!"

"What about Japheth?"

I stood silent and trembling until my rage had washed through me. "Forgive me, Ham. You are no demon."

I looked at each of them. Shem, with his big adoring eyes; my scowling second son, Japheth; and Ham, who exhausted me and also caused me to smile and laugh more than anyone else. "You are the greatest blessings I have ever received. I want to be a mother to you, and to be a mother to you for a long time to come, so you must be quiet and listen."

"When will you answer my questions?" Ham asked.

"I will tell you all you need to know, and what you need to know is only this: If the people of the town know for certain that there is a mark upon my brow, I will be burned alive."

Six eyes widened, and no one spoke. Ham opened his mouth, then closed it.

I did not tell them that they too might be burned, but perhaps they knew this. I did not hear them speak of my mark again.

. . .

By the time Ham was ten, my boys had taken to wrestling beneath the trees for many positions of the sun. Ham was easily held down in a wrestling match. Perhaps this is why he became more of a talker, and why the things he said were not always kind. He used his tongue to keep his older brothers from pummeling him, or worse, giving him lesser parts to play in their games.

"You will play the dead man," Shem told Ham one afternoon, "and Japheth and I will fight for your teeth."

"Why must I be the dead man?" Ham asked.

"Do as you're told," Japheth barked. "I could beat you black and blue without causing a single drop of sweat to form upon my brow."

"But Japheth! That would be as close as you have come to washing in many moons!"

I was watching from the tent window, as I often did since Ham had returned from town speaking of my mark. Whenever they started away, I secured my head scarf over my brow and chased them. Giving birth had left me with stiffness in my right hip, and when I ran after them, my joints creaked. This embarrassed them so much that they usually turned around. Also, they had surely not forgotten my mark and the danger I would face if it were discovered. That year a baby with a stain over half her face had been fed to a huge fire. It was said that the flames were red but that they spat thick green blood for twenty cubits in all directions. My sons did not like for me to stray from the tent any more than I liked for them to do so.

As I watched Japheth and Ham argue from the tent window, I saw Japheth make a fist. Japheth punched Ham in the face often enough that I studied Ham's nose daily to make sure it was not crooked.

I ran from the tent. Though I was not as strong as I had been before giving birth, I pushed between my boys quickly enough to stop Japheth's fist from flying. Despite his rage, I knew he would not risk harming me.

"Why do you always take up his cause?" he asked.

"Do not threaten to beat your brother again."

He turned his head to spit upon the ground beside us before unballing his fist and walking away.

"One day you will get yourself a broken nose," I told Ham. He started to open his mouth, so I clasped my palm over it to keep him from replying. The edges of his smile peeked around my hand.

Ham used his tongue on the rest of us as well. Of my stew, he said, "What creature's afterbirth is this?"

Of his father, he said, "He looks like a man who has just stepped in donkey dung." I was glad he did not say this when Noah was near.

To Herai, whom he adored, he said, "I do not know what makes you so slow, but it surely does!"

I could not bring myself to punish him. I loved Ham so much that every time I looked at him, my heart swelled. How had such a delightful child come from *me*, a marked and nameless girl? Ham made each day feel like a festive occasion, which must have bothered Noah even more than Ham's insults. Ham interfered with the spell of gloom Noah tried to cast over us.

CHAPTER 14

HERAI AND MY SONS

"It is a sad day on God's Earth when His creatures have forgotten their Maker," Noah said one evening as he entered the tent. Herai was helping me mend tears in the boys' tunics, and she did not look up. Only Japheth listened respectfully. He was fourteen years old. "The town has become so densely packed with prostitutes that the contagion has spread to the peoples of the surrounding towns. God cannot set His gaze down anywhere among us without getting man's filth in His eyes."

In mock outrage, Ham cried, "The town is knee-deep in man's rash-infected seed!"

This delighted Herai, who let out a loud wailing sound—her laugh—which I was sure Noah could hear. I suspected the reason that Ham loved to make Herai laugh was that the sound was loud and strange. People for a hundred cubits in any direction could hear it and know Ham had made a joke.

Noah narrowed his eyes. He also knew that Ham had made a joke.

I rushed over to Ham, held one hand against his cheek, and slapped it loudly with the other. Noah could not see well enough to know that I was not really slapping the boy. I often pretended to slap Ham to prevent Noah from actually doing so.

When I did this, Herai smiled and clapped her own hands together, causing Ham to burst into laughter.

"*Boy!*" Noah said. "The Lord can hear you. Your mouth is dirtier than a flesh tent. Take care you do not end up numbered among the wicked."

Noah did not chastise Herai. He considered her to be beyond the reach of salvation. At over twenty years of age, she was neither married nor a prostitute. She was the only woman my sons knew besides Javan and me. Her breasts were as large as her mother's but did not sag. Her face, though flatter than most, was pleasingly round, and she had a trusting nature. I was sure that if it weren't for Javan, Herai would not be safe from men. I often caught Shem looking at her. I feared that one day two of my sons would desire her, and their desire would tear our family apart.

CHAPTER 45

HUMBLED

Noah did not seem to notice our sons growing to manhood. He thought only of the sinners, who continued to sin loudly and long into each morning. When Noah was not riding through town at night, instructing them to turn their eyes to the Lord and mend their ways, he was tossing and turning upon his sleeping blanket. He was exhausted but often could not sleep.

Occasionally, I placed my hand upon his back to comfort him. He was too tired to be surprised by this. A couple of times it seemed as though he wanted to say something to me. His gaze started to move toward my eyes but then wandered back to the ground or up to the heavens.

I told myself he did not say what was on his mind because his voice was hoarse from yelling at the sinners. But I did not really believe it. He trusted no one but his God, and perhaps not even Him. As for his faith in himself, it was dwindling.

One morning he returned from riding through town and fell heavily upon his sleeping blanket. "Lord," he cried, "I am utterly humbled by this task."

CHAPTER 46

SHEM

Though Shem had been clingy as a child, as a teenager, he was sometimes a mystery to me. He would sneak away too quickly for me to notice and run after him.

Early one morning I woke up with Noah sleeping fitfully beside me and Ham and Japheth fast asleep on my other side. Shem's sleeping blanket lay bare. Beside it were his club and his sword but not his dagger.

Ham also had a dagger, and Japheth a sword that prevented him from squatting with the rest of us when we gathered around the cookfire for lentils and goat meat. Shem could not choose between several weapons, so he had three. My boys were never without their weapons.

As much as I feared that someone would pull off my scarf and call me a demon woman, having children sometimes left me no choice but to go into town. I pulled my tunic over my sleeping garment, secured my head scarf, and picked up Shem's club.

I noticed the vultures circling overhead as I followed the footprints from Shem's sandals. Once I got to the flesh tents, the footprints disappeared. There were too many tracks to separate them. Raucous laughter and yelling made it hard for me to hear my own thoughts.

"We have been waiting for you," a voice called out from one of the tents. I turned to stare into the kohl-ringed eyes of a woman who once was a beautiful girl. The patch of hair had long since grown back, but she was not half so beautiful as she had been when it was missing. Javan kept the difficult women and girls drunk, and there was a mean set to this one's mouth that she could not hide with a playful voice. I did not know if she recognized me or if she said the same thing to everyone who passed.

I quickened my pace, angry at Shem for leading me into the sinners. There was nothing but flesh tents and drunks stumbling in and out of them.

And then I saw him. "Shem!" I called. He was coming toward me down the road but had not seen me because he was staring at one of the tents. "*Shem!*"

He looked horrified to see me. "Mother!" He glanced nervously at my head scarf. "What are you doing?"

"What does it appear I am doing?"

"You did not need to come looking for me. I could not sleep, so I took a walk."

"Why did you walk in this direction instead of the opposite one?"

"I did not want to come upon any wild animals west of Father's tent." I let the silence work on him a few breaths. "Mother, do not worry."

That seemed to be all I would get out of him. I turned toward home. He looked back over his shoulder when he thought I could not see him. But I could, out of the corner of my eye. What was he gazing at? There was nothing for many cubits in all directions that he should have an interest in.

"Hurry. We must be home before your father wakes."

He smoothed his hair with one hand. Was it disheveled from tossing and turning upon his own sleeping blanket, or someone else's?

"Yes, Mother."

It was not only for fear of someone seeing my mark that I wanted to hasten our steps. I could not help hearing the voices that called from the tents as we walked away. Coy, beckoning voices. Calling my son's name.

CHAPTER 17

JAVAN'S PROPOSAL

Javan sometimes stopped by with wine and lewd remarks. "You grow more handsome each day," she told Shem. "Soon you will not be able to walk down the road without girls throwing themselves upon their backs in front of you."

Shem looked at the ground as though he had dropped something precious there. He was not modest, so it did not seem a good sign that Javan's remarks humbled him.

"Best to marry him off before he gets into trouble," she said to me.

It would have pleased me greatly for Herai to marry one of my sons. I cherished her company, and I wanted to make sure she would be safe even if something happened to Javan. But Noah would not allow it—not only because Herai was slow but because he had decided that Javan was a demon. "What mere woman could kill so many people, including men who are stronger than she?" he asked.

"What man can live for over five hundred years?"

Fearing the back of his hand, I stepped away from him. But though his lips trembled with rage, he did not strike me. In fact, he had never struck me. He said only, "The God of Adam has given me each of those years."

Perhaps He has given Javan her strength as well.

Noah was never within the tent when Javan came over, so I was left the task of telling her that Herai could not marry into our family.

This was not easy. When Javan was not jovial, the sight of her face quickened my pulse. She had a bump on her nose from where it had been broken the night we tried to save the three sons of the one-handed girl. She had never been able to straighten it all the way, and so it sat slightly crooked upon her face—not enough to look comical and not so little as to escape notice. What once was a gash running from her brow to her chin had turned into a scar. Yet somehow she had survived to become the oldest woman for leagues in all directions.

Our matriarch.

I often wondered about the X upon her forehead. Perhaps she had taken a heavy hand to someone. Rare was the man who was able to escape quickly enough to enjoy a girl's comforts for free. If a man bruised a girl's face or bloodied her nose, Javan sent out boys with spears. "The girls are mine," she told the men who came to her flesh tents. "Treat them accordingly."

Her girls did not elude her heavy hand either. She poured strong wine down the throats of any who became picky about which men they would lie with. And those who let themselves become undesirable suffered any number of insults and threats. I often heard her screaming from her flesh tents, "No wonder men never come to you more than once! What is this? *Is it your face?* I can hardly tell for all the dirt! Wash it, or I will use my fists to fashion you a new one."

. . .

One day Javan and I watched Herai as she stood beneath a tree Ham was climbing. Herai held her hands out for fruit. "Ripe for bearing sons," Javan said. "Look at her breasts, so full of milk. If childbirth undammed her nipples, she could suckle a whole village."

I had already planned what I would say, but my excuse sounded false even to my own ear. "She is too old, Javan."

"Let her and Shem lie together, and Herai will grow fat with Noah's grandson. Then she and Shem can be married."

"Noah has decreed that two who are unmarried should not lie together. A son must obey the word of his father."

"Instead of his mother? Was Noah nearly ripped apart getting this son out into the world? Did he suckle the child and wipe his backside?"

I didn't answer. But her words stayed with me that night when I could not sleep. It was I who had cared for our sons while Noah thought only of his God and the sinners. Noah did not even show any interest in Japheth, who wanted so badly to be as righteous as his father. The boys were more mine than Noah's.

The next day Javan brought over a thin tube of clay. "So that they do not need to lie together. Shem can spill his seed, and it can be sucked up into this. Then it can be blown into Herai. I will do all of this."

Though she did not laugh or smile, I knew she mocked me. My anger at her, Noah, and most of all myself overtook my fear of her. "The child she would bear might be slow, and this is why they cannot marry."

"What's so good about being quick?" Javan demanded so swiftly that I knew the question had been sitting on her tongue, waiting to leap off. "For instance, I am quick, and so it is dangerous to be within arm's reach of me." She came so close that her hot, sour breath entered my mouth. "If you displease me." She balled my tunic in her hand, tighter and tighter until I could not help but stumble into her solid, immovable bulk, which stopped me as completely as if I had run into a tree. For some reason, I was not afraid. My heart ached for her, Herai, and even myself.

"I am sorry," I said.

"Do not apologize to *me*," she replied, and looked out to where Herai stood by our trees. Herai was laughing like a strange and charming girl who had taken the form of a woman. "Noah might be wise in many things, but not about my daughter. She is more pure than Shem." Javan returned her gaze to my face. "You know this is true."

"Yes," I said, "I do."

That night I tried to sway Noah. "Herai is the only pure girl in all of Sorum. The God of Adam must be watching over her."

"She is not as sinful as most," Noah said.

This encouraged me to press further. "In what way has she sinned even the slightest bit?"

"She is the daughter of Javan."

"Is that all?"

"That is a lot."

"But what of how Javan has helped the one-handed girl, the one who bore three sons at once?"

Javan had tried to sell the girl's comforts. But word of the three demons had spread for leagues in all directions, and Javan could not entice anyone to lie with the girl. So she had offered wine and bones to the first three men who were willing to have the girl, in order to prove she was not a demon. One man died in battle soon afterward; one was killed by his son, who was yet a boy; the other moved on, and no one knew what happened to him. All of these things were commonplace in Sorum, but they did not bode well for the girl's prospects. Javan finally told the girl, "You will be better off where no one knows you," and traded her for dried goat meat and cosmetics—kohl for her girls' eyes and olive oil for their hair.

"What has become of you, woman, to say something so wicked?" Noah demanded. "Javan made the girl a prostitute. She and the girl are both corrupt in the eyes of the Lord and in the eyes of all good people."

"Of which good people do you speak?"

He flinched as if I had struck him. He said only, "Javan sold the girl's virtue and then sold the girl. The God of Adam will punish them both, and Herai as well."

"What will He do to them?"

"I do not know, but He will do it soon. He will not let this evil go on much longer."

CHAPTER 48

MUTTERING

Noah's eyes grew heavy with sadness. New wrinkles formed in the wrinkles already dividing his face into a hundred small parts. His footsteps slowed, and one day I realized he did not walk but shuffle.

He did not speak to me of his sadness. He moved back and forth in the tent, his gaze dragging along the ground or looking to the heavens, not noticing anything around him. I do not even think he saw my sons and me.

"Husband," I said one day, "you are brought lower each year. You do not sleep, and the corners of your mouth draw your face down. I am your wife. Will you not unburden yourself to me?"

He did not answer.

"Hus—"

"My duty is fastened upon my back no less than my own skin. I cannot set it down."

But husband, unlike your skin, you stumble beneath your duty. I am afraid you will fall and find that you are unable to get up again.

It was too late to say anything; he was gone. I stared at the tent flap, watching it sway back and forth and finally go still. Then I stared at the empty space where he had been. Everything blurred until I did not see our stores of food, the loom, our sleeping blankets, knives, spoons, rugs.

I thought, *This is what it is like to be him.*

There are many things I would have told him if he had let me:

You have taken on a burden no lone man could carry.

Look instead to your sons. Are the words you waste on the sinners not better suited to them? Take the sharpness from your voice, and bestow your wisdom upon your own flesh and blood. My own flesh and blood.

I knew there would be no use in saying these things to Noah. He listened only to the God of Adam.

. . .

He returned later and later from town each afternoon for supper. His stew often grew cold in front of him while he muttered to the heavens.

One night his bowl shook in his hands, steam seeming to follow his gaze upward. "They sin morning to night and night into morning. I have not words enough to convince them, and all I have are words."

I watched with our sons while Noah rocked back and forth upon his feet, slopping his stew over the edges of his bowl. Shem was the least troubled by Noah's rants. He continued to slurp his stew and look off toward town, hardly thinking of Noah, just as Noah hardly thought of him.

"My eyes are worn from all they have seen," Noah muttered. "I feel I can look no more, yet still I go to them." Suddenly, he threw his bowl onto the ground, splattering stew onto his sandals. "I did not ask to be the one to convince them of You. Perhaps you have chosen the wrong man."

Yes, husband! I thought. *Surrender this impossible duty, and do what I cannot—show our sons how to be men.*

"Is not there someone cleverer?" he continued. "Someone with a voice that could find its way to their souls?"

"No, Father," Japheth whispered through trembling lips. "There is no one above you."

But Noah did not hear his son over his despair.

His despair did not let up for any part of the night. Sometimes I felt the air swish past, and I knew he was waving his arms around, much more alive than anyone should be in the dead of night. I had to roll off my sleeping blanket, away from him, to avoid his flailing. "They think me a madman. They laugh at my donkey, they laugh at my words, they laugh at my face. I thought one day their laughter might end. But each generation laughs louder."

I wanted to reach my hand out to him, but I was afraid of his flailing limbs.

"They are full of evil, every one. Not a man, woman, nor child has heeded my words."

What of our middle son, husband? I did not speak aloud. Noah probably would not hear me, and I was afraid of what he would say if he did. Our sons did not concern him.

.   .   .

In the morning he did not eat his porridge.

"Each day I learn the same lesson—I am of no use. You have given me only one task. And in that I have failed."

"Husband, you will grow weak. Please, you must eat."

He stood and walked away, yet still I heard him:

"You have given me many powers—the power to easily make fire, to live hundreds of years, to go unscathed through a mob. But I would trade any of them, or what is left of my sight, or even, Lord, my sons, for the one power I most desire. The power to convince them of You."

.   .   .

One day he finally gave up. He was certain that he had done all he could on his own to sway the sinners, and He called upon God to do what he could not.

"If You would somehow fill them with awe at Your power, surely then I could lead them to righteousness. Please, *show them a sign.*"

I wondered how the God of Adam might do this. Turn a raven into a dove, a cloud into a star, wind into sunlight?

Though Noah pleaded for a few moons, God did not show the

sinners a sign. Noah began muttering not only to God but also to himself. "The Lord has given up on them. Only I can hold on to His faith in His creation. I can do nothing wrong. *Nothing.* Or He will give up on us all."

A couple of times he whipped around while he shuffled through the tent, as though looking for someone. "Can I ever talk only to myself, or am I always talking to God? *Who am I speaking to now?*"

"Please, husband, will not you squat and have some goat's milk and barley cakes, or recline and let me rub your feet?"

"They have not listened," he cried. A vein pulsed in his brow. "*I will plead for them no longer!*"

He stopped riding through town yelling at the sinners. He sat beneath the date tree with his donkey, ear cocked to the sky as if listening for something.

One morning he leaned his head all the way back against the rough bark of the tree and tilted his face to the heavens. Tears streamed down his face. "Very well, Lord," he said. "It is settled. I will prepare."

. . .

That night I dreamt of him as he was that day, his face tilted to the heavens, tears flowing from his eyes. In my dream, the tears puddled around him, and the puddles grew into a shallow pond. He began to cry harder, and the pond spread beyond the reach of his arms and then rose.

I felt it lapping at my toes from where I stood and watched it rise over his legs.

Now the tears did not so much flow as pour out of his eyes. The pond became a lake. It whipped back up at his chest. I looked to either side of him and could see no end to them; they stretched out over the desert in all directions.

I gazed down and watched my ankles, then my knees, disappear into them.

He must stop crying.

"Husband!" I started toward him, but the sea was heavy and held tightly to my legs. *"Husband!"* The sea rose over his beard to his lips, and still he cried. I called out to him again and again. I begged him to stop crying.

But he did not stop crying, he did not stand up, and he did not float.

CHAPTER 19

DAUGHTERS-IN-LAW

The following day Noah told me, "I am going away. I will be back by the next moon."

"Where will you go?"

"Wherever the God of Adam commands me."

While I was glad to think of the sleep my sons and I might get with Noah away, I did not like to think of him riding aimlessly, waiting for God's command. Yet he did not seem aimless. His voice had none of the uncertainty I had grown accustomed to. He was resolute. He did not look around; he looked only where he intended to go.

Still I worried. What if the God of Adam did not keep up His vigil over Noah? Though I did not always like my husband—in fact, I rarely liked him—I could not help but love him. He had taken a marked woman for a wife and given her a home and three sons.

I gathered together provisions for him while he readied the same donkey we had ridden across the delta eighteen years before. The animal was even lazier and more densely covered in flies. He had outlived many people of the town. He was over a hundred years old.

"Perhaps you should seek out a younger animal," I suggested.

"The Lord will leave the animal here on earth for me to use as long as I live."

"If that is so, husband, I fear you do not have much longer."

"Hush."

One of the vultures circling above screeched. *Is my sight warped by fear, or are they flying lower than usual?* "Don't go," I said.

"Be righteous, wife. See to the uprightness of our sons."

The donkey was on his feet but would not move. He might have guessed at the journey to come by the weight of the saddlebags. He hung his head as if praying.

"Please, husband."

"The sooner I go, the sooner I return."

As if the animal understood Noah's words, he began walking.

. . .

That evening Javan appeared at the tent's door flap. "Where is he?"

I did not reply at once.

"Where's Noah?" she asked.

"On a mission from the God of Adam."

"He has gone to find a wife for Shem, hasn't he? It is too late for Herai."

I was afraid that what Javan said was true. I did not wish for my sons to take wives and leave our tent.

"She is more suited to Japheth, anyway," Javan said. "He is a handsome one, with all those little points of light in his brown eyes. He should have a good woman by his side, and a mother-in-law who makes grown men tremble with fear. Otherwise, some man might think to have your son for himself."

Ham came up behind Javan and hit her lightly on the backside. Without looking, she grabbed his wrist, then turned around to twist his arm so that he fell to his knees.

"Hello, beautiful," Ham said. "Good to see you."

She released his wrist. "You will never know how good it is to see me," she said, "because I am too old to show you."

"What is the rough spot that nearly cut my hand on your rump, if not a ground sore from all the time spent on your back?"

He was flattering her. I doubted any man had wanted to climb on top of her since she fought for the three boys who were born all at once. She was too scarred.

"Take a closer look," she said, grabbing Ham's head and pressing it toward her flank. "See how old it is."

"Please!" I rushed forward, thinking of Noah's command to take care of the uprightness of our sons—a cruel task to have given me. It would have taken at least three of me to keep our boys out of trouble.

Javan let go of Ham. As she often did, she went from jesting to serious in less than a breath. "I have come to tell you I'm gathering a dowry," she told me. "Our families will make a lucky match."

"If Herai's luck gets her Shem or Japheth for a husband," Ham said, "I cannot think of anyone luckier. Except perhaps all those who have died of plague."

"Dip your tongue in dung," Javan said. "Herai and I *are* lucky—her to be a virgin and me to be alive. If we merge my families' luck with yours, the offspring will be more powerful than any who have come before."

"Herai is too good for either of my brothers." He said it without his usual playfulness.

"For Shem, perhaps," Javan said. "She will marry Japheth."

"Japheth?" Ham said. "She would be better off marrying my father's donkey. He is less haughty and attracts fewer flies."

"Japheth has the musk of a man," Javan said. "It is fortunate that so far it has attracted only flies and not other men."

"The only man Japheth cares for is Father," Ham said. "In fact, the only person he cares for at all is Father."

"Do not worry, son. Herai is not going to marry Japheth."

"You will change your mind when you see the dowry," Javan said.

"I am just a woman, and a nameless one at that," I said, unable to keep the anger from my voice. "It is not my mind that matters."

Javan came to stand so close to me that the pink gash running the length of her face was not more than a hand's width from my nose. "You can wait for a name," she said, "or make one for yourself."

Make one for myself? This had never occurred to me. I wanted a name almost as badly as I wanted the mark to disappear from my brow. And there was no one I would rather have as a daughter-in-law than Herai. But could I marry a son off without Noah's blessing?

"Perhaps you do not have the courage," Javan said. She spat on the ground near my feet. "I will need some sustenance for my journey back into town."

I hurried to get Javan some dried goat meat—something she could take with her. I wished for her to leave before she filled me with any more silly ideas.

"Good-bye," I said as I placed the meat into her greedy hands.

Half a moon later, I awakened to sounds of stamping and snorting. I got up and lifted the door flap. No fewer than five donkeys stood roped together in the road. My boys came up behind me. I stepped out of the tent, and they followed.

Now I could see that they were not donkeys but mules. Herai was stroking the muzzle of the first one.

"Herai's dowry," Javan announced.

"Mother?" Shem said. I turned around to look at him. He was staring steadily at the ground, and I knew he was going to say something I did not want to hear. "I cannot marry Herai. I am already married."

"No," I said as if I could keep it from being true. "No, you are not."

"A mistake, but it cannot be undone," he said. Then he buried his head in his hands.

This angered me as much as the fact that he had done something so stupid in the first place. I grabbed his hands and tore them from his face. It was trouble of his own making, and he would have to face it.

"It was a mistake, indeed," Javan said. "You have ruined Ona and must buy her from me now. She says she is with child."

Upon hearing this news, I did something I had never done before: I smacked my son hard across the face. "Your father has gone to fetch you a wife. How will you afford more than one?"

"These mules . . ." Shem said. He started to cry.

"Has she any family?" I asked Javan.

"Ona's mother is a whore with almond-colored eyes that she no longer bothers to ring with kohl. She is the one whose beauty stilled my sword when I traveled through town avenging the three boys born all at once. I could not waste the girl's value on death. Yet her value was as fleeting as a shadow at dusk. There is not a drop of sweetness on her tongue, and she does not fear my fists. No man will suffer her insults more than once. Her daughter is even more beautiful and now even more worthless."

I turned again to Shem, and he stumbled back. "Your father will punish us both for this. Get the girl and bring her here for me to look at. We will bathe her and make sure she holds her tongue tighter than"—I was thinking of Javan and Ham—"some."

Javan turned her attention to Japheth and pointed toward Herai. "This girl is already clean, and she comes with five mules."

"What will we do with five mules?" Japheth asked. "And what will I do with a slow girl too old to bear me many sons?"

"You will figure out what to do with a girl as quickly as any man does," Javan said. "Though perhaps not as quickly as your brother."

"I do not want her," Japheth said. "Even if her father were a good man—which he is not, for he laid with *you*—she would still be half evil."

"Then what is your brother? Is he not also evil for impregnating one of my hardest-working whores? I admire the strength of his seed in overcoming the herbs the girl was given, but he has cost me enough goods to supply a small army."

"She is not your whore," Shem said. But he did not say it with much conviction.

"Then whose is she?" Javan asked.

"If she is so hardworking, then how do you know the child is Shem's?" I demanded.

"Ona *used* to be hardworking. But for the past few moons, Shem has come to her almost every day, and she threatens to cut her face when I bring another man to her. Her face is even more valuable to me than her body. Men come from many leagues in all directions to see it."

Japheth sneered, and I feared Ham would say something cruel. But no one said anything; to the east, a spot on the horizon was slowly coming closer. So slowly that I knew it must be Noah on his donkey.

"I will sell these mules in five days," Javan threatened.

No one responded. My boys and I were straining to see if Noah had anyone with him. I did not take my eyes off of him, even when I heard Javan hitting the mules' flanks, followed by the heavy *clomp-clomp-clomp* of their hooves against the ground.

"You see how well trained they are," she called. I glanced around to look for Herai and was sorry to see her leaving with her mother.

Though perhaps it was best that she did not stay to witness Noah's fury when I told him of Shem's new wife. If I were going to insist that Noah allow one of our sons to marry Herai, this was not a good way to begin.

Shem alternated putting his head in his hands with looking up in despair. Perhaps that made it seem to him as if Noah were approaching at a decent pace. I no longer had the heart to deny him this indulgence. I secured my head scarf and started walking out to meet Noah. Japheth and Ham followed.

From the slight angle at which I approached, I could see a little leg behind Noah's. "The good Lord has provided," Noah said. His voice contained the same certainty as when he had set out on his journey.

"Provided what?" Ham asked him.

"First son's wife."

The little leg belonged to a little girl. She was short, or perhaps she looked that way because she was hunched over. And unless her dowry were small enough to fit in a saddlebag, there wasn't one.

"How old?" Ham asked.

The girl did not wait for Noah to answer. "Twelve!" she said. Her voice was not that of a girl. As they got closer, I could see that her face wasn't either. She was perhaps the oldest woman I had ever seen.

"Husband," I said. "I must speak with you."

"Speak."

"*Alone*, please, husband."

"When we are home," he said.

133

What felt like a whole moon later, yet before the donkey came to a stop, the little woman started to struggle down from the animal's back. She did not look like she had enjoyed many meals lately. Her skin was slack not only from age but also from the lack of flesh inside it. "Let me help you, Father," she said to Noah.

But for him, it was no great distance to the ground, and he stepped off easily. He was tired and hungry and seemed to have forgotten that I wanted to talk to him.

After I prepared a stew, we squatted around the cookfire to eat it. My sons and I stared at the little woman crouched next to Shem. Her name was Leah. She ate large amounts and somehow managed to smile as she did so.

"Let us retire before the sun does," Noah said. "First wife and I are tired from our travels."

Seeing that I was not going to be alone with Noah, I asked him, "Husband, where will Leah sleep?"

"On Shem's sleeping blanket."

"Where will Shem sleep?"

"He will sleep on his blankets as well."

"Father," Shem said, "I must speak to you."

"Tomorrow."

"I do not think it can wait."

"Son, cannot you see that I am tired?"

. . .

I left the cookfire burning bright and tied the window's goatskin covering off to the side; I didn't want to leave Shem and Leah in the dark together. On my sleeping blanket, I did not shut my eyes. I kept raising myself upon my elbow to peer over Ham and Japheth at Shem.

Shem was on his side facing me, with Leah behind him. Her withered hand was draped, unmoving, over Shem's neck. Shem stared back at me with horror-filled eyes.

"Mother," Ham said, "I cannot sleep with your goat's breath hanging over my head like a stink cloud."

Japheth slammed his palm on the ground and sat up. "Father! Father, *wake up*! Shem has impregnated a whore and now lies next to another woman!"

Noah stirred and opened one eye.

"I am sorry, Father!" Shem said. "I do not know how it happened."

Ham laughed.

Noah opened his other eye. Both were wide with fear as he sat up. "Be quiet, or God will hear you!" He seemed more scared than angry. I would have thought I'd be happy to know that he was capable of feeling something besides anger and righteousness, but the fear in his voice rushed into my heart. He glanced around as if someone might be sneaking up on us. "Middle son will marry Leah. We will not speak of any of this again."

"Husband," I said quietly, "there is much to discuss."

I looked back at Leah. She was sitting up behind Shem, but at

Noah's words, she rose and stepped over Shem. I held Shem's gaze so that he would not glance upward as she crossed over him.

"Husband," Leah said in greeting as she lowered herself down behind Japheth, bracing her hand against his shoulder. He didn't respond. Perhaps he was thinking that five mules would not have been such a horrible dowry.

Noah laid his head down again, said, "Sleep well," and closed his eyes.

I stared at him until he opened one eye. "Good night, husband," I said. "We will speak tomorrow."

. . .

In the morning we were all more exhausted than we had been the night before. This was when Noah announced that the world was ending.

"The people have not heeded my words," he said. "They have neither changed their ways nor repented of their sins."

We were crouched around the cookfire, eating millet porridge and barley cakes. As his words were no great revelation to us, we continued to slurp and chew. Noah must have realized he needed to speak more plainly. "The Lord has seen man's wickedness on earth and has decided to destroy him."

Was this what Noah had been speaking of the night before he went to find a wife for Shem, when he had leaned his head back against the date tree, raised his face to the heavens, and said, "Then it is settled"? Perhaps he truly had gone mad.

"*Which* man?" Shem asked anxiously.

"All men, my son. The sky will rain down on us with all God's fury for forty days and forty nights. We must make an ark of gopher wood, covered inside and out with pitch, so that we alone may be spared."

"You need some rest, my good husband," I said. "You have had a long journey and are overtired."

"We cannot rest. There is not time."

No one moved except Leah, who set down her bowl.

"Where will we go?" Japheth finally asked.

"Wherever the Lord chooses for us to go."

"How big is this ark?"

"Three hundred cubits long, fifty across, and thirty high."

Ham laughed. No one else joined in.

"How will we carry it to the sea?" Japheth asked.

"God will gather up all of the seas into His arms and rain them down over the whole Earth."

In the silence that followed, I aged many years. Finally, Ham said, "I think I will take my chances here on land, Father."

"There will be no land other than that below the great depths of the sea."

"Husband, what of *our* land and our herd?"

"After the sea washes away everyone else, we will have all the land in the world."

All the land in the world.

"How big is the world?" Japheth asked.

I had never wondered before, though now that Japheth asked, I needed to know. I felt I could not breathe until I did.

Noah would neither lie nor admit that he did not know. We sat in silence until he said, "First son, bring your wife to me." He turned to Ham. "In my travels, I have found a wife for you as well. She will arrive within a few days."

Leah had looked shocked about the end of the world, but as Noah spoke, her thin lips pulled taut around a toothless grin. I feared who Noah had chosen for Ham.

"She needn't," Ham told Noah. "I will find my own wife."

"It is already done," Noah said.

. . .

Shem wasted no time in setting off for town. I doubted he would hasten back. Even Japheth did not hurry to help his father. Out of the corners of my eyes, I watched Noah squatting in the dirt, drawing with a stick. He was drawing the ark that we did not have tools or timber to build. Leah lay nearby. She had fallen asleep on the patch of ground where she'd eaten.

"I need a better wife," Japheth said quietly.

"We will speak to your father after he has gotten some rest," I said.

I went in to clean the tent. As I swept around the sleeping blankets, Ham came to stand beside me. "Mother," he said, gesturing toward where Noah squatted outside the tent, "I think we have lost him."

I hoped it was only Noah we had lost. I could withstand losing a husband but not a son.

That night Shem did not return. After Noah, Japheth, Leah,

Ham, and I laid our heads down on our sleeping blankets, I felt a hand upon my shoulder. I recognized the inadvertent roughness of the touch. "Yes, husband?"

"First son."

"He must be having trouble finding his wife."

"He must repent, or we cannot take him with us."

"He said he was sorry."

"Yet where is he now?"

"Finding—"

"He must repent."

Noah rolled away. My heart started to race, and I could not force my eyes to close.

In the middle of the night, I heard shuffling, and I rejoiced that Shem had returned. *Thank you, God of Adam and all other gods!* But the shuffling moved off the sleeping blankets, and I knew it was not Shem that I heard. Pot covers were lifted and set down upon the ground. A couple of nuts were dropped, and dried fruit was sifted through. I did not move or speak.

Not long after the shuffling began, it disappeared out the tent's door flap.

When the sun rose, I went out to the cookfire. Shem was sitting there, alone. "Javan will not let me see Ona."

Then where did you spend the night? I said only, "Maybe you will need to take another. Perhaps even one who is not a whore."

"You said we cannot afford two, and Javan has already told me I must bring goat meat and fruit for the child in Ona's belly. She says he is an insatiable beast."

"What have you done, Shem?"

"All will be well, Mother, if only Japheth marries Herai. You know Leah will not bear sons. I have never seen a woman so ancient. She must be eighty years old."

"And many years wiser. She has left."

Shem looked to see if I was serious. When he saw that I was, he said, "Then it is settled: Japheth will marry Herai."

"Tell this to your father."

"Cannot you?"

"No, but I will try anyway."

.   .   .

"Where is first wife?" Noah asked me when he woke.

"She is gone, husband," I said. I did not mention that much of our dried fruit and nuts was also gone.

"Gone where?"

"Away from us." I did not want to give him time to come up with a different plan. I hurried on, "Japheth is in need of a wife. Unless—"

"At what position of the sun did she leave?" he interrupted.

"She was gone before first light. It is too late to catch her now. The girl you have gotten for Ham can be given to Japheth."

His eyes seemed to draw deeper into his skull. I was afraid he was considering going after Leah. Finally, he said, "Then who will Ham take for a wife?"

"Herai."

He banged his staff against the ground. "Speak no more of Javan's daughter. I will find Japheth another wife."

"There are few righteous and pure girls in the world, and here is one within reach. We must be practical. Javan has gotten five mules for a dowry."

He came close and squinted into my eyes. "Wife," he said quietly, "Be careful. *We are watched.*"

. . .

Javan returned five days after bringing the mules. I had tried to sway Noah, then to scare him, then to wear him down. Each time I had spoken to him, he'd seemed more certain of Herai's unworthiness.

I was crouched by the cookfire and did not stand up to greet Javan. Just the sight of her wearied me. Before she had come within ten cubits, I said, "No."

"*No?* So where is Japheth's wife?"

"You know she has left."

"The will of the gods," she said.

I was too tired to think of any reply.

"Shem told me Noah believes the world will end and only his family will be spared. And you are at the mercy of such a man?" She spoke with so much scorn that for the blink of an eye, I hoped Noah's prophecy would come true. Then, without warning, and as quickly as always, she became serious. "You have more sway than you know. My girls can teach you things—"

"No. I have done all I can. Leave me alone."

Every time she started to speak, I said, "No," until finally, she kicked the ground near me and left.

CHAPTER 20

THE CARAVAN

The next morning, Japheth stepped in a pool of blood outside the tent's door flap. He looked back into the tent at Noah. "Father," he cried. "A sign!"

Noah got up from his blanket, put on his tunic, and went to crouch in the doorway.

"Most people sacrifice animals for God, but Father, God has sacrificed one for us!"

"Keep talking," Ham said, "and one day you are bound to say something that is not foolish."

"God does not sacrifice goats," Noah said. Japheth's zeal did not please him. Quite the opposite.

All of us besides Japheth knew that the blood was a threat. Javan was not going to take no for an answer, and Noah was not going to say yes.

"Attend to this," he told me. To Japheth, he said, "You will help your mother. It will be good practice for the cleaning to come. Our ark will be full of two of every unclean creature and fourteen of every clean one."

"*Every* creature?" I asked.

"Every creature."

"Biting flies?"

"The Lord has commanded me to take clean animals, animals that are not clean, birds, and things that creep on the ground," he said.

What about the Nephilim? I wondered. They would not fit in an ark. Was their great height enough to keep their heads above water?

Without further explanation, Noah wandered out to the road and stood absolutely still, listening. For what, I did not know. Clean animals, unclean animals, birds, and bugs? Or perhaps he was listening, as he usually was, for the voice of God.

I gathered a bowl of clay, a waterskin, and a small shovel, which we would use as carefully as possible so as not to create a ditch, and took them to our doorway.

"Did you think three hundred cubits were only for us?" Japheth asked scornfully. He crouched over the blood, his expression a mix of insolence and awe. He was the strongest of my sons and, though he did not seem to know it, the most handsome. Men and women alike turned to look at him when he ventured away from Noah's land to catch a loose goat or yell at a sinner about God's wrath.

Suddenly, Ham stood up from his sleeping blanket and ran from the tent, splashing Japheth and the tent with blood.

"Curse you," Japheth cried.

Noah broke from his stillness. "Hush, boy!" He made his way toward Japheth, his staff hitting wildly from side to side upon the ground. It hit the little pool of blood, and he stopped. "Do you so quickly forget the things I tell you? How will you grow into a man if you cannot contain the recklessness of a boy? You will not speak again today."

Japheth glared at Ham, who had turned around to enjoy his brother's chastisement. Since Noah had started using a staff to make his way around, the boys had gotten bold with their looks and gestures. Sometimes, when Ham wanted to goad Japheth, he even grabbed his tunic where it covered his loins.

. . .

Japheth was still crouched in front of the tent when Noah called, "Ham! Your wife approaches."

I looked to find a man riding upon a beast larger than any I had ever seen. It was taller than one man standing upon another and weighed enough to shake the earth as it came closer. Huge tusks protruded alongside a trunk that could have wrapped itself ten times around me. A cloud of dust hovered around its knees but did not rise up high enough to obscure the man on its back—a man who rode so upright that I imagined his flanks were riddled with calluses or open sores. Behind this beast were others. They advanced from the north in a single line, one animal following the one before it so precisely that head-on, you might not have known there was any more than one man upon one great beast.

Ham was impressed by neither man nor beast. He looked hate-fully at the caravan.

"Ham, go help Japheth clean," I said.

"But my beloved approaches."

"At least stop frowning," I said. Though he obeyed me, it did not improve his countenance. In fact, it made it worse. He stared coldly at whatever it was that approached.

As if just realizing someone had gotten the better of him in a deal, Noah muttered, "*She* is the seventh saved. Not one of my sons but her."

"What is the importance of seven?" I asked, thinking that I wanted the very best for Ham and wondering how I could arrange it.

"Seven is God's number and represents perfection. He made the world in seven days."

He made it in six, and He does not seem to think it is so perfect, seeing as some of His creations have fallen so low in His favor that He wishes to destroy them. But I knew better than to argue with Noah.

Japheth looked like he wanted to say something, but he could not disobey Noah by speaking. Perhaps he wanted to point out that he was *seven*teen. Poor Japheth. Maybe it was not his fault that he was so fervent about God and the sins of others. Shem's wayward-ness drove him to it, and this self-righteousness of Japheth's forced Ham into a rebellion of irreverence.

Though I loved Shem and Japheth, I was glad Noah and I had not stopped son-making after Japheth. I hated to think of how miserable we might all be without Ham. Even Japheth. Without Ham, he would have only one brother to look down upon.

I went to my favorite son and put my hand gently upon his arm. I could think of nothing comforting to say except, "She looks like she comes from a powerful family."

Ham's bottom lip was trembling. He did not respond. I knew he was thinking of Herai. I was not sure if there was any other boy in the world who would cry because he could not have a girl so much older than himself, one who was thought to be slow because of demons or God's punishment. But I hoped so.

"I am sorry," I told him. "I wish Herai could be yours." And by "yours," I meant "ours." Unfortunately, neither Ham nor I held sway over Noah. But Ham at least would one day have his own family, and then he would make decrees instead of following them. It seemed I never would. I wondered who had more control over her life—one of Javan's prostitutes or me. At least none of them would be forced to put their sons on an ark with a bunch of animals many leagues from the sea.

I had thought myself into a dark state by the time the caravan was within a hundred cubits. Ham, on the other hand, no longer looked like a mixture of emptiness and fury. He was straining to see what approached as if he could not wait until it arrived to know what it was.

At last I could make out the man at the head of the pack. *Surely this is a mirage*, I thought. A mirage so powerful, everyone could see it. The man appeared to be as old as Noah. His beard was so thick that it covered half of his torso and so long it rested on the strange beast he rode. On the beast behind his was another man, also ancient. And behind him, a little girl.

A little girl. Reins in one of her little hands.

Someone sat behind the girl, holding a parasol between her and the sun.

After this came two more men. All in all, from the tusks of the first beast, to the tail of the last, they were quite a solemn procession. Not a sad sort of solemn but an important sort. Noble men on a noble errand. Their tunics billowed out behind them in the wind like banners, as if they ruled over every place they traveled.

Do they mean to rule over this place?

Though Noah had invited them, he stood stock-still in the middle of the road as if he were going to confront them.

"Cousin," the first man greeted Noah.

"Welcome, Manosh," Noah said. The way he said it was not very welcoming. By his tone of voice, I would have thought he was speaking of a great stench. Then his intonation became hopeful: "Did you have any trouble with the sellswords?"

"No. Just as the God of Adam watches over you, so does He watch over us." Yet a sword hung from Manosh's belt—sheathed but with blood on the handle. It seemed God had given these men steady hands and swords and left the rest up to them. I wondered how many fewer sinners there were now in the towns to the north.

The girl on the third beast looked young—seven or eight— except that the stiffness of her spine was too great for a child's.

"Which of these is my wife?" Ham asked.

I did not think the blood on Manosh's sword bode well for Ham's insolence. I moved to step in front of my son, but he held his arm out so that I came to a halt.

Manosh did not move or speak. He and Noah's other cousins stared at us without emotion, letting any fear we might have mount in the silence.

Then Manosh laughed. "You cannot tell which of these is your wife? You must have inherited your father's sight." This caused the rest of Noah's cousins to laugh as well. You would not have been able to tell they were laughing by their chests or bellies. Only their faces moved. I thought: *They are too controlled to be trusted.*

In almost perfect unison, they dismounted their beasts. Age did not seem a hindrance to their strength but, rather, an explanation of it, as if their great stature was due to growing taller each year of their lives. Their noses and ears were not out of proportion to the rest of their bodies, as with most old men.

I realized the woman behind the little girl was a slave. She struggled to hold the parasol over the girl even as one of the old men lifted the child off the riding blanket and set her gently on the ground. Much more gently than Noah had ever touched me.

Even in the shade of the parasol the slave held over her, I could tell that the girl's skin was as light as any I had seen. Not deep olive, dried brown, or glistening black but a color like sand that had taken in a whole summer of sunlight. I wondered how it was possible for her to be even lighter than the parts of my body that were hidden. Had she never walked out into the sun without a parasol? Had she never seen the sky?

My eyes were filled with the old men, the little girl, and the huge beasts. But when the slave glanced up for half a breath, I nearly forgot all but her. She had a mark upon her brow. I felt a confounding mixture of compassion and revulsion. I reached up to make sure my head scarf was secure.

When I realized I was staring, I hurried my gaze off the slave's face. I did not want the others to wonder at any connection between us. Instead, I looked at the men and the little girl. The girl pressed her cheek to the tusk of her great beast, which had lowered its head, as though to be nearer to her. Then she walked, as slowly as if she were floating, to stand with the old men, two on either side. The wind that billowed our tunics and blew our hair into our faces seemed not to touch her. She waited with the men for Noah to approach.

These men looked as commanding as any army. The source of their power was not their stature or the great beasts they rode. It was how they seemed to move as one body. One large body with four sharp swords and eight steady hands.

No one scratched an itch or cleared his throat or shooed a fly from his neck. We were as still as if the next movement might determine all that was to come. Then Ham shook my hand off and began walking toward the girl.

"Son," Noah said. "*Stop*."

Ham halted. He had some loyalty to his father in the presence of strangers. But he did call out: "Have you torn this little girl from her mother's breast in order to make her my wife?"

"This is the daughter of the prophet Kesh—our cousin, favorite grandson of our beloved, ailing Methuselah," Manosh said.

Noah's face took on the expression of a man being bitten by

gnats and trying not to show it. "Three hundred goats do not make a man a prophet," he said.

Manosh smiled. "Three thousand."

"The God of Adam told him of the end of the world before He told you," another of the old men said to Noah.

"But the Lord has left me here to survive it."

"He has left Kesh's daughter Zilpha as well," Manosh said. He looked at the girl, and she smiled faintly up at him. "We are entrusting you to her and her to you."

"As a wife or a ward?" Ham asked. I had never once raised my hand to Ham, and right then I thought this a terrible mistake.

They were not accustomed to being mocked. "Ahh!" one of the old men cried. Another banged his staff against the dust.

Manosh looked to Noah to chastise Ham. Noah said nothing and perhaps tilted his nose a bit more toward the sky after this insult to Zilpha. Manosh placed his hand upon the bloody handle of his sword and took a step forward.

Zilpha reached up and lightly touched Manosh's hand with her own, bringing him to a halt. I wondered how such a little hand could still such a large one, though I noticed that he did not take his hand off his sword.

"Lay down your fear," she told Ham. Her voice sounded like it contained apricots and cream and all other manner of good things, and after it left her mouth, it seemed to float above us. "My father said I would marry a difficult man, and we would be as happy as two people born of prophets are allowed to be. Though this amount of happiness is small, it will be all we need."

Ham stared at her as if she had grown a second head, but luckily, he said nothing.

This speech and Ham's reaction seemed to meet the quota of awe that the girl needed in order to leave her place beside her second cousins. She raised her arm. (I would come to see her do this a hundred times over—every time she was about to walk.) The slave hurried to hold the parasol between the girl's newborn-looking skin and the sun.

To my surprise, the girl and the slave came to me. Because of the parasol, which was level with my chest, the little girl was not able to come close. The slave raised the parasol above our heads, nearly scratching my face, so the girl could walk forward. As the girl placed her arms around my waist and pressed her head gently to my belly, I stood as still as a stone, unsure what I should do.

The girl stepped back and took one of my hands in both of her own. "Mother," she said.

Perhaps she called me "Mother" because she had nothing else to call me, but I do not think so. I had never wanted a daughter. A daughter would remind me of what I had made myself forget: My own mother had left me. And I was afraid if I had a daughter, she would be marked and there would be no old man righteous or blind enough to take her in. But I would not need to worry about this with Zilpha. She was more powerful as a girl than I ever would be as a woman. This did not please me.

She let go of my hand and turned to Noah. In coming to me, she had already walked over half the distance between them, and she must have thought she had done her part. She waited for Noah to come to her.

He did not move a hair's width in any direction. Even the shock of hair on his head was so stiff that not even the desert wind could stir it.

Enough. Though the land we stood on was Noah's, along with the food, the cookfire, and even me, and though it was Noah's right to invite guests to eat, seeing the girl's sway over so many men made me bold. As if Zilpha and her second cousins had just arrived, I said, "Welcome! Won't you gather around our cookfire and eat with us?"

Before anyone could answer, I ran to gather goat meat and lentils.

CHAPTER 24

THE OTHER PROPHET'S DAUGHTER

Zilpha and the slave were the first to come to the cookfire. Everyone except Noah soon followed. He remained in the road in the same place where he had stood when the caravan was barely discernible on the horizon. He stared in the direction his cousins had come from, as if he had no interest in us and were waiting for something more important to appear. He looked so ridiculous there that I felt both pity and anger.

The rest of us crouched around the cookfire, all except Zilpha. The slave laid a blanket on the ground for her. "You will know," Manosh said, "that Zilpha must not go unprotected from the sun."

"My father gave me this parasol, which he has blessed. It will keep the sun from stealing my years."

"Have you never seen daylight?" Ham asked her.

Manosh ignored Ham's question. "You will also know," he said, "she does not—"

"I saw it once," Zilpha said. "Surely I will be blind a few years before I would have had I never looked at it, but I do not regret it. Now I have seen it and do not need to look again."

Manosh continued. This time he spoke too loudly to be interrupted. "You will also know that she does not squat or needlessly tire herself in any other way."

"My strength must be preserved for the many years to come," Zilpha said. She propped her head up on one little arm and tried to drink her stew in this position. It slopped onto the blanket. Surely it would have been easier to drink in a squatting position, but she remained prone on the wet blanket, surely getting no less hungry than she had been when she arrived.

I looked over at Ham to make sure he was not about to say something cruel. He was staring at Zilpha. I could not tell whether he was staring in awe or disgust.

Watching her go hungry caused my jealousy to recede a hair's width, which was enough that I got some bread for her. "Thank you, my good mother," she said. Again, "mother." Perhaps even the daughter of a prophet needs one.

Without Noah near, Manosh looked from one of my sons to another, deciding which one to address, before grudgingly settling his gaze upon Ham. "Zilpha's father was a great prophet. He told us of this drought we are in now, and of a great struggle between mankind and the God of Adam. Zilpha is his one remaining child. The rest grew old and died, as most people do. Zilpha must carry the blood of Kesh to many sons."

Though it was considered bold for a woman to ask questions, I ventured, "And Zilpha, how old is she?"

"I am seven," she said, "and I will live for seven hundred years. This is why Noah wants me with you when the end of the world comes. If I am going to live through it, there is a greater chance that the people around me will too."

Finally, I had met someone as mad as Noah.

"Blaspheme!" Noah cried from his place in the road. He did not address Zilpha directly. "The girl is a virgin, and that is her worth."

"Then if I tell you I am not a virgin, you will not want me on your boat?"

Manosh raised one bushy eyebrow at Zilpha but did not chastise or strike her. He also did not give anyone else time to do so. "She is the only chance that Kesh's blood will be carried on to a son," he said, "and her father prophesied that in this, she will be successful."

Zilpha would not be ignored. She raised her arm. The slave lifted the parasol slightly, and the girl calmly rose up and turned to Noah. "If I tell you I am not a virgin, you will not want me on your boat?" she repeated. The apricots and cream had not left her voice.

When she first arrived, I'd thought that Ham had met his match. I now saw that it was not Ham who had met his match but Noah.

"The girl is untouched, and that is her only value," Noah said to his cousins, his sons, and me. I am certain none of us believed him. If that were his only concern in choosing a daughter-in-law, and seven-year-olds would do, he could have found count-less others.

His distaste for his cousins and Zilpha increased the suspicion I'd had ever since we rode into town on the back of his goat-sized donkey: He *liked* living among sinners. He did not care for anyone's righteousness but his own.

· · ·

"We are still one wife short," I told Noah. In fact, we were two wives short; Javan had not let Shem's wife leave her tent.

"God will find another," Noah said.

Noah, my sons, and I were in our own tent. We had just lain down on our sleeping blankets. Zilpha and Noah's cousins had made camp on the other side of our herd. I heard laughter, and I feared they were talking about us.

Japheth looked at Noah but remained silent. The sun had not yet set, and Noah had not told him he could speak. Ham, for once, was quiet as well. And Noah. Noah was as grouchy as the grievances of half a millennium could make a man.

"Kesh had wealth enough to buy himself the title of 'prophet.' He is not a prophet but a murderer of shepherds and a thief who steals from the dead."

I did not know how to ask him why he wanted to make Zilpha Ham's wife without sounding as though I were questioning his wis-dom. But I wanted to know. I said only, "Zilpha?"

"Ham's marriage to her will bring us many of the spoils they inherited from her father. They have goats enough to pay men to bring the animals God has commanded us to take onto the ark, and lumber enough to build it."

"What do they want in return?" I asked.

"A place on the ark. They believe that Zilpha secures this place for them."

CHAPTER 22

THE ARK

Make yourself an ark of gopher wood; make it an ark with compart-
ments, and cover it inside and out with pitch. This is how you shall
make it: the length of the ark shall be three hundred cubits, its width
fifty cubits, and its height thirty cubits.

GENESIS 6:14–15

"Three hundred by *fifty*?" Ham complained to Noah. "Does God want to tip us over?"

"That is plenty wide, fool," Japheth said. "Besides, you will be lucky if He lets you on at all." Japheth should not have said this aloud, knowing how Noah considered talk of luck to be blasphemy.

But Noah did not waste time chastising either son. He said only, "Hurry."

This was what he said each morning before the sun came up as well. "Hurry. There is not much time." The hard work helped keep us from thinking of the ridiculousness of our undertaking. We were much too tired to question Noah.

Our first task was buying three hundred by fifty cubits of land, which was possible only because of the hundreds of goats, dyed fabrics, and gems Manosh had brought from his home in the fertile north. Noah wanted to be the one to present these riches. He made sure to stand in front of his cousin as they bargained the neighbors off their land. But people gazed right over the shock of hair on top of Noah's head, sometimes even standing on tiptoe to behold Manosh.

My sons pulled out stakes and took down the neighbors' tents, letting the patched-together goatskins fall to the ground as they hurried on to the next plot of Noah's new land.

Zilpha had left with her second cousins. "Now you have seen her virtue and her youth. We will give her to you when we all return to board the ark," Monosh had said. This left only me to do all of the women's work. I alone cooked, cleaned, and helped the neighbors fold their tents and pack their stakes. But I did not feel like I was helping them so much as I was helping my family to their land. I did not ask whether they had somewhere to go.

One woman kept looking at the sack of gems her son was holding. When my boys came to take down her tent, she cried, "Wait!" She ran to open the sack and gaze inside it for a few breaths, allowing herself to be convinced. She turned to my boys. "Very well," she said, "go ahead."

· · ·

Once there was a space large enough to construct the ark, Noah drew an outline, counting paces as he dragged his staff through the sand. Some of the townspeople came to watch. They did not enter the space where the ark would be, and I was surprised by this show of respect until I saw that they were running their feet back and forth over the lines Noah had drawn. Almost as soon as he completed a section, another was lost.

On the third day, people tired of this game. Or perhaps they wanted Noah to finish the outline so they could see it. Noah did not need light to work, and sometime in the early morning of the fourth day, he completed his drawing of the ark.

When the sun rose, we stood with the townspeople, staring at it. The outline was so big that we could see it only in parts. We could make out more as it stretched away and got smaller. Then the impression of Noah's staff in the dusty earth seemed to fade away, leaving the ark open at the far end. If the wind picked up, our ark might disappear. That may have been a relief, except for the towns-people's unending ridicule.

We walked the length of it, weaving through the people of the mob. They were so taken with the drawing that they did not bother us. We saw that everywhere the ark was the same size, it did not get smaller at the far end, as it had appeared to. It was a long narrow rectangle with three levels.

"A flat bottom?" Ham asked. "Are not boats supposed to be pointed at the bottom?"

"And are *you* going to hold it balanced while we build it?" Japheth sneered.

"It will be weighted on the lowest level with the large beasts," Noah said. He explained that the diagonal line between levels was a ramp, and the two lines near each other toward the top were where a long window would be all around the ark.

Not that there would be much light to let in.

Long into the night, I lay awake on my sleeping blanket. I could not sort the dread from the euphoria from the exhaustion from the feeling that already one world was ending and another beginning. Maybe the sea really would spread to our ark. If not, perhaps we could take the ark north in pieces and put it together right beside the sea.

I had never been on a boat before. In fact, I had never seen the sea. My father's tent was half a league west of the Nile, and the closest I'd come to witnessing a great sea was being near the river during the hottest moons of the year when it rushed over its banks faster than man or beast could run. Once it even rushed over the mud dykes that men had built around our village to stop it. Though the water came only as high as my sandals, my heart pounded hard enough that I feared it might burst. I did not know how to be in the water—how to keep it from swallowing me. I had heard that people could survive in it for short periods if they kicked it with their legs and hit it down with their hands. They called this battle "swimming." I hoped never to have to engage in it.

One night while my father snored upon his sleeping blankets, I had used a meat knife to cut off a lock of my hair. Then I slipped quietly from the tent. Some villages sacrificed virgins, but I prayed that the lock of hair I threw to the Nile would sate the hungry waters within.

. . .

The morning after Noah completed the outline of the ark, we were awakened by shouting. It was so many voices thick I could not separate one person's words from another's. The people sounded as incoherent as a distant mob, yet too loud to be distant.

There was no use in speaking—no one would hear, least of all Noah. I looked at him, and he squinted back at me. Then he took a deep breath and rose from his sleeping blanket.

My boys and I followed him to the tent's door flap, and peeked around his bony shoulder at the mob. They were staring at the outline of the ark. Children, and even some adults, stood on each other's shoulders, pointing, shouting, and laughing so hard they fell to the ground.

They were not looking at us. Yet I knew that it was us they laughed at.

Noah rushed from the tent without his staff and elbowed his way through the horde. I checked that my head scarf was secure and followed. "What is it?" he asked.

He seemed so helpless with neither his staff nor his sight. I had never seen him this way, and I was certain my sons had not either. I wanted to get him back to the tent before they did. The crowd had quieted to watch us.

I could see the part of the outline closest to us. Or rather, I couldn't see it. The ark Noah had drawn in the sand was covered in rocks. At least one day's work would be lost clearing all of them away. A man picked up one of the rocks and threw it at us. It landed with a *clack* against the rocks in front of our feet.

"Husband," I whispered into his old ear, "let us return to the tent."

"I do not understand," he said.

I grabbed his arm and turned around. Someone blocked my path. "It is your boat, sunken to the bottom of a sea of rocks," Javan said.

There were so many people gathered that I hadn't heard her sneaking up behind us. The townspeople had let her through, her and her brutes. She smiled threateningly at Noah, and then—for much longer—at me. Perhaps I should have been flattered that she refused to believe what was so obvious to me: I had no say in the matter of Herai's marriage into Noah's family. *I am not like you,* I wanted to say to her. *I am a good, obedient wife.* But maybe the real difference between us was that I lacked courage.

Javan raised her hand and I flinched. The flinch was good enough for her, she did not strike me. She stepped around us, and her boys followed. They admired their handiwork for a few breaths before leaving us with it, and with the laughter of the townspeople, which began again with even greater fervor.

If we could not do something as simple as keep Javan from destroying an outline in the sand, how could we hope to build an ark?

As though Noah could hear my thoughts, he said, "We do not need an outline. God will guide us."

. . .

Whole forests of gopher wood were dragged through the desert sand, pulled by oxen and great beasts. Noah had told me the beasts were called mammoths.

As soon as whichever cousin brought the wood had left with his slaves and mammoths, the onlookers came and hauled it all away. Noah yelled about God's wrath, but this did not concern the people as much as jewels.

"Have you any more gems to buy this wood from us?" a man asked.

Noah had no more jewels, so they kept our wood and mocked us.

"What do you need this wood for? A ship to sail across the desert dust? We will put this wood to better uses—brothels and taverns."

"Why don't you build a ship of rocks? You can give it a rudder of sand and a sail of air."

Someone threw a stone at us. Another soon followed. Noah did not seem to notice. "There is more gopher wood in the world," he told his sons and me as a stone flew right under his nose.

More rocks rushed past us. They came close enough that I felt the air move, but they did not hit us. Noah's God was great indeed.

Yet He did not hinder the skill of Sorum's thieves. Even if one of Noah's cousins brought more wood the next day, we would lose a day's work. And what good would more lumber be if we could not keep hold of it?

"Javan could help us," I told Noah. I was thinking that her protection of our ark could only truly be repaid by allowing Herai to marry one of our sons.

Noah knew my thoughts. "Herai can never be part of my line," he said.

"We still have no wife for Japheth. The God of Adam has instructed you to put your sons *and their wives* on the ark. How will we repopulate the world with only a whore and a little girl?"

"When the flood hits, we will have our pick of every girl who wants to live."

I did not know whether there would be a flood, but it would not help my cause to say so. "With no lumber to finish our ark, we will drown." Because not being special to his God would seem many times worse to Noah than death, I added, "Like everybody else."

"My cousin will leave us a mammoth tomorrow, and we will lose no more lumber."

The cousin came not only with his slaves but with Zilpha. It was her mammoth that was left to protect our lumber. "When I heard about the loss of our lumber, I insisted I return to you," she said. "My beast has been trained his whole life to guard me. Methuselah has bestowed upon him a blessing of wisdom and strength. No one can take anything the beast watches over."

ZILPHA'S BELOVED MAMMOTH

Zilpha loved her beast. She often stroked his trunk or had her slave help her onto his back while she held the parasol over her head herself. She stayed up there for many positions of the sun, looking down on the world as she had done when she traveled with Noah's cousins to our camp.

Great and much loved as the mammoth was, I feared for his safety. While it was true that the stones flying past Noah, my boys, Zilpha, and me never once touched us, the mammoth was not so lucky. Fortunately, hitting a beast that large with a stone is like striking a grown man with a date seed.

But the would-be thieves continued to search for ways to bring the mammoth down.

. . .

Early one morning, as the sun had only just started to reach across the desert, there was a ground-shaking *THUD*. Japheth rushed to peek around a large mound of gopher wood. Ham and Shem came up behind him. When Noah tapped on Japheth's back with his staff, all three boys moved to the side to make way for him; they had to do their best to believe in their father and the flood he prophesied, or feel like weaklings and fools for obeying him. None of us wanted to think about what the mob camped all around the ark would do to us if the flood never came.

Zilpha walked as quickly as she could without moving ahead of the parasol the slave held between her and the sun. "No," she said when she saw the mammoth lying on the ground. She rushed to kneel beside it, and the slave followed with the parasol. She caressed the beast's tusk and pressed her head against his cheek. Instead of lying with his legs tucked under his large body, he lay completely on his side.

People were taking our lumber. I recognized a few of them as Javan's brutes.

"What have you done?" I yelled at them. "The brothers, cousins, and uncles of this beast will come back to trample you like tiny ants beneath their giant feet."

"We will soak them with wine too," one boy said.

"Do not worry, old hag—he is not dead," another boy offered. "He only needs some water and a little rest, perhaps a whore or two, and he will be ready to celebrate again tonight."

The mammoth did not rise by nightfall. Zilpha and I stood staring into his shiny, fear-filled eye.

"I have never seen one on his side before," Zilpha said, "and now I know why. Once they are on their side, they can never get up."

The weight of the beast was already carving a shallow ditch into the ground. I did not like to see something so big be afraid. "If we feed him and give him water, we will figure out a way to help him stand."

My sons tried to push him off the ground. The beast was too heavy; we could not raise him even a hair's width. He drank little and would not eat.

"If we can just keep him alive for a few days, he will grow light enough for us to lift." I was deceiving myself and nobody else, except perhaps Zilpha, whose eyes clung to mine to make sure that I was certain.

The beast never slept. His visible eye stared around him at the place he would die, until finally the sight left his gaze, and we knew he was gone. Ham pressed his thick eyelid down over his eye and said, "He is at peace."

Zilpha went into the tent and lay upon her sleeping blanket. Even there, she made her slave hold the parasol over her. It was no longer the sun that she wanted to be shielded from. It was us.

She despaired too greatly to journey back to her home with one of Noah's cousins who came with more gopher wood. The cousin made six of his men ride back upon three beasts so that three could be left. Not even Javan could get enough wine to inebriate that much flesh.

THE TOWN'S LAUGHTER

Within a few days of measuring and cutting the new lumber the cousins brought us, it was not just the townspeople who came to jeer. Soon there were more faces I did not recognize than those I did. The small mob turned into a crowd and then into a throng many times larger than that which had gathered outside my father's tent.

"Only I will speak to them," Noah told us, and glared at where he thought our eyes were.

We obeyed. Even Ham. But being ignored did not seem to have any effect on the hecklers.

I had never known what a terrible sound laughter can be. It is many times worse than the sound of hammers banging away day and night. After a while you grow accustomed to hammering.

I stuffed wool in my ears, but their voices found their way past it.

"Where is the sea you will sail?" yelled a man with two black eyes and a dagger twice as large as Ham's in his belt.

Noah heard the man, and he answered: "It waits in the sky for the ark to be finished." Had he given up on the sinners, or did he still hope to sway them to righteousness? Though he was my husband of nineteen years and I usually knew what he was thinking, this time I could not tell from the tone of his voice. Perhaps he himself was just as uncertain of the flood as I was.

His response caused the crowd to become even more unruly. Someone shouted, "Then put down your hammers and leave the sea where it is!"

If they had truly believed the unfinished ark was delaying the rain, surely they would have helped build it. This would have been a great relief for Shem, Japheth, and Ham. But it was hard to believe there would ever be rain. The sun beat down like fists of fire upon the backs of my boys as they did what Noah commanded from sunup to sundown. Sometimes I could see Ham's lips moving, and I knew he was cursing under his breath or uttering insults he did not speak aloud. Japheth scowled at the more blasphemous shouting, and Shem only looked into the crowd if he heard a woman's voice.

Noah was consumed with thoughts he did not share. He was the first to rise each morning, and even after the sun went down at night, he would talk quietly to himself until he fell asleep. Because he did not see as well as he had when we first met, I could not watch to see where he looked in order to better know what was on his mind. He might be gazing upon one son, thinking he was gazing upon another.

When the time came to knock copper into nails, Noah did a demonstration for the boys. I heard the banging of hard, heavy objects. Not long after this, I heard another sound—a single bang that was muted. Then Noah's voice, not at all muted, calling out to God not in praise but in anger. "God of Adam!" he cried. I looked over to see him holding his thumb.

He knew how a ship should be built, but he could not have constructed one without my sons. He could not see well enough—not even as far as his own thumb.

"Will you sail as keenly as you wield your hammer?" a man yelled.

"Maybe you should build yourself a new thumb!" cried another.

"Or a pair of eyes!"

This last voice I recognized: the drunken whore who had been an unusually beautiful girl, Shem's mother-in-law, stood heckling the boat that her daughter should rightly be on when the flood hit. That is, *if* the flood hit. Which I was beginning to hope it did. It seemed the only way to put an end to the laughter.

I thought of setting down the lentils I was sorting and hurrying over to bribe the woman with food or goats. But I did not dare hazard the crowd. I was afraid my head scarf would be ripped away and my secret revealed. Besides, the woman likely held little sway over Ona. Javan was the one—the *only* one—in charge of her girls. She had not returned since covering the ark Noah had drawn in the sand with rocks, and I was grateful for this. Perhaps she was too busy with all of the travelers. Though I was sure she had not forgotten about us.

THE RUDDER

A merciful thing happened to my sons. They stopped hearing the laughter. In fact, they stopped hearing anything, and they saw only lumber, saws, hammers, and nails. They did not flinch at the insults thrown at them like sharp rocks from sunup to sundown. They did not even hear when I called them for supper. I had to step over wooden planks, watching the ground for nails, and stand in front of them waving my arms. Perhaps the hammering had rendered them temporarily deaf. Or maybe it was the exhaustion. They appeared to be in a trance. Only occasionally did one of them seem to startle awake, as if at that instant the banging of hammers had entered his ears. He would go still, all but his eyes.

Of my three sons, it was Ham who gazed up the most, searching for clouds. After one of these futile searches through the sky, he jerked his gaze back down and stared in dismay at the vast mounds of gopher wood that were turning into a ship and at the three small shapes dwarfed by these mounds—his brothers and father. Perhaps he was thinking they were all mad. Or maybe he had just realized how tiny we all were. Laboring to build the ark left no strength with which to defend against not only the immensity of the cloudless sky and the great ark, so far from the sea, but also whatever lay ahead. The future had opened before us like a crater whose size and depth we could not know until we fell in.

Though Ham's arrogance seemed to fall away a little more each day, Noah went unchanged. "When will you instruct our sons to build the rudder?" I asked him.

"The Lord is our rudder."

Once in a while, if I did not guard against it, my eyes moved like Ham's—with greater and greater disbelief—over the great long skeleton of the ship. Sometimes when this happened, my legs forgot to hold me. I felt both elated and terrified. *If Noah is right, once we get in, we will never see the world we know—both good and evil—again.*

But we did not know if he was right. We were following a blind man into the unknown. And so it was that even before getting into the ark, as my sons constructed the ribs and cross braces, already we were floating without a rudder, not knowing where we were headed and whether we were obeying a prophet or a madman.

CHAPTER 26

HELPING HANDS, STRANGE TONGUES

The more our lumber began to look like an ark, the more numerous were the people who came to laugh at it.

Noah snorted when the new arrivals yelled to him, asking where the sea that the ark would sail upon was. He told them that God was holding the sea in the sky. This caused the men to mockingly hurl their spears at the cloudless sky in order to pierce it.

"The clouds will come," Noah told them. "They will come for all of your lives."

"Then we had best make our lives good. Fill them with battle, wine, and girls for the God of Noah, who does not come down and take these things for Himself, like a real god."

"Yes," another man shouted, "if Noah's God is too old and weak to enjoy the flesh of young girls Himself, we must do it for Him!"

Soon there were as many people as I had ever seen in my entire life standing around the ark. Men came from farther and farther reaches of the desert. This was good for the trade in town, for Javan especially, but not so good for us. Not all of the men spent the night in flesh tents. Some had families, and they put up tents all around the ark. My sons had to build a little round wall of stones to keep me safe while I cooked and wove blankets for our journey.

One day Manosh himself came with his slaves and mammoths pulling yet more gopher wood. By this time the path to the ark was gone. People, tents, and animals covered every cubit. The people were drinking, shouting, and sometimes swinging at each other with great force but little accuracy. A few of the children were not drunk, and they must have felt the ground shaking when the mammoths approached. The shaking grew more violent and then, suddenly, stopped. The children looked back to see why.

They watched Noah's cousin carefully rise up on the back of his mammoth, with the reins in his huge hands. Manosh steadied himself and stood as tall as possible. "Disperse!" he cried.

The whole crowd turned to look at him. I don't know if they would have moved of their own accord. Manosh did not give them a chance. He stomped his foot upon the back of the mammoth, and it started walking. He stomped with more force, and it walked faster. The mammoth was too large to run but large enough that it didn't need to. It easily gained on the people who could not get out of its path quickly enough to live. The ground trembled as if thousands of lightning bolts were falling from the sky. People screamed and pushed. Men, women, children, mules, donkeys, and goats were trapped by tents and fences and even by each other. What little there was of the ark did not move a hair in any direction.

Manosh came to a halt in front of it. Behind him lay a trail of huge hoofprints full of blood. "Cousin! We have generously brought more gopher wood for our ark. This is the last from our lands, but we can get more."

What was Noah to say? He needed the wood. He could always tell himself that the people Manosh had trampled would otherwise have died in the flood. "Very good," he said stiffly.

After this episode, there were a few days when he did not meet anyone's eyes. He became quite occupied with supervising his sons and rarely looked up from their hammers.

Manosh never again had any trouble bringing lumber through the crowd. People cleared a path while he was half a league away. Though the crowd was quieter when he was around, my heart beat wild and panicked in my chest. I had a bad feeling about him—not just about what he had done already but about what else he might be capable of.

"Surely Manosh and his cousin do not need to bring the lumber themselves," I said to Noah one night when I couldn't sleep for fear that Manosh would return soon. "Cannot they just send the slaves?"

"No. They come to see the ark."

.   .   .

"What is this?" Manosh asked us on one of his visits, looking at the ark as if he had never seen it. And in fact he never had seen it as it stood that day, with the entire skeleton stretched long over the desert and part of one side built up so that it looked like something a family might be able to live in someday. I could not help but feel proud of my sons.

Manosh continued, "Our lumber has only been molded into the barest ribs? Ribs as bare as those of a carcass that the flesh has completely rotted off? Ribs scrubbed barer than time and sea and man can scrub them?"

The sun was directly overhead so the ark did not cast a shadow over Manosh. I hoped one day it would. I looked up at him and tried to keep my voice steady. "You are free to bring a hammer with you the next time you come."

"This is the ark exactly as God commanded," Noah said. I could hear that he also was straining to control his voice. "It is built in His time and no one else's." After this, he did not let more than a few breaths go by each day without saying, "Hurry. *Hurry!*"

The ark was already being built as quickly as any three humans could build it. Even without perfect vision, surely Noah could see this. Otherwise he would not have said that the God of Adam was the hammer in the boys' hands and the strength in their hearts. Sweat poured in torrents down their thickening backs. Calluses formed on their fingers, thumbs, and palms. Aches and pains tossed them around at night as if they were many times older than they were.

Only when the sun disappeared, taking every last drop of light, did they put down their saws and hammers. By this time they were empty of all feelings besides hunger and exhaustion. They raised their dinner bowls to their sun-chapped lips with shaking hands. Then hands, bowls, and bodies fell to the ground. My boys slept so deeply, I worried they would never wake. At least then they would never have to see for themselves what was already clear to me: The ark would take years to build, many more than any of us would live. The flood would carry us away, along with the skeleton of our salvation.

. . .

It took two moons for Manosh to return. When the townspeople abruptly picked up their tents and hurried from their positions around the ark, I looked to the north. There were men with him— men who did not ride mules, men who had no sandals and walked barefoot across the burning desert with heavy sacks slung across their backs. Their chests were bare and divided by muscles more rounded than any I'd seen. Some had skin the same desert-dusk color as that of most people I had seen in my life, and some were a color that made me think they had never known the merciful shade of a tree.

As usual, Noah did not journey far to meet his cousin. He walked no more than a few cubits from the lumber pile. He glanced unhappily at the slaves and then up at Manosh.

"They will build our ark," Manosh said.

Noah pressed his lips together before whatever words had gathered on his tongue could leave his mouth. After a few breaths of silence, he said, "We do not have food for so many mouths."

"What little they need, I have brought."

Shem came up beside Noah and began to whoop. "Hallelujah!" he cried. "Japheth, Ham! Put down your hammers—put them down for good! *We are saved.*"

Japheth was so tired that when he looked up, he seemed surprised to see the many men standing on either side of Manosh. Ham was tired as well, but it did not weigh down his tongue. "Perhaps one day we will be slaves too, Shem. If so, I hope we will not know the language of our captors. Surely it's better not to hear people cry 'hallelujah' at the thought that you might break your own back doing their work."

"Better their backs than ours," Shem said.

"God blesses us," Japheth said. "May I rest now, Father?"

"Sleep, son," Manosh said. "Your burden is lifted."

Japheth did not move from his place beside his father. Everyone waited for Noah to decide whether he would accept the labor of slaves.

I did not like the thought of slaves being forced to build our ark, but neither did I like to think of my sons working themselves to death trying to complete such an impossible task. "Husband," I said, "there is no other way."

"Do not tell me what I already know. Make use of yourself. Go look at their rations, then count their heads and tell me if it is enough."

"No need to weary your feet, *woman*," Manosh said to me.

I could have almost forgotten that I had no name. I had grown accustomed to Zilpha calling me "Mother," and the people of the mob would not have called me by a proper name even if I'd had one. They preferred "old hag," "wife of the madman," and "sea woman." I liked all of these more than "woman," because they did not remind me that I had no name.

I looked to Noah to see his reaction to the insult. I hoped it might convince him that it would be better for me to have a name than to give his cousins a means of disrespecting him. Is not the wife of a great man worthy of a name? Then again, perhaps Noah's greatness was the reason he thought I needed no name other than "Noah's wife."

But his face showed nothing besides his usual disgust with Manosh and perhaps also with himself for accepting Manosh's help.

Manosh clapped his hands, and overseers brought forth a large flock of goats from the rear flank of his procession, along with three oxen pulling carts full of nuts and dried dates. I looked over the flock and carts and counted as many slaves as the fingers of twenty-one hands.

"Yes," I told Noah, "there is enough for at least three moons."

"Three very large moons," Manosh said, "or several of the usual size."

·   ·   ·

That evening, while Zilpha lay in the tent with her slave holding a parasol over her, Noah called his sons and me around him. "Manosh's slaves will help us build the ark, but they will not finish their work. Before the hull is complete, we will send them away. Do not think to put down your hammers while they are here."

"Father," Shem said, "why wear down our own strength when we have theirs?"

Noah continued, "Do not allow a day to pass in which you build less than the strongest slave."

"Father," Shem implored, *"please."*

"Do not recline while the sun is in the sky."

"It will take years—"

"And do not question my decisions."

. . .

Besides the overseers, only one of the men was able to keep any meat on his bones, and this was the cook. The rest toiled for no more reward than the smallest amount of goat and nuts it took to keep a man alive. They did not speak much, but when they did, it was in a language I had never heard.

"Do you understand any of their language?" I asked Ham.

"Enough to know that there are at least three. Some greet each other by touching their own chests, others by mouthing something they never say aloud."

I watched more carefully. Only some of the dark men had rings in their ears. These and the men who were the same color we were squatted while they wielded their hammers, while the others labored on hands and knees. They all starved and sweated beneath the pounding sun.

Once they discovered Noah did not hear well, the men with rings in their ears sang together in low voices. Every time Japheth told his father of this and Noah came to listen, the men went silent.

"Mother," Japheth insisted, *"tell* him."

"I am sorry, son, but I heard nothing of the noise you speak of."

When Noah turned away, Japheth spat at the ground near my

feet. It was so hot and dry that I feared the ark would catch fire, yet Japheth had brought forth what little moisture was left behind his parched lips to show his scorn for me.

.   .   .

I was carrying a pot of lentils to the cookfire one day when the desert seemed to wave in the distance. The wave came closer, as if a pack of animals was rushing toward me beneath the sand. I tried to move from its path, but the sun had taken my strength.

The wave hit me, sending the hidden fire in the sand burning up the length of my legs, through my body and all the way to my head. I started to fall. Before I landed upon the ground I was lifted off my feet and carried to the new patch of shade the ark had given us. First my backside, then my back, and last my legs and head were gently laid upon the ground. Sweat that was not my own tingled on my cheek and arm.

Suddenly there was a great commotion. Japheth was yelling and I heard the smack of a stick against flesh. "Leave him be," I tried to say. But when I opened my mouth my throat seemed to crack in half.

"Enough, Japheth," Ham cried. "Mother has sun sickness. The slave has done yet more of our work for us and brought her to the shade. Now we must bring her water. *Put down the stick.*"

"Shut up and draw her scarf down over her forehead," Japheth commanded.

I felt the scarf being pulled lower over my brow. I opened my eyes and there was Ham's face before me. Not more than ten cubits from us Japheth beat the slave, who did not make a sound; it was not the first time he had been beaten. Japheth's stick broke, and he hurried to the pile of lumber to get another. Noah followed him back. "What goes on here beneath the eyes of the Lord?" he demanded.

"Mother fell beneath the sun's strength, and this slave rushed her to the shade. I will fetch Mother some water."

"This slave saw Mother's brow, and cannot be left to spread word of it," Japheth said.

I knew from trying to rescue the three boys born at the same time that once you help someone you do not want any harm to come to him. "No," I whispered. "He will tell no one of my mark."

Noah held his hand out for the branch Japheth had brought back.

Japheth kept hold of it. "It must be done, Father."

"This slave does not speak our language and Manosh would not heed his words even if he did," Noah said. "He is no threat to the God of Adam or His plan for us. When the hull is complete Manosh's slaves will leave this land and never return." He took the branch from Japheth's hand and threw it into the desert. Then he walked away.

The stick lay more than thirty cubits from where Noah had thrown it. I was glad to see that though my husband's eyes and ears were worn down by his many years, his strength remained.

I was about to close my eyes again when I caught a glimpse of the slave's back. I wish I had not. My son had raised welts high up from the man's flesh.

The man did not look at me, and he did not rise. When Ham came back, he handed me a waterskin, and then handed one to the man. The man would not take it. This seemed to be at least some consolation to Japheth who snorted and stomped away. The man had a pink scar above his right eye. Besides the scar, his skin was so dark and wet it was like someone smeared olive oil across the night sky.

When I had drunk enough water to find my voice, I told the man, "I am sorry for my son's foolish temper." I hoped my tone would convey the meaning of my words. But the man's face did not change, just as it had not changed while Japheth beat him. He rose slowly, backed away a few cubits, and went to pick up his hammer.

"Bring him the waterskin, Ham. Then he will know he did nothing wrong, and we will not appear unjust to the rest of the men."

"If we appeared just," Ham replied while he did as I instructed, "they would get up and leave."

. . .

When the hull was almost complete, Noah told Manosh to take the slaves away. "We will finish the ark ourselves," he said.

Manosh's eyes widened. "Have you other slaves?"

"God requires only my sons' hammers to complete His ark."

"Six hands cannot complete this task in only one lifetime."

"I can see why it is me He chose," Noah said as if he were speaking to himself but loudly enough for Manosh to hear. "Those who do not know His might will learn soon enough."

He beckoned to our sons and turned back to the ark.

. . .

It did not take long for the overseers to start yelling commands. The slaves quickly set down their hammers and gathered together what was left of the rations. *Do they never think to turn upon their masters with those hammers they so easily set down?* Perhaps the mammoths scared them. Or perhaps their spirits had been broken.

"Have them bundle the timber too," Manosh told his men.

"No!" I cried. No one paid any attention to me.

I hastened from the cookfire and ran ahead of the slaves to where Noah stood directing our sons, who by this point needed no direction in what length to cut each piece of gopher wood. "Husband," I said, afraid that he had not heard.

But Manosh had spoken loud enough for even Noah to hear. Noah slowly turned to face him. "You have already given us this gopher wood."

"And *this* gift you do not wish to return?"

Slaves surrounded the pile of wood Japheth was measuring. Japheth glared up at them.

"It is owed me, for taking Zilpha on board the ark."

"The ark is made by my slaves and of my lands—the lands I have lived on for six-hundred years. It will not forget me now. I will leave the lumber with you, for the girl, daughter of the prophet Kesh. But I do not leave it for good. Do not think to board the ark without us."

One of Manosh's men shouted at the slaves. They lined up on either side of Manosh, facing the ark. It was time for Manosh to receive our thanks. He looked patiently down at Noah from where he sat upon his mammoth. I wished my husband would be quick about it so Manosh would take his eyes and his anger and his half-naked slaves away, and I could return to preparing the evening meal.

"My sons have appreciated the help of your slaves," Noah said stiffly.

Manosh continued to stare down at him.

"If we said 'thank you' a hundred times it would not be enough," Shem said from where he stood beside Noah. "You have saved us many moons."

Manosh looked hard at Noah. "I know you would do the same for me. We are family, bonded by blood and the Lord's blessing. We will journey together into the new world." He walked his caravan in a tight half circle and turned back toward his home.

If there truly was to be a flood, then the men who had built the ark had saved our lives. I wanted to thank them, but they did not know my language, and I did not know theirs.

CHAPTER 27

A SIGN

With construction of the hull almost complete, we could have spread out our sleeping blankets. Yet we never did. Zilpha and her slave slept next to each other on one end of the hull, while Noah, my boys, and I slept not more than a few cubits from one another on the other end. But I did not sleep much.

After Manosh's caravan left, people gathered around us once again. They seemed to sleep neither day nor night. The jeering had a new intensity. They called us mad, but they said it with such desperation that I began to think maybe we were not mad. I knew their secret; I could hear it in their voices. They were afraid.

Rocks hit the side of the hull with so much force that each morning I expected to find holes in the wood. I might have assumed it was the children who threw them, except for the strength with which they hit. On the end, where there was only a skeleton of the great ark to come, we would occasionally see a stone somehow balanced upon the tip of a crossbeam. Noah called this a sign.

"Of what?" I asked.

"How perfect God's aim will be when He hurls death upon the earth. He will drown the whole world except us."

To Noah and his God's credit, we remained untouched by stones, despite that there were so many of them, we had to clean the hull multiple times a day. If we had been on sea instead of sand, we would have sunk.

CHAPTER 28

COUNTDOWN

It took seven moons to build the ark. Once it was finished, you could not help but believe in the flood. As the ark's shadow slowly passed over the crowd with the rising and setting of the sun, everyone must have known that they would die.

My sons' jaws were set as if in stone while they applied pitch—twice and sometimes three times—to the same section of gopher wood. Surrounded by desert drought for many leagues in all directions, we had begun to fear the sea.

Noah tried to ease our dread. "It will rain not even two moons. Only forty days and forty nights." To Japheth, he said, "I am entrusting you with slaughtering the herd."

Japheth went straight to work. He did not hesitate between slitting the throat of one goat and another except to wipe off his knife. The animals bleated, bled, lost control of their bowels, and died. My chore: to cut, clean, dry, and salt their meat.

Zilpha would not rise from where she mourned her great beast. Noah stood over her and commanded her to help me.

"No," she said calmly from beneath her parasol.

Noah did not have time to argue, so he turned to me and said, "*Wife.*"

I knelt beside Zilpha's sleeping blanket. "Daughter, I am sorry for the loss of your mammoth."

"Good," she said.

I asked if she would help me with the meat we needed for our journey.

She did not want to damage her skin in the sun or roughen her hands with washing and scrubbing. "You are already worn," she told me. "This skin"—she lightly touched her arm—"these eyes, and the bones of my fingers need to last me another six hundred and ninety-three years. The flood is only one tiny piece of my journey. I cannot spend all of myself on it."

I did not know how to argue with her and did not have time to figure it out. She seemed completely unconcerned about the end of the world, and this bothered me more than her refusal to help.

. . .

Finally, it came to pass that the one-eyed boy who had threatened to tell the world of my mark came back as a man whose arms and calves bulged with muscle. He had one green eye and one black and red eye socket that he uncovered for a moment when he saw me look down upon him. I quickly moved to the other side of the deck. "Grandmother!" he called after me.

Noah did not leave the ark unless he had to relieve himself. None of us ever went far, and we seldom went alone. And so Jank camped near the ark and waited.

I did not know if I should alert Noah. I considered telling Japheth, but I did not want him to come to any harm. Jank was a more formidable opponent than a starving, overworked slave.

One afternoon when Noah walked onto the deck to survey his sons' work, Jank called up to him. "Father! You must remember me."

"No, I mustn't," Noah said irritably.

"I have come to ask for your blessing."

But Noah no longer seemed to hear him. He had finished looking over the deck and walked away.

The next day Jank yelled, "The God of Adam has sent me here with a message for you. I must speak to you at once."

Noah and I were again on the deck. Noah briefly squinted down at Jank, who lifted the cloth tied at a steep angle around his head to show Noah his eye socket. I doubted Noah could see well enough to recognize the boy, or that he would remember him even if he could clearly see him.

Noah easily ignored him. His hearing was fading almost as quickly as his sight. I envied him. It seemed as though God were shielding him from the world with the loss of his senses.

But the one-eyed man could not have known this. Especially not after one day when he managed to get Noah's attention. Noah was testing the side door of the ark, opening and closing it as if he had never seen a door before. I do not know why Noah stopped and squinted out at the man below.

"Hello, my father! It is Jank. I spared your life. Can you spare your ear for a few breaths?"

Without responding, Noah turned his attention back to the door.

"God commands it," the one-eyed man said.

Noah's nostrils flared. "Blasphemy! God did not send you to speak with me. He speaks to me Himself."

"I come bearing the knowledge of your God that you gave me nineteen years ago. I let you live, and your God let me live. *And I told no one of what you now keep secret.*" He looked hard at my head scarf. "Please repay my kindness by preserving my life. God asks that you take me with you on the ark."

Noah did remember Jank. I could tell by the blood that surged into his temples. He was coming alive as he used to when he yelled at the townspeople about the wrath of God. He had the look of a man in front of whom a large meal had just been placed.

"You could not kill me, and that is why you believe in the God of Adam. But He does not believe any more in you than He does in all the other sinners whose evil He will drown along with their bodies."

"But Father, how did I get so old if He is not watching over me?"

"You have gotten as old as you will."

"Why would the God of Adam save a man who is going to die?"

"We are all going to die, child."

"Maybe it is you who has gotten as old as you will and will be the first to die. I think you can hardly see me at all."

"And yet I know who you are."

The one-eyed man spat, and despite the distance between us, I saw the canines he had sanded into sharp points. "Do not test me as you test that door, old man. I will tell people what I saw upon your wife's brow. Then you will be killed, and God will be wise enough to give this ship to a younger man—one who has his sight, his hearing, and seed young enough to populate the new world."

Noah was unmoved by Jank's threat. "The God of Adam will not let you on this ark even if you are the last man left alive. Your blood is unholy, and there is no place for it in the new world. God would rather begin all over again than begin with you."

"But God commands—"

"Good-bye, boy," Noah said, and closed the door.

"Do not walk away from me!" Jank threatened the door. He waited, as if it might answer him. Then he yelled, "*Do not make me reveal what I know!*"

"I have a bad feeling about this," I told Noah that night. "Perhaps we should take the one-eyed man on the ark."

Noah refused.

.   .   .

The next morning, when I went to the cookfire, he was there. His green eye flashed at me, and before I could say or do anything, he began screaming, "This woman is a demon! Tear the scarf from her head, and you will see!"

I ran back into the ark. "What is it?" Ham demanded.

"We are doomed," I said. I could still remember my father saying this nineteen years earlier, but it had not seemed true until only a breath before.

.   .   .

The crowd screamed day and night for me to reveal myself, so they could know whether Jank spoke true. Fires were carried in from the town, and on Manosh's first visit to the ark after taking away the slaves, he had to leave not only mammoths but also several overseers, to throw sand into the flames before they reached the ark.

Manosh lowered his gaze onto my head scarf. "What is this talk of a demon?" he asked.

"There is no demon among us unless you have brought one," Noah replied.

Manosh continued to stare at my head scarf. But he did not ask me to take it off.

.   .   .

The jeering became nastier, and I became less afraid of being adrift in the darkness with three hundred cubits' worth of bugs and wild beasts.

So perhaps I will be forgiven this cruelty: When the flood swelled inside distant clouds, I looked to them and tried to draw them near with my gaze. I hoped that Noah's prophecy was true, despite all the people who had to die in order to make it so.

I was not the only one who lost my reason. People made claims of thunder and lightning that only they could hear or see. Little girls pointed to bird droppings and swore that they came not from any bird but from the cloudless blue sky. "White rain," they called it.

Other clans were starting to build ships as well, and I was afraid they would tear our ark apart for wood.

. . .

It was a relief when one morning, after praying all night, Noah announced, "We must hurry to prepare. We have only seven days."

That evening Ham came to stand inside my little fence of stones. I was roasting goat meat and the smoke was so thick I could hardly see his face. "What of how Father told Manosh only a few days ago that the flood would not come for another moon?" he asked.

"Perhaps the God of Adam has changed His plan."

"Or perhaps not. Father did not tell Manosh this until Manosh had said good-bye to Zilpha. She thinks Manosh and his cousins will be back soon enough to board the ark."

I did not want to let go of my relief. "I can worry only so much, son. I will not add this to my list."

CHAPTER 29

FLESH

*And of all that lives, of all flesh, you shall take two of each into the
ark to keep alive with you; they shall be male and female. From birds
of every kind, cattle of every kind, every kind of creeping thing on
earth, two of each shall come to you to stay alive.*

GENESIS 6:19–20

We could take only two of each unclean animal, yet many came in packs. All but two of each were slaughtered. We were allowed seven pairs of every animal that chewed its cud and had fully cloven hooves: oxen, sheep, goats, deer, gazelles, ibex, antelope, and mountain sheep.

"Why do we take more of those who chew their cud, husband?"

"Because those are clean animals. Their meat will sustain us."

"What is so clean about chewing, swallowing, and bringing forth the same straws of wheat over and over?"

"Wife, do not speak ill of God's laws."

He hurried away, staff swinging wildly in front of him. I looked silently into the sky. *Why do You make strange laws? And why have You called so many animals to Japheth's knife?*

Japheth snorted gleefully as a herd of camels appeared on the horizon. Though camels chewed their cud, they did not have fully cloven hooves and were therefore unclean. "More meat," Japheth said as Manosh's overseers escorted the beasts through the horde. Some men threw stones, but these fell a couple of cubits from the beasts, as if they had hit a wall.

Japheth was not awed by the spectacle. He thought only of slaughter.

"Son," I told him, "these animals are not clean. We cannot eat them."

This didn't stop Japheth's knife.

"I do not know how you manage to keep your blade so sharp, considering how generously you wield it," I said.

"It would not be right to do God's work with a dull one."

Though Noah had instructed Japheth to complete this bloody task, I trusted that if he knew the joy with which Japheth went about it, he would be as displeased as I was.

Japheth continued, "The more lives I take, the less of this chore I leave to the God of Adam."

To keep the animals from running away, he tied them together. He unsheathed his knife while I was standing in front of him. I averted my gaze, but I had no way to keep out the animals' panicked cries.

"We must burn them, Father, to make a sacrifice," Japheth told Noah one evening.

"Do not tell me again that we must do something. You will remain silent until the sun has come and gone once more."

So Japheth let the animals' screams speak for him. He must have believed that they told of his righteousness, but the voice that went up from the beasts testified only to his ruthlessness.

Of those left alive, many were hobbled. A great number of birds lost their wings. "Mother," Japheth called. "Come sweep these away! I can barely see my sandals."

Cages had been made for the animals, and they were herded onto the ark bleating, snorting, and roaring, and locked inside them. "You are Chosen," Noah told them as he walked the dark paths between the pens, waving his staff on the floor in front of him so that it hit the bars of the cages. The lowest level of the ark had no window, but Noah did not carry a candle. "You are Saved," he called into the darkness.

It took many positions of the sun to coax Noah's donkey into the ark. "Husband," I said, "I am afraid there will not be another generation of donkeys if this is one of the two we take." Though I was not fond of donkeys, they could be helpful for traveling and farming when they wanted to be.

"He is as virile as oldest son but more virtuous. He will do God's work when the time comes."

After all the animals were loaded into the ark, Noah ordered our sons to dismantle the ramp. "And you are never to leave the rope ladder down."

Soon people brought their own ladders. My sons were kept busy pushing them back to the ground. "No one but us can come aboard," Noah said, "or we will all die."

Zilpha preferred the animals' company to ours and was with them belowdecks. I was glad she was not around to hear this. I knew

Manosh and his cousins were no exception to this decree, even if they made it back before the God of Adam unleashed the floodwaters upon the earth.

.   .   .

"No!" I cried when Japheth cornered a dove on the deck near the bow of the ark and poised a small blade over its wings. I could not bear to see another pair of wings on the deck floor.

"Then how will I keep her on the ark?"

"The world will be covered in water. Where else will she go?" I did not know if even the tops of the trees would be covered. But if they were not, the bird would be better off in them than in an ark with Japheth.

He did not lower the blade.

"The God of Adam wants the animals exactly as they are. Do not anger Him any further," I said.

Japheth glared at me. I did not look away. After what felt like a long time but was likely no longer than the blink of an eye, he released the bird. She flew past me, the tip of one feather flapping against my cheek.

I walked toward Japheth and held my hand out for the little blade. When he did not give it to me, I reached for it. It slashed the tip of my finger as he yanked it away.

"Son!" I cried in surprise. "What has happened to make you so cruel?"

He laughed. His laugh was as far from happy as the earth is from the stars. Then he turned and walked away, which was merciful. I did not want to see his face for a while.

Ham came up beside me and took my hand in his own. "You got off much easier than most of the animals." He gently squeezed my finger to stop the bleeding. "Japheth is an animal worse than any other."

Ham's hatred of his brother had begun to weigh upon his brow. It hurt me to see it. "No," I said, "he is not. Perhaps if you had gone into town more . . ."

"The whores are not murderers, and at least the thugs and mercenaries murder people for some gain—spoils of food and riches."

"Noah has instructed him—"

"Cannot you see I am upset enough, Mother, without having to think of Father's madness as well?"

"We are doing what we need to in preparation for the flood."

"Noah's God is saving the wrong people."

My heart dropped into my belly. I took my hand from his. Ham had a sharp tongue, but it had never truly cut me before.

"I am sorry, Mother," he said. "I did not mean it."

"If He saves you and your brothers, I will worship Him gratefully in this life and the next."

I stepped forward and embraced him. He let me. Then we returned to our tasks. I cleaned the animals Japheth had slaughtered and prepared the meat for our voyage. Ham fed the animals, stroking the coats of those who would still allow it.

CHAPTER 30

A QUESTION, A DEAL

The animals were not the only ones I mourned. I missed Herai. I missed her nearly as much as I missed my father. When we had only one more day before the flood was to come upon us, I decided I must see Javan.

Ham tried to talk me out of leaving the ark, but he relented when he saw it was futile. Though it was night, he rubbed desert dust from his sandals over my forehead to cover my mark, then helped secure my head scarf. But at the last instant, when we had lowered the rope ladder and I had climbed over the wall of the deck and taken hold, he said, "No. *No!* Do not go."

I loosened my grip on the rope, and instead of using the rungs, I began to slide. I ignored the burning in my palms. Ham tried to pull the rope ladder back into the ark, but it was too late. When I reached the bottom, I let go and fell to the ground. In case anyone who had made camp around us had heard me, I quickly moved away from the ark.

"The demon woman!" a boy shouted. Luckily, children screamed "demon woman" so often that no one believed them anymore.

"Shut your brat up," someone yelled toward the boy's camp.

I hurried toward a clan with no tent and lost myself among them.

In town there were people enough that even if the boy had come looking for me, he would have little chance of finding me.

One of Javan's brutes guarded her tent.

"She asked to see me," I lied.

"Go rut yourself."

"You will be in mortal danger if she finds out I was here and you did not summon her."

He hesitated for only a breath before calling into the tent, "A dusty hag comes to see Jav—"

Javan appeared. She laughed. "Then you are a demon woman. It is the only way you could have made it here alive." She beckoned me inside.

I did not wait to be offered refreshment or a place to squat. "There is not much time left before the flood comes. It will be upon us tomorrow."

She raised an eyebrow. She still didn't believe in the flood. "Then do not delay. Say what it is you've come for."

"I have come to ask you a question."

"Why should I answer it?"

"For Herai. If you bring her to the ark tomorrow, I will throw down the rope."

"What will she do on the ark when the rains do not come?"

"Be wife to Japheth. We will need Shem's wife as well."

Her eyes gleamed. Though surely she didn't want me to know it, I could see that the thought of Herai finally marrying one of my sons brought her great happiness. "Ask your question."

"Before I came to Sorum—perhaps nineteen years before but maybe less—were there ever any here who looked like me? Either branded with an X or not?"

"What are you asking?"

"I am asking of my mother."

Javan looked at me. I did not know if the pity in her eyes meant that my mother had not come to Sorum or that she had. "Not a one," she said.

I did not ask if she spoke true. She was a murderer, but she was not a liar.

CHAPTER 34

THE SLAVE WOMAN

Javan's brutes saw me back to the ark. Ham threw down the rope ladder, and shortly after climbing it, I was fast asleep on my blanket.

I was awakened by the tap of Noah's staff against my leg. He stood over me. "The slave woman cannot come to the new world," he said quietly. "You must tell her to leave and see that she does."

For an instant I was filled with fear. I thought he somehow knew of the promise I had made Javan, and was speaking of Herai. My confusion quickly cleared. Still, I did not like Noah's words. I sat up. "Husband, the woman is no trouble. She eats little and never speaks."

He lowered himself to my ear, perhaps hoping to speak softly enough that God would not hear. "I do not like it either. She seems a good slave, without sin." He quickly added, "But the God of Adam comprehends things we cannot. There is a reason, even if we cannot see it."

I thought of the woman's mark and how it could only be by some miracle that both she and I had survived. Should not we honor this miracle? "She is a hardworking and obedient woman."

"God has commanded that I can take only you, my sons, and their wives."

I started to shake. "Does He have to know? There is much hiding space in the ark."

"Do not blaspheme, wife."

"I am sorry," I said, lowering my head to give the impression that I was ashamed. I waited a few breaths, then said, "Ham can take both Zilpha and the slave woman as wives. The new world will need slaves even more than the old one. How will we harvest the whole world without help?"

"Our blood and the blood of our sons cannot run through the veins of slaves."

"Then where will slaves come from?"

He did not answer. He said only, "Someone else will carry out this task."

LAST LIGHT

Black clouds hovered in the distance, casting night below. Towns-people pulled up their tent stakes and rushed south, away from the sea. But black clouds rose up from that horizon as well. People searched frantically for a patch of blue in the sky, turning round and round and round.

The wind and the clouds had come for us from all directions, pressing the darkness closer until only a small circle of light was left. A shallow coat of water, littered with the things it had destroyed and the lives it had taken, rushed up over the desert through the town. Bowls, sandals, empty sacks, feathers, goatskins, and even a lifeless infant were visible upon the ground. The darkness that sur-rounded us was rain.

The frenzy began. People fought to move to the middle of what light remained. Some were trampled. A little girl tripped over them, and—beneath the feet of her neighbors—joined her body to the mass grave piling up upon the road. No one stopped to pillage teeth or jewels.

Wind struck from one direction and then another. It seemed to me that all the winds of the world were competing to take what was left of our lives. Objects began to hit the hull—blankets, tent poles, even a ram's horn that traveled up the deck wall and flew close to my eye.

"Where are my second cousins?" Zilpha asked.

Despite the pounding of the rain upon the deck, the howling of the wind, the crying of the sinners, and the softness of Zilpha's voice, I heard her. She had been on her sleeping blanket, but now she hurried onto the deck, and her slave hurried after her. I noticed she did not have her parasol. Perhaps the screams of the sinners had woken them.

I had been waiting for everyone to go below so I could stand near the rope ladder, ready to throw it down to Javan when she brought Herai and Ona. But I had to make sure Zilpha returned safely to the belly of the ark. Japheth was also on deck, eager to use his spear on anyone who tried to climb the hull.

"We must get belowdecks," I yelled. Japheth gave no sign that he had heard me.

"Manosh was here only a few days ago," Zilpha said. "Surely Noah told him the flood was almost upon us."

"Almost" encompasses a few days and a moon. "Yes," I said. "But we must get below."

"They will come," she said. "Of this I am sure."

"Come now," I said, moving toward the hatch.

"My parasol is missing. Has someone brought it up here as a shield from the rain? It is meant for sun. Rain will ruin it."

"As it will ruin us. I do not know where your parasol is. But gopher wood will shelter you better than your parasol." I looked up at the black clouds, hoping her eyes would follow mine.

Though she did not glance up, she did not argue. She and her slave followed me below. I worried for the slave. Had Noah changed his mind about telling her to leave the ark?

Japheth would not follow us belowdecks to the gathering place, but his voice soon came down the hatch. "I see the parasol! It has blown from the ark and drifts along the ground."

"Do not concern yourself," I said loudly. "We can make another."

"That one is mine, given to me by my father," Zilpha called up to Japheth. "Please get it for me, brother."

"Send the slave," Japheth said. "And hurry! I will take up the ladder when she reaches the ground and wait to send it back down when she has the parasol. I will make certain no one climbs aboard."

"No, Zilpha," I said. "You will lose your parasol *and* your slave if you send her."

"I cannot throw away the years the parasol will add to my life. Go," she told her slave. "The spirits of my father and grandfather will watch over you."

Slaves are trained with quick hands and whips to neither smile nor frown. The slave woman's face showed nothing as she went to retrieve the parasol.

I started to follow, but Noah stopped me. "Wife. Let us all pray together"—he must have sensed my restlessness—"briefly, as soon as Japheth returns."

Noah, our sons, Zilpha, and I waited for Japheth on the second level, where the lesser beasts were caged. A little piece of gray light streamed through the window, so I could see that when Japheth returned, he was alone.

"Let us take a few breaths to praise God that we are all here," Noah said, closing his eyes.

"Where is my slave?" Zilpha interrupted.

"She fell and was trampled," Japheth said, "and your parasol along with her." There was satisfaction pulling at the edges of his mouth. It caused a knife to twist in my belly. Zilpha surely saw it too, with her almost perfect eyes that had seen the sun only once.

She turned from Japheth to Noah. Spots of red flared in her pale cheeks. Other than that, I would not have been able to tell that she was angry. The apricots and cream had not fully left her voice. "I suppose I will have to get used to people dying," she said, the words floating from her lips and hovering over us, "since I am going to live for seven hundred years. *With or without the parasol.*" She turned to Noah, whose eyes were closed and whose lips moved with silent prayers. "More years than you have lived, dear Father. My children, grandchildren, their grandchildren, and all of you"—she looked at each of us in turn—"will die while I live."

As she walked off toward the animal cages there was a violent *Thwack!* Someone hit the hull. *Whack thwack thwack!*

I ran toward the hatch. "Wife," Noah called. This time I did not stop. My sons followed.

From the deck, my sons and I watched the horde crashing against the hull. I prayed that my father had died peacefully of old age, so he would not have to die in this storm. People were trying to climb over one another. Men even stepped upon children in their attempt to be at the top of the mob. Hooks with ropes attached were thrown on deck. Most hit the hull and fell down, but a few made it over the deck wall. My sons threw them off, all but one, which Shem would not let go of. The people holding the rope below were fighting, hitting, and kicking, and then there was a breath in which no one held the rope. Shem pulled it on board. Then he moved a few cubits to the right and lowered it again.

"What are you doing?" Japheth yelled.

"We need wives."

"Shem, you already have a wife," I told him. "We must watch for her."

He did not seem to hear me. He gazed at a girl trying to claw her way up the ark while dodging the objects hitting the hull. A piece of a clay pot sliced her cheek open. I did not know why this caused my heart to ache. Around us, people were trampling and fighting one another. All of them were going to die. But as the blood gushed from the girl's cheek, I wished I could bandage her wound.

Shem struggled to bring the rope to her. He quickly realized it was better to use the wind than to fight it. The rope whipped diagonally against the hull while Shem tried to position it so it would be within the girl's reach, if the wind did not change. He waited until it hit the girl in the head. "Hold tight!" he called. She had come out of her daze enough to wrap her hands around the rope when a boy knocked her out of the way and took hold of it.

"Let go of the rope," Japheth told Shem, "so the sinners below can die, as God has commanded."

"I must have a wife, and you must too. Our happiness lies at the end of this rope. We will knock the boy off and send it back for wives."

The boy managed to climb up the hull, bloodying the rope where his hands came apart on it. Shem hit him with a plank of wood, and Japheth jabbed his spear at him. The boy screamed and grasped the spear in both hands. He fell to the ground, taking it with him.

"My spear!" Japheth cried. He swore.

"I am sure that is what he would say if he could," Ham said.

Japheth swung around and struck Ham straight across the face. He had the wind behind him, and Ham was knocked back upon the deck.

I hurried over to my favorite son. He rolled away from me onto all fours. He was breathing hard. *Thank you, gods,* I whispered, *for not taking his breath.* Then I thought of Noah's God, the God of Adam, Who I finally understood was all-powerful.

I knew I would never again pray to other gods. If they actually existed, still they did not matter. They were no match for Noah's God.

"Mother of Shem and Japheth!" a familiar and welcome voice called from the ground. "I have your daughters!" Javan wore a halter of metal spikes and carried a sword. Pieces of cloth, fur, and blood were on the tips of the spikes. She held a girl by the hair. The girl was huge with child. She was tied with thick leather straps to Herai. Unless Javan untied them, they would not be able to climb the rope ladder.

"Ona, my love!" Shem cried. He threw down the simple rope he held. I hoped it would be enough.

Though the girl was small-framed, with a belly large enough to contain three children, she managed to catch it and knot it around the leather straps securing her to Herai. She gripped the rope and yelled for Herai to do the same. Men tried to hold on to the girls, but Javan sliced their legs until someone clubbed her in the face. She fell down and was lost in the crowd.

Herai started screaming. She let go of the rope. Because it was tied to the leather straps around her and Ona, she did not fall. I silently begged Noah's God to make sure the straps withstood the panicked weight of the girls. I am sure it took many moons off my life to help Shem and Ham drag them up onto the deck. As soon as we wrestled them over the wall of the ark, I fell to the floor and continued to gasp for air. When I had caught my breath enough to speak, I turned my head toward Herai's sobs. "Your mother is strong. There is no need to worry," I lied.

Japheth stepped over me. To keep him from tossing the girls back over the deck wall, I grabbed his ankle. I did not need to. As he looked at Ona, his strength fled his body like a ghost. His mouth went slack and then fell open. His hands dropped limply to his sides. Even in the gray light, tied to Herai with ropes, and more pregnant than any woman I had ever seen, Ona was beautiful.

"*Oh,*" Japheth said.

He took hold of a saw and put it to the straps that held the two girls together.

Herai flinched away from the blade. I held her hand tightly in my own. "Careful for your wife, Japheth," I said. "You are sawing too close to her body."

When the rope was cut, I pulled Herai against my breast. She struggled free and went to look over the wall of the deck at the ground below.

Without even half a breath's hesitation, Japheth grasped her from behind and hoisted her over the side of the ark. Herai fell into the mob of people trying to climb up the hull and disappeared.

"Did you really think your dirty whore spawn was good enough for me?" Japheth yelled. Neither Javan nor Herai was visible, but Japheth gathered saliva into the corner of his mouth and spat at the crowd where Herai had vanished. "God will wash you both to death!"

My eyes moved over the people below. "Herai?" I yelled. "*Herai!*" No answer. "Javan?"

The wind howled louder than all the wolves in the world put together. Bits of rain from the clouds that lay less than a league in every direction hit my face. Above us, the sky turned from blue to purple and then to red. It began to bubble like a pot of water left too long on the cookfire.

I looked at everything—tents flying blindly through the air; people pushing and climbing, fighting and dying; the beauty of the girl who carried my grandchild; the mix of sadness, anger, and courage upon the face of my favorite son. I tried to absorb it all one last time, to memorize it, before the world went black.

{ BOOK TWO }

CHAPTER 33

DARKNESS

All the fountains of the great deep burst apart,

And the floodgates of the sky broke open.

GENESIS 7:11

Thunder booms and the sea falls from the sky. Out of the bowels of the ark come bleating, braying, and almost human-sounding cries. We are blinded by darkness for a breath before lightning streaks the sky and sea with white fire. Then the whole world is drowned again in black.

People scream as they fight to keep their heads above the sea. Some scream for help; some scream because they know they are going to die.

Still, the ark remains fixed upon the earth. All else is chaos. Some of those who haven't built ships have made rafts of tent poles—more tent poles than one family would have, yet there is not enough room for more than a few people on each. In a lightning flash, I see children throw a woman, maybe their mother, from their raft. In another flash, I see a man using his arms to try to stay afloat near a raft carrying a young woman and a child. When the lightning illuminates the world again, the man is alone on the raft.

If there is anyone in the world who has a raft while Javan does not, I am certain that fortunes will change. Otherwise, it will be up to me to change them. With Ham's help. He has brought up planks coated in pitch, and I am ready to throw them into the sea if I spot Javan or Herai below.

Noah struggles against the wind. He has come up to see the world end. But he watches it with his eyes closed while rain pounds against his eyelids. I am close enough to see his lips move. He is praying to God while God destroys the life He put upon the earth. I hope He has not yet gotten to Herai.

During the next flash, I will find the rope.

The sea lifts the ark. I stumble for a breath before the wind—or perhaps the God of Adam—knocks me down. Lightning cracks the sky and illuminates the deck. It seems to me that it lights the rope brighter than all else. The rope is like a small, solid line of sunshine. The God of Adam must have heard my thought and mistaken it for a prayer.

I start crawling. The last layer of pitch has not fully dried, giving me the tiniest measure of traction. Enough that I am able to make my way, ever so slowly, toward the rope.

Noah stops praying. "Wife!" he yells at me. "Get below!"

There are many reasons why I should obey my husband. But then there is Herai. God must want her on the ark. Why would the rope glow brighter with each flash of lightning if not to beckon me closer? I try to dig my nails into the pitch, but the sea throws the ark up in the air, and when we land, someone smacks into me. We hurl against the wall of the deck.

The ark rights itself, and the body pushes off of me. "Father?" Japheth calls as he stands up. "Father?"

I rise onto all fours and then onto my feet. The wind is at my back. Lightning flashes, and I run toward the rope faster than my own legs could possibly carry me. The hook attached to the rope is cold and slippery. "Ham!" I call. Though there is no reason he should hear me amid the screaming, the crashing of the sea, and thunder, he does.

His face turns toward mine. "Herai," he says.

"Yes."

Together we secure the hook to the inside wall of the ark.

When lightning flashes, we look into the sea at the multitudes of people on rafts. One of the rafts bursts into flame. I do not know what happens to the people on this raft; I can make out no one amongst the flames. But I can see Herai crouching on the raft nearest to the one that burns. With one hand, Javan grips her daughter's arm. With her other hand, she tries to hold on to both her sword and the raft.

The fire beside them is starting to smoke. It will be out soon, and Herai and Javan will be cloaked in darkness.

"Javan!" I call. She does not hear me.

Ham is yelling her name too. "Together," I tell him. We call her name, and she looks up at us.

Ham casts the rope into the sea beside them. Though it is at most five cubits away, the water is too rough for Javan to reach it or to go into the water to retrieve it. We pull the rope back up, and Ham casts it again. It lands a few cubits from the raft. The fire is giving way to smoke. Dimly, we watch Javan let go of her sword, jump in, and grasp the rope. She swims back to the raft and beckons to Herai.

The fire dies.

Below us, caged and uncaged animals crash from wall to wall. But now I hear thuds not just below but sounding across the deck toward us. I fear some animal has escaped and is coming to punish the human flesh that caged him. Zilpha's voice reaches out from the darkness. "Here," she says, though no one can see anything in the dark, "tie the rope around his chest."

Flash.

I see Zilpha on the back of one of the mammoths. Ham and Shem rush toward it. After a breath, the beast's heavy footsteps sound slowly across the ark. I pray to the God of Adam that the beast is pulling Javan and Herai closer to safety.

Flash.

Japheth is beside me. "Sinners!" he cries.

"Let them on," Shem says. Even without seeing his eyes, I know he is looking at Herai.

"Father," Japheth yells. "Come stop this wickedness!"

Ham and I pull Javan and Herai over the side of the ark as they choke on swallowed pieces of the sea. The sea inside them has made them as heavy as men. I get behind Herai, and though my joints ache and my arms are shaking, I press upon her stomach until I feel her lean forward and give up the contents of her stomach. The darkness and the rain fall over us like a tent that has collapsed wetly down upon our heads. Javan is alternating between choking and speaking in short, panicked bursts. I cannot understand her. I have never known her to be scared.

Flash.

Japheth and Javan are wrestling. I try to run to them, but the ark is tossing, and my feet slip out from under me. I drop to my hands and knees and crawl toward them through the dark.

Ham yells, "You rotting goat's cock!"

Flash.

Javan is nowhere in sight. I look over the side of the ark, and she is there, bouncing on the sea. In the distance, I see a large ark-shaped piece of darkness—a ship—that there is no time to worry about now.

"The rope!" I cry.

"I have made it so she cannot grasp a rope," Japheth says. When the next flash comes, he holds a thumb out to me. "She can only die, as she is meant to."

"I'll cut off *your* thumbs," Ham yells at Japheth. "Even the little one between your legs."

The world goes black again. I should not have let go of Herai.

"God commands," Japheth announces from somewhere nearby, "that I throw this sinner's spawn over too."

Noah's voice twists out of the darkness, enraged. "God does not waste His time speaking to you. The girl will stay. She is your wife."

"Praise You, God of Adam," I whisper.

THE GIANT VERSUS THE SEA

I do not know if it is day or night, or if day and night exist anymore. I do know I am dreaming, because I am surrounded by grandchildren who have not yet been born. I tell them of the flood and the tragedy I witnessed after Herai boarded the ark. I tell them of the nephil. I say nothing of the people who tried to climb up the side of the ark and what Japheth did to them.

"God was drowning all the beings of the world from weakest to strongest. First pregnant women, and infants and toddlers who had been separated from their mothers, were knocked down by the sea. It covered the ground and rose so quickly that you would have thought countless days of unbroken downpour had passed between the flashes of lightning. People were swallowed whole. When the tenth flash of lightning lit the world, all the pregnant women and motherless infants and toddlers were gone.

"The next people taken by the sea were those who fought each other for the trees and clung to them like lovers. Men and women alike were layered upon their bark, holding on to each other's hair, backs, and legs, their feet not more than a few cubits off the ground. The water came for them: injured mercenaries, whores, and children just like you, who were probably strong enough to have climbed higher, if only there had been time.

"By the twentieth flash of lightning, the sea had eaten the tree trunks and all those who clung to them.

"A few people made it to the very tops of the trees. Their fate was cruelest of all. They could climb no higher; they could only wait. Wind pruned them from the treetops until just the strongest remained. They heard people below screaming, and then they heard the crashing of the sea. Worse than hearing the people scream was listening as their screams were abruptly silenced. With each flash of lightning, those in the tops of the trees saw the horrible power of the sea. And yet they may have welcomed the lightning. More terrifying than watching death come for you is knowing it is coming and having to wait for it in darkness. The sea reached up from the earth and consumed the trees and all of the people without rafts.

"Rain continued hurtling down from the heavens. It hit us so hard, it felt as if it were being thrown. I never knew how sharp water could be. When the lightning came, we opened our eyes to see what was left of the world, and the rain slashed us nearly blind. On deck, the sea mounted our ankles and rose to our knees. Yet the ark remained on the ground even as people on rafts floated past.

"Soon though, the sea started to come not just from the sky but from the center of the earth as well.

"Children, the ark was huge, three hundred by fifty cubits. Can you think of anything heavy enough to lift that much gopher wood, filled with all the species of the world, off the ground? No number of men or beasts could have raised the ark from the earth. Yet as easily as a strong wind lifts a feather, *the sea lifted it*.

"The wind and the dark carried us we knew not where but far. Our eyes were of no use in the darkness, even when we dared to open them against the blades of rain. Everything was black, even us. I did not believe that we would ever emerge.

"But then flashes of lightning started coming closer together, one flash quickly mounting another. I risked my sight in order to open my eyes. The lightning was unlike any you should ever hope to see. From unbearable darkness, we had entered into unbearable light.

"That was when I saw one of the Nephilim. His torso was larger than twenty men across and ten high. It looked as if he were wearing a skirt of thrashing water. His eyes were black with rage as he smacked at it. The sea turned a few of his nails backward and ripped them from his body. But still he slapped at it, bloodying it with his leaking fingers. Turning it pink and then red.

"How must this grandson of God have felt, dying at his grandfather's hands? I doubt he had ever encountered anything he could not smack away, anything he could not hurt or kill. There is no sound sadder than a giant crying. We are used to babies and women and sometimes men crying. But when a descendant of God cries, the world cries with him. The clouds shook from the strength of his sobs. His tears were added to the water that sought to drown him.

"Would it drown him before he could pull the ark into the sea or punch a hole in the hull to drown us? Our ark had no sail, no rudder. We thought we were taking our last breaths as the wind began to hurl us toward him. Uncle Ham was yelling at me to join Shem, Ona, Herai, and Zilpha belowdecks, but I could not take my eyes off the giant.

"'Take up your weapons!' Uncle Japheth yelled.

"Your grandfather knew there was no use in trying to fight one of the giants with weapons, so he prayed. He prayed for our lives and the nephil's death. I prayed for all of our lives. 'Two of *every* creature,' I cried up at the God of Adam. Perhaps He did not hear me over the pounding of the rain.

"As we came within thirty cubits of the giant, I could sometimes see his face through the rain. It looked like separate pieces of clay slapped together. His nostrils flared five cubits in either direction, and each of his eyes held enough fury to win a war. But maybe not this war. The sea he was smacking away fought against the sea that carried us toward him.

"Waters clashed beneath the ark, raising us as high into the sky as the top of the tallest mountain. The goat meat in my stomach rose into my throat. For an instant, we were perfectly balanced on the wave.

"Then the giant started losing; the sea he was smacking away could not hold back the sea that rushed toward him.

"'Hold on!' Uncle Ham cried.

"I still remember the blink of an eye in which I was suspended in air before we started to fall. It was the feeling I'd had in my head since Grandpa Noah started speaking of the flood, and finally, it had spread to my body.

"Then the bow of the ark tipped toward the giant, and we were falling face-first into the sea. As we plunged, I gripped the hatch's handle with my hands. The rest of my body lifted into the air.

"I had never swum before. I had never even been in water up to my knees. The sea slapped my eyes harder than hands can slap. It entered my nose, mouth, and ears, and filled the inner passages of my body. I could not breathe; there was no room for air.

"When the ark righted itself, water from the bow spread across the deck. The sea fell from my back, and if I'd had the strength, I would have stood up. But the water in my body did not go anywhere except deeper. My lungs were drowning inside me.

"Footsteps splashed over the deck. Uncle Ham lifted me and pressed his fingers between my ribs until I gave up enough of the sea to gasp for air. Ham tried to open the hatch and push me down the ramp to the second level, but there was a sudden thwack upon the hull. We were thrown against the wall of the deck where the giant's hand had hit it. He drew his hand back to strike again.

"'We mean you no harm,' I called to him. But the waters and the wind were hurtling us toward him again, and Uncle Japheth gripped a spear that was drawn back as purposefully as the giant's hand. The giant looked at him with bloodshot eyes and hit us, once more knocking us against the deck wall. Somehow Uncle Japheth kept hold of his spear.

"'You'll get us killed,' Ham yelled.

"'Is no one else man enough to defend the ark?' Japheth yelled back. He was as enraged as the giant.

"'You cannot defend the ark with spears or swords or daggers,' Noah said. 'We must pray.'

"I took my eyes off the giant to look up at the sky. *Why do You pit the ark against the nephil? Do You mean to save only him or us?*

"When the giant drew his hand back again, the waters were crashing higher against his chest. He did not know how to swim; there had never been an opportunity to learn. Until the flood, water probably never reached waist-high upon any giant. His great chest was heaving with anger and exhaustion. This time, when he hit us, the sea caught his elbow. Instead of winding back his arm to strike, he reached over the wall of the deck. His fingers were wrinkled prunes of flesh, and they bled where the sea had torn his nails from his body. The fingers were coming down onto the deck. We rushed from their path. All but Uncle Japheth. He bent his knees deep and braced his spear against the deck.

"Children, you see the lines on your own little palms? They crisscross and form triangles. The lines of the giant's palm seemed to form a perfect target in the center. This was where Japheth jabbed the spear with all his might.

"The giant's lower lip fell so that his huge mouth lay open, yet no sound issued from his throat. A tear big enough to drown any one of you rolled from the outer edge of one eye. He raised his hand up, with the spear stuck through the palm.

"Japheth kept hold of the spear and was lifted off the deck. He jerked his body around, trying to free the spear. Blood poured not just from the giant's fingertips but from his palm as well. I yelled at Japheth to let go of the spear. When he didn't, I grabbed his legs—no easy task, considering the force with which he kicked them. I was lifted from the calf-deep water on deck, almost ten cubits into the air. My weight was not enough to unhook Japheth's fingers from the spear or the spear from the giant's palm.

"He drew his hand back, and Japheth and I dangled over the sea. It smacked up at my feet, then rose to my legs and then to my waist. My tunic tangled around my thighs.

"'Please,' I called to the nephil.

"My father, your great-grandfather, said that Nephilim do not see well, but the giant's eyes met mine and gripped them despite the tossing of the sea. He lifted his hand higher and raised it above his head to get a better look at me. Japheth flailed his legs. 'Let go so I can kick him!' he screamed at me. If I let go, I would fall into the thrashing sea. But I could not keep hold of Japheth's wet leg as he tried to shake me off.

"I did not have far to fall. A wave rose up to meet me and carried me with it as it crashed down to rejoin the sea. The cold knocked the breath from my body and seized my heart. The deep pulled me near."

I do not tell them that the sea wanted me the way a man wants a woman—I could not rise, I could not breathe.

"I knocked into something solid, and small enough that my arms could encircle it. The giant's littlest toe. I tried to travel up along the slant of his foot and climb the hair on his legs. But the sea would not let me, and the sea had become master of everything on earth.

"You might not believe me, children, and I hope you will never know for yourselves, that the sea's greatest weapon isn't its violent crashing or its depth. It is the cold. My mind was losing its sway over my hands.

"If you have ever been underwater for long, you know it's as hard to keep your mouth closed as it is to swim through the center of the earth to the other side. Without my permission, my lips unlocked and my jaw stretched wide, seeking air and whatever warmth the air could provide. This time the water did not stop at my lungs. It filled every organ, every space, every passageway, even my veins. *The God of Adam is going to let me drown*, I thought.

"I knew I was the least needed of all those God had put on the ark. Noah was the prophet of His word, and our sons and daughters-in-law were tasked with repopulating the world. I could clean and weave. But so could everyone else, even Noah and my sons, if they could bring forth the necessary humility. As for cooking, we had dried meats, dried fruits, and nuts—foods that needed little preparation. Perhaps my rations should have been divided among Noah and the children instead.

"My body panicked, but my mind was done fighting. *Please, keep my sons and daughters-in-law healthy*, I said, *and spare this giant.*

"Red descended through the swirling sea. The giant's hand, the one without the spear in it, was coming closer. Then the giant lowered his head into the waters as well. He looked down at me, and our eyes met again. I was too cold to be afraid when he pinched me between his thumb and forefinger, cracking one of my ribs as a man would accidentally crack the shell of a small beetle he picked up, no matter how gentle he was.

"The giant's balance was unsteady. Giants are known for stumbling and sometimes taking out whole villages beneath their feet. Yet he was able to bring me toward his face. He began to choke, just as I was. *Why has he lowered his head into the sea?*

"A current caught him and smacked him sideways. Without his feet on the ground, he could not regain his balance. Still he pushed me toward the surface. But the sea refused to let me leave. My giant struggled to his feet, his footfalls raising the deep. Sand swirled around us. The sea was growing taller, rising over my giant's head, but he refused to fall. He lifted me up, and I broke the sea's surface.

"Air—there is nothing so delicious in the entire world.

"The currents grasped him now. They jerked him first in one direction and then another. Still he kept me above the surface of the sea.

"Ham, Shem, and Herai were pressed against the wall of the deck. Ham and Shem screamed, 'Mother! *Mother!*' My whole body choked on the sea and the cold, and I did not know if I was going to survive, yet I felt a speck of joy to hear my sons calling to me. Ham held one end of a rope and tossed the other end toward me. The wind knocked it back into the ark.

"He tried again, and again the wind returned the rope to him. I leaned toward the ark, stretched my arms in front of me, and prayed. My giant heard my prayer. We began to move toward the ark. The faces of my family became clearer to me and all seemed to contain the same emotion: hope.

"As we came within ten cubits, their expressions changed. Though they were happy that I was near, the giant's arm came near as well, and it would smack against the hull in the next few breaths. My body was trapped in his fingers, but I leaned my head back to signal him to slow down. By this time, though, he had little say where we went. The water climbed higher in search of me. I suddenly knew what the people who had made it to the tops of the trees felt: a breath of utter helplessness, followed by the wailing of a small wild part that refuses to give up.

"The wailing unleashed itself into my limbs. My mind had taken hold of them again. Even before the water reached me, I began beating my arms as if I could push it back down. My head was not far from the hull, my feet not far from the sea. Both closed in on me. The giant did not let go of me as the sea rushed over my legs and mounted higher to suckle at my breasts. The side of my head knocked against the hull, and I felt what little warmth was left in my body bleed out of the gash in my ear. That gash turned into the scar you see now. My arms and legs stopped moving. As the water rose over my nose, I said good-bye to my family.

"Then I was buoyed up and tossed skyward. The giant released me into the air. 'Grab the rope,' Uncle Ham called down to me. But my hands no longer worked. I was at the mercy of the sea, and the sea has no mercy.

"*God of Adam, before you kill me, please, let me see my family one more time.* And then I grasped the rope.

"A rope burns without flames but burns nonetheless. I did not feel it at the time. I felt the wind and the cold, and the smacking of my body against the hull, and then the hands of my family pulling me over the deck wall. Fingers pressed into my aching ribs, and my stomach heaved and sent up pieces of the sea.

"'Japheth?' I asked.

"'We pulled the fool from the sea, and now he sharpens another spear,' Ham said.

"*For what?* As soon as I wondered this, the giant must have pushed off the bottom of the sea. The surface of the water, already greatly chipped from the rain and heaving in the wind, now shattered. The giant's hand reached toward us, trying to grasp the wall of the deck. *Can the ark keep us* and *the giant from drowning?* That was a question for which I did not have an answer. The side of the ark tipped toward the sea with each attempt the giant made. When he finally gripped the wall, his bloody fingertips touching the deck, Japheth rushed forward and stabbed the giant's wrist.

"First with a spear, then with a dagger, then with a sword.

"The huge hand released the ark. Japheth tried to reclaim his weapons. 'I command you, let them go,' Grandpa Noah said. This time Japheth listened. My sons joined together to hoist the giant's half-lame hand over the wall. The God of Adam must have helped them.

"Now both of the giant's hands were wounded. I peered over the wall with what little strength the sea had left me. I saw only waves crashing. When the waters stopped thrashing, I knew they had digested the giant. If they could bring down the nephil, I knew that not only he but all the world outside the ark had been murdered by the sea.

"I lay down on the deck. The rain was like a stampede, and I wanted it to trample upon my head until I could not feel my heart. For a while I did not want to be awake to witness any more tragedies. I heard someone telling me to get up, then telling someone else to get me up. Then I heard nothing.

"But children, I must wake now. There are animals to tend and water to bail. I just wanted you to know, in case I do not make it to the new world, of the great giant. He saved my life. He and all of his kind are gone now.

"Or maybe not. The world is bigger than we can see all at once. Big enough, perhaps, to hide a giant."

CHAPTER 35

LIFE ABOARD THE ARK

When the sea is rough, you do not wake up in the morning and wonder what to do. You bail water, eat when your stomach allows, and most of all, hold on for dear life. That is, if you are lucky. Or blessed. Often there is no sleep to wake from. Just a long spell of darkness broken only by lightning.

If there is a chance to catch your breath, that is all you do: breathe. There is no time to worry about the ship you have seen in the distance. Well, not usually. When you do think about it, you wonder if it was your imagination, driven by fear and by hope that the eight people on board the ark are not the only ones left in the world.

When it is safe to feed the animals—some of which are injured from the force your sons must use to return them to their cages whenever they break out—you feel a flicker of sadness for them. You do not have the energy to feel it much. You are mildly grateful that when your oldest son corrals the animals too violently, your second-born—despite his bloodthirst—stops his older brother's whip because he fears what the Lord will do if one of the creatures He has chosen to save is killed.

You see in flashes. You forget how your husband walks or how your children's expressions change. Only Zilpha seems the same: nearly motionless, calm.

The one joy God has left in the world is being near Ona when she is on deck and lightning strikes. Her almond-colored eyes are slightly too big for her face, and this awkward, girlish feature makes it hard to look away. We are all in awe of her—all but Shem. Though he grabs at her when she's nearby, he rarely looks at her. He may not even know that sometimes her eyes turn brown. Her lashes are the longest I have ever seen, shining and black because of the rain. She seems like a creature not altogether human—queen of an unearthly species that is more attractive than ours. One that is more beautiful when wet.

The rest of us are as pleasing to look at as orphans left overnight in the rain. When we are belowdecks and the rain does not fall upon us, still we are wet. Our bones seem to be made of water; the sea tosses inside our heads. I think I am wet down to my very soul.

. . .

After Japheth slaughtered the eighth ram that came to the ark, Noah had him take the beast's horn. Its sound is the only one that can be heard throughout the ark over the bleating, braying, screaming, and roaring. Noah blows it to call us to the gathering place, on the second level near the lighter beasts, in a corner where a wall half the width of the ark has been erected to create a room that is open on one side. We burn incense to cover the smell of wounded and infected animals, urine, and dung.

"Not you," Noah tells Ona one day after sounding the horn. I can see in the dim light from the oil we are burning that her wide eyes are not as wide as they were when our journey began. She's exhausted, yet still too remarkable to look away from. I suspect that Noah does not want to struggle for our attention. "You will lie on your blankets, so my grandson can take his afternoon nap in a restful belly."

No one actually knows whether it is afternoon or midnight. Herai's moon cycle is our only source by which to tell time. She was bleeding when she boarded the ark, so we will know when one moon has passed.

Ona's moons have deserted her. She should have given birth at least two moons before boarding the ark, yet her belly continues to grow. She cannot balance for more than a few steps before reaching for the bars of a cage or one of us—usually Herai—to keep from tumbling to the floor.

Through the smoke that rises from the oil we are burning, I watch her shuffle away with her hand on the lowest part of her back.

Ona prefers Herai's company to all of ours, but Herai is falling into a trance of sorrow. She has stopped pressing against the wall of the deck, eyes trained on the waters below, waiting for lightning to illuminate the people floating upon the sea. There are no more people floating upon the sea. I wonder if I really saw a ship in the distance. No one has mentioned it, and I will not be the first.

Before Noah begins on whatever it is he wants to tell us, I move to squat next to Herai. My hips pop, and my knees feel like they have swollen to the size of my head. To steady myself, I gently place a hand upon Herai's leg. Shem pinches his nose. As if he smells any better.

"Animals—human or otherwise—do not give off a pleasing smell when wet," I say.

Noah's brow furrows. "We are not animals."

"Some of us are not," Ham says. He turns to look up at Japheth, who is standing because he cannot squat with a sword in his belt.

I let go of Herai and move between Ham and Japheth. Ham pretends to choke on the smell of me. "Mother!"

I am tired but cannot sleep, starving but too nauseated to eat anything more than a few nuts here or there. Every last shard of me aches more deeply with each breath. The gash across my ear, where the side of my head knocked against the hull while the nephil held me, throbs day and night. "How do you expect me to smell when I alone must shovel all of the lighter beasts' dung?"

"What sons has the God of Adam saved, who let their mother break her back while they play in the rain?" Noah demands.

"Father," Japheth says, "I guard the ark at every—" He was going to say "position of the sun." But there is no sun.

"You will shovel no more dung," Noah says to me. "Ham and Shem, you will help your mother."

Ham likes to feed the animals but does not like to deal with what results. Still, I know that if I had asked him for help, he would have taken the shovel from my hand and bent his own back. I hadn't wanted to trouble him. As he lowers his head in shame—something I have never seen him do—I regret my words.

We are silent while we wait for Noah to tell us whatever is important enough that no one has been left on deck to guard the ark.

"We must protect the ark at every breath," he says.

"Good idea," Ham mutters.

"Neither the sea nor the sinners are done with us." Noah quickly adds, "God is protecting the ark, but sometimes He does so using our flesh. We must always be ready."

Maybe the ark in the distance was not just my imagination. But Noah is nearly blind. How could he have seen it?

"And we must keep watch for my second cousins," Zilpha says. "I do not know why they did not come back to board the ark before the flood came, but I can feel that they are still alive. Have you ropes in place for them to climb aboard?" She has not gone on deck since bringing the mammoth to help save Javan and Herai. She does not clean up dung, and she does not help me prepare and serve dried meat and fruit. She is still, except when she feeds and pets the animals. But because she helped save Herai's life, I do not think there is anything she could do that I would not forgive her for.

Noah says nothing, but Shem does not miss the opportunity to please one of the few girls left in the world, even though she is many moons from ripeness. "Yes," he says, "I have seen to it."

There is actually only one rope. What feels like a whole moon past but may be only yesterday, Noah wanted to throw it overboard. "Japheth could fall into the sea while defending the ark," I protested. Noah sighed and walked away, leaving me with the rope and the small hope that if Javan is alive, we can rescue her.

Zilpha looks gratefully up at Shem. "Thank you, brother."

Noah bangs his staff against the floor to get our attention back. "When Japheth needs to rest—"

"I do not need to rest, Father. God keeps me awake."

"I am sure He does," Ham says.

"When Japheth needs to rest," Noah repeats, "Ham or Shem will be lookout and will alert me at the first sign of life on the sea."

Everyone goes about his or her business except Ham, who comes and puts a hand on my back at the lowest part. The part that aches worse than any other. He rubs gently before going to shovel dung.

. . .

Later, the horn sounds one long note. Noah has a special pattern of blasts for each of us, and this one is mine.

I come to sit beside him, each of us on our own sleeping blanket. Together we listen to the beasts and to the crashing of the sea all around. He does not speak. Yet I do not think he has called me here because he wants company. He has always preferred to be alone.

"Wife," he begins, "I am sorry."

"Do not be. Our sons will help me now, and I will no longer have to bend my back over the animals' dung."

"I am sorry for much more than this."

It feels as though a hand has suddenly gripped my heart. *What has happened?* Or worse, *What is going to happen?*

"You see, wife, after the first two hundred years, I began to get tired. All those I loved died, and the newness of life wore off; little brought me joy. Since then it has seemed that I watch life but am not truly a part of it. I do not remember what it is like to be in the center of it. Each year I observe from a greater distance.

"And what I observe above all else is evil increasing upon the earth. It spreads from one person to the next like a plague—the worst plague I have ever seen, and I have seen many. There were a few good people, but they have long since passed.

"Then one day God called to me, telling me to rectify the evil upon the earth. I was to call the people to the Lord the way I had been called, except He would not speak directly to them. He would speak only to me, and I would deliver His words.

"I did as He commanded, yet still evil continued to dwell in the heart of man.

"Though people have sinned since the time of Adam and murdered each other since the time of Cain, it has gotten worse each year. People are—*were*—wickeder than their parents, and their children were wickeder yet."

He leans toward me, trying to see my face. Our noses are not more than a cubit apart. I feel as though I can smell each of the years he has been upon the earth. His skin smells of dirt, desert, sorrow, and the smoke of a thousand fires.

Still we are too far apart for him. He leans even closer and squints at my face. Has he ever truly looked at me? And when I looked at him, did I really see him? His eyes are full of tiny red veins the same shape as the lightning that cracks around the ark. They have seen enough of what they have seen already. Now they want to see me. I did not realize how much I wanted him to *really* look at me until this moment, when it is too late. I am certain he can no longer truly see anything.

"Wife." He reaches his old hand, which is as steady as a young man's, out toward my leg and sets it upon my knee. Even through my tunic, I can feel the cracks and calluses on his palm. "I feared finding wickedness in our sons, so I could not bear to look too closely at them."

I am too shocked to reply. I thought he did not care very deeply for our sons, but perhaps the opposite was true. He cared too much.

"I was not present for their boyhoods, and you were more alone than you should have been."

Husband, it is you who were alone. I do not say this aloud, because I do not wish to wound him. He is wounded already. Yet I cannot stop myself from saying, "Do not worry for me; I was far from alone. I was with our sons."

He does not flinch at my words, and he does not look away. "You were. And so it brings me a hundred years' worth of happiness to tell you that since God has seen fit to save our sons, I have hope that they will not be wicked after all. And we must make certain of this, or God may decide to start again."

"Start again?"

"Kill us all."

CHAPTER 36

BEYOND THE REACH OF LIGHT

Most of the animals on the ark are too shaken and disturbed to mate, but no matter how pregnant Ona is, or how violently the sea rocks the ark, Shem slinks away from his tasks and goes to her. He pulls her deep down the rows of caged beasts, beyond the reach of the light from our little flames. Deep enough that our ears cannot separate human cries from those of the animals.

Ona's belly continues to grow, and one day she can no longer fit between the cages.

I am feeding the chickens when I hear Shem coaxing her: "This is far enough. No one will see."

I am glad for her that the sea is calmer than usual. I hope the ark will remain steady until they are done.

Noah climbs down the steps from the deck and sounds the horn. Two short blasts and a long one, the signal that we are all to come to him. "Gather with the lighter beasts!" he calls. I get more oil for our lamp and walk with Herai and Ham to the meeting place. I notice how gaunt our faces are and how big our eyes look. It is as if our eyes have eaten our cheeks. Zilpha is already there, reclining on some blankets that have been piled up for Noah to kneel upon when he speaks to God.

Japheth appears, chest pressed proudly out in front of him as he declares, "I am here, Father."

"I know," Noah says. "Do you think I am blind?"

No one answers.

"Now that we are all here—"

Japheth interrupts, "Shem is not here, Father."

"I can see that." Noah sounds the horn one short blast for Shem, but he does not come. "Well, go get him," he commands Japheth. Then, as if it is Japheth's fault that we are being delayed, he adds, "We will wait."

Japheth returns alone. "I cannot bring him, Father. He is with Ona."

"I ordered Ona to rest until my grandson arrives. Tell Shem not to speak with her; she must sleep."

"He is not speaking with her."

"Stubborn child, go get him at once!"

"He is lying with her."

Color flares in Noah's cheeks. He swings his staff back and forth on the floor before him to clear a path. He moves more quickly than he has in many moons. It is hard not to fall behind.

When we reach Shem and Ona, Shem is just rising up from his knees. Noah uses his staff to knock Shem away from Ona. Her backside is red from the force of Shem's attentions.

"Ignorant mule," Noah yells at Shem. "This is the first son of the new world! I will lock you in the bowels of the ship if you go near him again."

Ona rises heavily, unsteadily, from her hands and knees. The thin blanket beneath her has not kept the floor from scraping her palms. She stands, and her tunic falls over her swollen belly and hips. She listens to Noah's words with her hand in its usual place upon her low back. Though her back must hurt even more than mine, her brow softens; she is relieved.

"I am sorry, Father," Shem says, "I did not know it was forbidden."

"Then why are you all the way back here instead of on your sleeping blankets?"

"I did not want to bother anyone."

"You have failed in this," Noah says, "as I know you will fail in many things. Only Japheth may lie with his wife, and only until she is with child." He does not chastise Ona. He raises his staff to point at her belly. "Herai will watch over you and the child," he says. "You must rest now."

"What did you wish to talk about at the gathering place?" I ask.

"The importance of appearing righteous before God." Noah gives Shem a thwack to the ribs before he turns and walks away.

I doubt a thwack from Noah's staff will keep Shem from the pleasure of women for long. He stares at Herai as she helps Ona back to her sleeping blankets.

CHAPTER 37

A SHIP IN THE DISTANCE

Whenever the storm subsides for more than a few breaths, our thoughts come back to us. It is not a happy reunion.

The quieter the sea, the more haunted we are.

Our heads are full of people who are not on the ark. We think of them more than we did when we knew them, and sometimes more than we think of one another. We find it impossible that they no longer exist in this world.

They are here, all the more so in their absence.

When I gaze at Herai, I think of Javan saving her from drunken mercenaries. When I look at Zilpha, I picture Manosh with his long fingers wrapped around the handle of his sword until Zilpha touches him and he releases his grip.

When I look at the sea, I think always of my giant.

Each time I hear Noah talking to God, I wonder if he too is afraid of the ship in the distance. Does he even know of it? I have started to think of that ship as much as the one that shelters me.

Sometimes we accidentally call out the names of the dead. One day Noah goes to the hatch to summon Japheth down from the deck: "Manosh," he yells impatiently. When Shem sleeps, I hear him muttering the names of women I assume are whores. I call Herai Javan so often that she comes to her dead mother's name.

It is not only by accident that we invoke the names of those who are not here. Zilpha prays aloud for her second cousins, perhaps so we will not forget our debt to them. She thanks them for the lumber they have given us, "without which we would all have drowned." Herai cries for Javan. She has someone to mourn, so she has learned to speak, naming her loss to keep from losing it completely. "Mwah-fah," she cries.

I cry too sometimes. I know with a certainty I did not before that my father has passed into the afterlife. A deep well of sadness has opened within me. Perhaps this is why I have started to think of the three boys that came out of their mother at the same time. I wonder if I will see them when I die, and if my sons are worthy replacements.

.   .   .

"Father," Japheth calls one day as lightning violently rends the sky. "There is a ship no more than half a league away!"

I hear Herai's eager, inflectionless wail, and then her footsteps sound up the ramp to the deck.

Together we look out across the sea. There is only darkness. The lightning has returned to the palms of God. He holds it there no matter how desperately we beg Him to let even the smallest spark fall so that we might see the ship Japheth speaks of.

Noah sounds the horn two short and then one long note. "Prepare," he says. We light the lamps. Shem and Japheth frantically sharpen copper swords and daggers. Zilpha brings a mammoth to the second level. She wants to take it on deck in case the ship in the distance is Manosh's. She says, "My second cousins are large, but we will have little trouble pulling them aboard."

"Wait at the ramp to the deck," Noah yells down to her. "You are not used to so much wind."

"I have traveled the desert. The only wind I am not used to is none."

"This wind is sharp and full of teeth. It will break your skin."

She hesitates, then steps away from the ramp.

Ham collects dung shovels and other tools that can be used as weapons. Noah asks for my meat knife. I retrieve it from under my sleeping blanket. It is a weapon small enough for me to wield, and I am used to the feel of it in my hand. "Will not I need it?" I ask as I give it to him. I have kept it hidden so Japheth could not claim it as a weapon that he, as defender of the ark, should possess.

Noah closes his eyes with the knife clutched tightly in his hand, trying to summon the answer. He opens them abruptly and holds the knife out to me. "I do not know," he says. I wish he had not chosen this time to be honest. I wish even that he had said "yes" instead of "I do not know."

I leave my hands at my sides. "There is something I need more than this knife."

"Right now there is not. Take it."

"Husband, *do not let me die without a name.*"

He presses his lips together. Has he not thought of a name for me in the nineteen years that I have been his wife? I will forgive him for this if he gives me one now.

Instead, he says, "*This* is your thought as we prepare to fight for future generations? You are the wife of Noah and mother to three sons. Is this not enough? Do not ask for too much, or God will see that you are ungrateful and take what He has given you already."

He lets the knife fall from his hand onto the floor at my feet. Then he walks away. I suppose he is going to find another place to pray, since I have ruined this one.

After a moment, I pick up the knife. If Noah and my sons die when we meet the other ship, *who will I be?*

. . .

I help Ona into the sheep cage and gaze with them at her strange, beautiful face before I cover it with straw. If anyone finds her, he will keep her, even if only to gaze upon.

She sneezes.

"Do not do that," I say.

She sneezes again.

The sheep are staring at where Ona's eyes were visible only a breath ago. The ewe comes and rubs her wet nose against the hay. Ona sneezes, then sneezes again. I unbury her face.

"Help me over to the large manlike creatures" she says, struggling to a sitting position. "If you do not, I will scream and punch my belly."

"There are other, more peaceful animals."

"Not huge furry ones I can hide behind."

"Ones that will not kill you."

She laughs. "They are gentle with me."

As soon as the words leave her mouth, I imagine they are true. The furry beasts are indeed like men, except that they do not ride donkeys or go on about God.

"They are not so fond of Shem," Ona says. "But they will not hate you."

I have been saving the majority of my rations of dried fruit. She waits until I return with them. Her stomach is so large, she can barely walk. We move slowly down the ramp to the bowels of the ark. I have been forced to come down here only once before, when Ham was throwing up too violently to feed the larger beasts and Shem was nowhere to be found.

A roar comes from a few cubits away. Another roar answers the first. Soon beasts on every side are joining their voices to the terrible chorus.

Ona talks as we make our way to the large manlike creatures. "They are all saying, 'I am alive!' Some are saying, 'Fear me, I am alive,' and others are saying, 'I am alive, please, look at me!' This little beast"—she points to a large fur-covered animal with stocky legs, a long snout, and thick claws—"who is pacing back and forth, says, 'I am hungry,' and this she-wolf says, 'Do not come any closer to my cubs, or you and I might both lose our lives.' This rough-skinned beast with a horn upon his nose is saying, 'I am grouchy again today,' and this great lizard wants to know where all the light went."

"I fear it is gone for good."

"God will tire of the clouds. He will wake up with them one morning and decide He no longer likes them. Then He will use the wind to smack them and send them away, like men do to the girls who lose their beauty while you lie with them."

I raise the lamp to look into her huge eyes. She ignores the lamplight and my stare. "What would you know of not being beautiful?" I ask.

"Well, nothing yet."

I am certain that as long as she can open her eyes, she will not know what it is like not to be anything but lovely.

I move the lamp in front of us again and look at the bars of each cage along our path, to make sure a paw cannot reach out from between them. Ona does not fit easily in small spaces. When we come to a narrow path between a cage of the beasts with horns upon their noses and another of llamas, I let her go first, and then I push while she curses.

I finally force Ona between the cages. I am breathing so heavily, I almost do not notice that the animals have gone silent in order to listen. Though I am faint, I am afraid to rest against the cages or place my hand on the bars to relieve the weight on my feet. Instead, I lean against Ona. She falls on her hands and knees, and I fall with her.

I see a fat ashy-gray hand several cubits ahead of us. The hand is turned sideways, reaching through the bars of its cage to secure the latch on the outside of the door. I wonder if the sea has driven me to madness.

The large manlike beast stands at least two heads taller than I do. He appraises me with a single sweep of his eyes, then reaches his ashy-gray hand back through the bars of the cage to unlatch the door. He holds it open, and Ona gives him the fruit. The she-beast, who is sitting at the back of the cage, makes a noise that sounds like a happy belch. When Ona lies beside the she-beast, it begins to sift through her hair. The male closes the door and drops back onto all fours to eat the dried prunes and apricots.

I have not been invited in. I would not go in even if I were, but still it would have been nice to be asked. I turn and go back the way I came. The animals look different to me now; their eyes seem more like people's. I wonder what they are thinking. They do not roar for me this time. Perhaps they were not roaring for me before but for Ona. I wish I too could rest with the manlike beasts and not worry about anything for a few breaths.

I return to my sleeping blanket to get the meat knife from where I have hidden it beneath my sleeping blanket. It is gone. Did Noah decide to take it after all? I go up on deck without it.

The rain is like little hatchets hurled from the sky. I could return to the second level and remain with Zilpha and her mammoth. But my feet will not move me from my place against the wall of the deck. I want to know who besides us exists in the world.

We wait for lightning. I have never been so cold in all my life.

I do not know if we will survive to see the new world. If we do, I hope there will be no more heavy rains or cold winds. Sometimes I think it is not how the ark tosses me around, or how I labor without sleep for long periods that makes me ache, but the cold. *Why did Noah's God create the cold?* Perhaps He meant only to bring forth a cool breeze to relieve us as we labored on the ark, but at some point—as with the sinners—He lost control.

Japheth begins to pace and then to mutter that we should hurl spears into the darkness below.

"Stop strutting about. Surely you have worn footprints into the deck," Ham says. "If we cannot see them, they cannot see us."

"Lightning will come, Japheth," I say. "Keep hold of your spear."

When jagged lines of white fire strike from the sky, we stare out into the rough sea, stumbling from one side of the ark to the other. There is only froth and what remains of the world that has been destroyed: bare branches, empty tunics, and sometimes tunics with bloated bodies inside them. *Why do the living sink and the dead float?*

"What did it look like?" I ask Japheth. "How big was it?"

"Big enough to see from half a league away."

"How do you know it was half a league away?" Ham asks. "Maybe it was just small."

"Exactly what a coward would tell himself. You are careless for a coward. Most would know better than to pronounce their cowardice aloud."

"I am even more cowardly than this, brother. I think there was no ship at all."

"When the rains stop, you will see that you are wrong, perhaps even before your skull is cracked open by sinners."

If only the clouds would part for a breath. I would rather know what is coming, and from what direction, than wait for the unknown. My heart squeezes painfully in my chest, afraid to beat because then I might miss the sounds of survivors—trespassers to the new world—who have come too close through the endless night.

I will not know a moment's peace until we meet the other ark and I find that the people aboard are friendly, or until they kill me. If they are friendly, what will Noah have us do?

. . .

When we give up and return to the second level of the ark, Noah gazes away from me. This is how I know he is not completely blind. He puts rations of dried meat into all of our shivering hands, even though it does not seem long since we last ate. Perhaps he does not think we will live long enough that we need to save our stores.

After we eat and the children return to their duties, Noah turns to me. "Wife, I . . . I did not want you to think you could die." He is embarrassed.

As he should be. Not that I do not feel moved by his desire that I live. But still, his feelings are finally known. He does not think I need a name. I will have to find a way to change his mind. "I did not plan to die."

He bows his head as if in thanks. Though surely he gives thanks to the God of Adam and not me.

"Did you want to use my knife after all?" I ask.

"No, my wife. You will keep it."

My stomach lurches as if the sea has just tossed us halfway to the heavens. If Noah did not take my knife, who did?

CHAPTER 38

A MISSED MOON

"Has it not been even *one* moon yet?" Ham asks.

"The girl does not bleed."

"Herai," Ham corrects Noah, as if speaking to someone from a distant land who doesn't know the language. Ham does not like for Noah to call Herai "the girl." Noah does not like being corrected.

"The seven ewes have already cycled twice," Zilpha says.

"How would you know this?" Japheth asks.

"You would not understand no matter how carefully I explained." She does not say it cruelly. She says it as if simply remarking that the wood is brown or the animals are in pairs.

"How many days are in two ewe cycles?" Noah asks.

"Thirty-four."

Ham looks at Shem, who quickly looks down. Japheth continues to listen intently to Noah, unconcerned with Herai's moon cycle.

Noah says, "Then we are near the end of the storm."

"Praise the Lord," Japheth cries, "for bringing us safely into the new world."

I guard myself against hope. There is nothing that breaks a heart harder.

"Does this mean that He has killed everybody else?" Japheth asks.

"I do not know," Noah says. This is the second time I have heard him say these words and, I hope, the last.

"Manosh is alive, and perhaps others too," Zilpha says. "I will tell my sisters the good news that the rains are almost over." She turns to go without waiting for Noah to excuse her. As usual, Ona has not gathered with us. Noah told her to stay on her sleeping blankets, and he ordered Herai to stay with her.

"I will tell them too," Shem says.

"You will stay where you are," Noah says.

All of us except Japheth stare at Shem. "Is there something of interest on the floor, brother?" Ham asks.

Noah takes his eyes from Shem's face to gaze at Japheth. "Have you lain with your wife?"

Now Japheth stares at the floor. "I am sorry, Father, I have not." Suddenly, his head jerks up, and he turns to Shem. "Snake!" He unsheaths a sword from his belt and takes a step toward Shem.

"Get back to your post on deck," Noah commands. Japheth stops advancing, but he does not retreat. Noah bangs his staff against the floor. "Go."

Japheth spits in Shem's face. There is blood mixed with his

saliva—he lost two teeth, falling upon the bars of the great lizards' cage when they tried to escape. Shem moves to wipe it away. But before his fingers reach his face, Japheth says, "Raise your hand any higher, and you will lose it."

"Son," Noah says. None one moves until Shem lowers his hand. Japheth holds his brother's gaze for a heartbeat before turning and walking away.

When we can no longer hear Japheth's footfalls, Noah raises his staff and points it at Shem. It shakes in his hand. "You," he says. "*You . . .*" His eyes are narrowed, and his brows arch above them. His lips tremble so violently that perhaps he cannot speak.

Abruptly, as though the staff has just grown unbearably heavy, his arm drops. I step out of his way as he shuffles in the direction of our sleeping blankets. Before he gets there, I hear him fall to the floor.

"This is what I have always feared," he says as I approach. "And why I could not bring myself to watch our sons too closely."

I kneel beside him. "Perhaps there is no sin, husband. Maybe Herai did not bleed because the moon is not visible through the clouds."

From the corners of his eyes, two thin wet lines have cleared the grime down the length of his face, revealing the sand color of his skin. His beard hangs in damp knotted ropes along the length of his chest and rests in his lap. His hands tremble; his eyes are fixed upon the wooden planks of the ark above us.

"You are just overtired. The rains have almost ended, and then all will be well."

"God has not spoken to me since the flood began, but it did not worry me until now. I think He has been watching to see if we are worthy. I have thought about it more often than I have wanted to, and I know now that if He is merciful, He will kill us instead of deserting us."

Now my hands begin to tremble as well. I want to shake him, to slap him, to squeeze his head in my hands, to make him take it back. "God cannot kill us or abandon us for this one sin. Our sons are not thieves or murderers."

"I do not blame only our sons. It is the girl who has compelled them to evil. See what has come of allowing her on the ark."

"God told you to take your sons and their wives on the ark, and that is what you have done."

Noah ignores me. "He has closed His ears to me. My prayers are as good as rafts that have sunk to the bottom of the sea."

I know how you feel, I think. I say only, "Surely He is very busy and cannot attend just to us."

"He has always been busy, and now there are fewer people to be busy with. If He returns to us, it will likely be to wipe away the last remnants of His mistake."

"Husband, you must try to call Him back to us."

He does not scold me for telling him that he must do something, which is not a comfort to me. "The only way to regain His favor is to right the evil on the ark. Shem must be beaten, and Herai will be kept separate."

"Please, husband, I am sure there is another way."

"If you knew Him as I do, you would know that there is not."

CHAPTER 39

THE BEATING

Before Shem's beating, Noah allows him to see Ona one last time. He does not want her to know Herai is pregnant. "Tell her Herai has plague," Noah instructs. He does not think this is a lie. He says she has the same plague Javan had: wantonness.

"Did she believe you?" Ham asks when Shem returns to the gathering place. "Or is she smarter than a piece of timber?"

Shem flinches as though he has never been insulted by Ham before. "I do my best."

"Do not speak so cruelly of yourself, brother," Ham replies. "Your best could not possibly be so pitiful."

"Silence," Noah says. "There is important work to be done." He holds a leather strap in each hand. "I will call middle son."

"No," Shem says. "Anyone besides Japheth."

Though Ham is angry at Shem for lying with Herai, he comes to his brother's aid. "I will do it, Father." He reaches for the leather straps.

Noah moves his arms behind him. "I must summon middle son; go get my ram's horn," he tells Ham. "It is on my sleeping blanket."

I know Noah is right. If he does not allow Japheth to give Shem the beating, Japheth will beat Shem later, when no one is around to make sure that he leaves a little life inside the flesh of his brother.

Shem pushes past Ham and flees deeper into the ark.

"Bring him back," Noah commands me, then glares at Ham. "I will see if middle son is on deck."

Since Herai missed her moon, Noah has forbidden her to be in the common areas. If Noah comes across her on the second level or on the deck, he prods her to the ramp and then swings his staff in front of him to make sure she is gone. "Stay!" he calls down to her.

Because Herai lives in the bowels of the ark, Shem is no longer allowed there. But that is where I find him. I do not see Herai; I see only my oldest son, crouched low, holding his head in his hands.

"Mother," he says when I approach, "you must help me."

My heart aches. For all his flaws, he is still my firstborn. His birth was the beginning of my happiness. Though it now seems his birth will lead to great sorrow.

I squat beside him. "Son, it is best to have done with it."

"Japheth is a madman. He is worse than Father. He will kill me."

"Your father thinks that God will kill all of us if we do not appear righteous. He will not let Japheth kill you. He wants only to show the God of Adam a few drops of your blood."

"Japheth will not be as easily satisfied as God."

"But he listens to your father, and your father will tell him to stop long before your spirit flees your body."

"Just because Japheth has listened to Father up till now does not mean he will listen to him forever. I will not return to the gathering place."

"It will go better for you if you do not fight."

"Mother, please," he says, and leans his head against my breast. I lose my balance and fall back onto my hindquarters. He stretches out along the floor to keep his head pressed against me. I am reminded of how, as a child, he always wanted to be held. I wrap my arms around his head, and we stay like that until I hear Noah yelling for us.

"Let us return," I say. "Japheth's fury will soon be spent, and you will be acquitted of your crimes against the Lord." I move my hands to either side of his face so he is forced to look at me. "Try to cry right away."

"That will not be difficult." He stands up. "Wait for me a moment. I must get something."

I do not like to think of what it is he might want to get. "No," I say, rising as quickly to my feet as the dampness in my joints will allow, "let us go. They will not wait much longer before coming for you."

"I just need a sip from my waterskin." He runs off behind the cages. When he returns, I am relieved to see him wiping water from his lips. "Now I am ready."

Noah and Japheth are waiting. Japheth is holding the leather straps, and Noah has brought the rope down from the deck. "We do not need the rope," I say.

"Do not bind him," Japheth agrees. "I will enjoy seeing him try to escape on broken legs."

I cannot think of anything to say that will not deepen Japheth's thirst for blood. I do not allow myself to hug Shem, or even to squeeze his hand, before I walk away.

I find Ham shoveling dung from the lighter beasts' cages. I take the shovel from him. "Go make sure you do not become my second-oldest son. And come get me when it is over."

He hesitates.

"Go."

I shovel with great fervor while I wait for Ham to return.

Half a pail full of dung later, screaming erupts from the gathering place. The screams belong not to Shem but to Japheth.

I let go of the shovel and rush to find Japheth on the floor, clutching his head. Blood streams between his fingers. "You *are* a demon woman," he yells at me. "You have cost me my ear."

Noah raises his staff slightly and points it at Japheth's head. "*Silence, boy!*"

My mark is the thing of which we never speak. None of us has ever wanted to draw attention to it, and I hoped that there was no one left in the world who would call me a demon. But I forgive Japheth, though he continues to gaze up at me with hatred. He is maimed, and I am not without guilt.

The staff shakes violently in Noah's hand. Does it shakes because of the strength with which he has to restrain himself to keep from striking Japheth?

I am beginning to worry that his heart will give out when, finally, he lowers his staff. He waves it in front of his feet to clear a path, and he leaves. Perhaps now he feels the same way about our sons as

God felt about the sinners before He wiped them from the face of the earth. The sinners besides us, that is.

Ham stands as far back as possible against the outer wall of the gathering place. As Noah walks past him, our eyes meet, and I see that Ham is sorry. I am sorry too, for the responsibility I yoked him with and the guilt he will always have with him now.

"I brought Mother's knife myself, little brother," Shem says, "and I would not have used it if you had not brought your own knife and tried to unman me." He holds my meat knife out to me. "Sorry, Mother." It is cruel to give it back to me with another son's blood upon it, but I take it anyway. I do not want him to have it anymore. Beneath his foot is another knife, this one made of copper, a knife Japheth did not tell anybody about.

Now Japheth looks back at Shem. "You have turned my wife into a whore. You can keep your cock and her too. At least for as long as you live."

Shem's eyes dart to something over my shoulder. Slow, unsteady footfalls approach. Ona stumbles against my arm and falls into the center of the gathering place. She does not acknowledge Japheth or his blood on the floor in front of her. Instead, she gasps loudly for breath. Perhaps she is choked with rage, or perhaps she is exhausted by the weight that the God of Adam will not let her put down.

She places one hand on her belly and the other upon her lower back. She straightens as tall as she can with the unruly burden inside her. I cannot see her eyes, but I can see Shem's. There is no remorse in them.

"I let you lie with me even when my hands and knees bled and I could hardly get up afterward because of the heaviness of your child in my belly," Ona says quietly. "Yet you could not wait even half a moon after Noah forbade you to have me."

"If you would not have stopped taking Javan's herbs, you would not be pregnant, and I would not have had to lie with Herai."

"I did not stop taking them. Though your heart is weak, your seed is strong."

"Then where are all my other children?"

"They bled to death after being cut by knives long enough to reach a woman's womb."

"Well, what am I to do? I am not limp, like my brothers."

Japheth throws something at Shem. It is covered in blood. It slaps Shem wetly in the face and then falls to the floor. Shem cringes, but besides this, neither he nor Ona seem to notice.

"You are nothing more than a child," Ona says. I know she speaks true. A man wants sons, but Shem wants only pleasure. "And that is as much as you will ever be." She turns to leave, and I look into her huge almond-colored eyes. Any man would have been happy to have her for a wife. Any besides the one she chose.

As she brushes past me, I see what has hit Shem in the face and fallen to the floor: Japheth's ear.

Japheth's ear.

I want to hold Japheth's head in my lap and bandage the place where Shem cut him, but when I go to him, he strikes my shins and I fall down beside him. I am little more than bones; he easily pushes me aside and rises from the floor, jaw clenched against the pain.

"Son," I call up to him, "we must wash it and make a covering—"

"Quiet, woman," he says. "I will take care of myself, *as I have always done,* and leave you to your favorites. A bloodless knife of flame will seal my wound better than you can."

He steps over me and disappears into the rows of caged beasts.

MEAT

Nothing but rain guards the ark. The only footsteps on deck are those of the clouds.

Japheth and Shem are lost in a darkness even greater than this. Noah has stopped sounding the one blast for Shem and the two for Japheth. A few times I blew the ram's horn myself, but it made no sound. I fear my sons feel forgotten.

Though I cannot find them, I have found what I think are human droppings on the floor. I leave meat out; I know that if the manlike beasts come upon this food while wandering outside their cage, they will not eat it. I place animal skins full of water around the ark. When I find these skins empty, I thank the God of Adam. My sons are still alive. Or at least two of them are.

· · ·

One day I come upon Noah kneeling on his sleeping blanket. His eyes are closed, but his lips are not moving. He is not praying. He is yearning.

I kneel beside him. He does not acknowledge me right away, but then, after a few breaths, he says, "I miss them." I do not ask of whom he speaks. He is speaking of the sinners.

I cover his shaking hand with my shaking hand. "I know."

Later, I lie awake on my own sleeping blanket, listening to an owl hooting, a large cat roaring, and the steady chorus of insects rubbing their wings together. I think not only of Shem, Japheth, and all of the sinners but also of Herai, and I begin to cry. I get up.

I walk to the ramp, hiding the light from my lamp behind my tunic. Light is something Noah can still see. In my other hand is my knife. I descend slowly, grateful for Noah's snoring, the sounds of the animals, and the pelting of the rain against the deck, which drown out the squeaking of the ramp beneath me. Or perhaps I no longer have enough flesh to make the ramp creak.

Herai is sleeping on the floor by the cage of the rough-skinned beasts with the horns upon their noses. I crouch beside her and put the knife behind me, where it will not scare her. Quietly, I say her name. She opens her eyes, then immediately shuts them and turns her head away. I brush her hair back from her face to look at her. "Herai."

She squints up at me as if staring into the sun. Her pupil takes up half of the eye she is able to keep open. I set the lamp behind me next to my knife and ask if she is well.

She smiles. "Mwahfah," she says, and points to herself. She

takes my hand and places it on her belly, which is no bigger than it has ever been. Yet I do feel warmth beneath my palm.

"Yes," I say, "a healthy child grows here."

I am startled by the loud, strange sound of her laugh. I had not expected to hear it. I quickly place a finger on her lips to quiet her. She brings my hand back to her belly. I have never seen her so happy. She is not sad that she has been banished to the bowels of the ark, or that she may have lost any chance of ever being with Ham.

She hits her chest. "Mwahfah!" she says again.

I am surprised to feel myself smile too. My face has not moved other than to speak or strain against my many aches in a long time. We clasp hands. She laughs again, and this time I join her. Our laughter grows wilder, until soon it takes hold of our bodies. We are elated. We wave our arms. I lose my balance, but she has hold of my hands and keeps me from falling. The male rough-skinned beast snorts, which causes us to laugh even harder.

I point to my chest. "Grandmother," I say. Then I think of Javan and wish I had not said it.

But Herai smiles. She points at me and says, "Grawdmwahfah!"

Her happiness has almost made me forget the true purpose of my visit. I reach for the knife and hold it up for her to see. It is hard for me to believe that I am arming a girl against one of my own sons. If it were Ham who wished her ill, I would not risk any harm that might come to him from the knife. But it is not Ham.

"I hope you will not need this," I say.

She pushes it away and pulls her tunic up. There, sheathed

in a belt he must have given her, is Ham's dagger. I am glad to see my favorite son has not deserted her, despite the pain she and Shem have surely caused him. I pray that if Herai is ever in danger, she will be able to reach the dagger quickly enough to defend herself.

I squeeze her hand and say good night. It does not matter that it might be noon. For us it is always night. Unlike all the others, though, this night is a good one.

As I return to my blanket, Noah is still snoring. I cannot help but be grateful for the loss of his sight and hearing. These losses have brought me a small measure of freedom.

When I wake Noah is squatting beside me. "The middle boy must return to the deck to guard the ark," he says. "Do not leave any more food for him."

"I do not . . ." I trail off before the lie fully leaves my tongue.

"What reason does he have to rejoin us if he already has meat in his belly?"

"I am afraid he would rather starve."

"Be afraid for yourself, wife. Creaking is one of the sounds that have gotten louder to my ears instead of softer. In less than these forty days that we have been on board the ark, the ramp has gone silent beneath you."

"I am not hungry." This is true. Though I am starving, I'm not hungry. The jagged pitching of the ark tosses my stomach even more violently than it tosses the rest of me.

Noah frowns. "From now on, you will eat all of the meat I give you instead of hiding it in the sleeves of your tunic."

I must admit that I am moved. With this demand, he has said what he otherwise would not be able to: *I love you.*

The power of meat does not stop there. Though we have an ark full of it, Japheth is afraid of God and will not kill a single animal. Only a few meals after I stop leaving meat for him, he emerges from wherever it is he was hiding and comes—palms up—to Noah.

"You have returned," I cry, as if he has been on a long journey. He has sealed the skin where not long ago there was an ear. I position myself on the unwounded side of his head and embrace him. I wonder if our wounds look alike. The scar where my head knocked against the hull during the drowning of the nephil cannot be easy to gaze upon, but at least I kept my ear. Still, I imagine that we look like members of the same clan. Will this somehow serve as a bond between us?

He does not put his arms around me, but he does not push me away. He says nothing more of my mark or demonry.

Though it has been too long for me to be able to smell his wound, I do. It is more nauseating and sweet than leather being tanned over a flame. I console myself that the agony he felt as he burned his own flesh likely was not as great as when Shem cut off his ear. Japheth surely prefers to be the one wielding the weapon, even when the person he wields it against is himself.

"Father," he says, "please, I am hungry."

I hurry to get a bowl. Though it has not yet been forty days since we have been on the ark, our stores have dwindled, and Noah has begun meting out our food. He does not greet our son with happiness, but he places at least two rations inside Japheth's bowl. "You will never again call your mother a demon," he says.

Japheth flinches at the memory. "I never will, Father. Please forgive me." This is as close as he will come to saying he is sorry, and I am not the one he says it to. Still, I am glad to hear his words.

As Japheth eats, the scar tissue tugs at the edge of his face. The flesh beyond his cheek is hard to look at, and the expressions that contort his face take what is left of his handsomeness. He hardly chews the lentils and meat before gulping them down. Twice he chokes and spits into his hand. Then he hurls the food as far back into his throat as he can. When he swallows, his eyes bulge as if the meat were a knife.

I wonder how I could let this happen to my son. And yet I think that if he tries to hurt Herai, I will let even worse harm come to him.

A DECEPTION

Noah is the only one who knows how to tie and untie the mysterious knots our stores are sealed with. If the God of Adam really has deserted us, He did not miss the opportunity to show us that our lives are in Noah's ancient hands first.

But God did not give Noah the power to provide Shem with what he most wants. Even after Shem emerges and eats the double portion of meat Noah gives him, he is hungry. He needs to be held. He puts his head against what little is left of my breasts. Though Japheth eats with his head bowed, out of the corners of his eyes, he looks at Shem and me with disgust.

Ona eats apart from us, but we know Noah gives her large portions. Whenever Noah returns from her chamber, there is still meat in the bowl. Noah divides it among us. Zilpha's only task aboard the ark is to bring whatever remains to Herai. Noah and Japheth always eat all of their meat and lentils, leaving nothing. Shem rarely leaves anything either.

One day when Zilpha has almost finished her ration, I say her name and stare sharply at the last few lentils in her bowl. She is small and rarely exerts herself. Surely she can spare something for a girl she calls "my sister."

The faint smile comes over her face. It hardly moves her mouth, but it turns the corners of her eyes up a hair's width. "I must keep up my strength so I can help my second cousins onto the ark," she says, and tips the bowl so the last lentils fall into her mouth.

She pours Ham's leftovers onto mine to bring to Herai. Noah has given us each a piece of dried fruit. Zilpha takes the halves of the dates that Ham and I have saved for Herai.

"Leave them," Noah says.

"Herai needs fruit," I say.

Zilpha seizes the opportunity to disobey Noah. She hurries off to bring the lentils and dates to Herai. To ease the injury to Noah's pride, I pretend he has given her his permission. "Thank you, good husband."

Shem does not like to hear the women's names. He slinks away, no doubt thinking of how cruel and unfair the world has been to him. Neither Ona nor Herai will let him come near. Herai guards the little life in her belly with both hands, and I am certain she would not hesitate to use Ham's dagger if she felt that her child were in danger.

"I have not decided whether the adulteress can stay," Noah says, gazing steadily ahead at the inner wall of the ark. He does not look at us, and I am afraid he means what he says. "It is probably a waste to feed her."

"You will repopulate the world with one child?" Ham asks. "Who will the child mate with? Himself?"

Zilpha returns from bringing food to Herai. "I have felt Ona's belly," she says. "Three children live there."

Hush, child!

"If Ona does not come into better spirits," Zilpha continues, "all three will be born into eternal sadness. Perhaps they will even die. We should have told Ona that it is Japheth's seed in Herai's belly."

Noah's eyebrows smack together in the center of his forehead. He lifts his staff and bangs it hard against the floor. Zilpha is cruel to use the word "should" when speaking to Noah. "The adulteress cannot stay on board the ark," he says.

If Herai dies, I will blame Zilpha as much as Noah.

Zilpha's face, as usual, is still. Is she pleased that Noah wants to cast Herai overboard? Perhaps she wants all of her husband's attentions.

Ham is the only one I can trust. Ham and myself. "I do not want to do it, husband," I say, "but I will. We must do whatever is necessary to bring God's favor upon us once again."

Noah narrows his eyes at me so that they are slits too small to see into. But he does not want to admit that I might question his decision or disobey him. Especially not in front of Zilpha. "Very well," he says.

. . .

I wait until the storm grows wild, until cages fly across the floor and sharp blades of rain divide the darkness into tiny pieces. Flashing lightning, booming thunder. Herai is wrapped in her sleeping blanket, securely tucked in with the manlike beasts. I have taken her tunic. It lies on the ground beside me as I straddle one of the seven ewes. I hold the meat knife out to Ham. Though we have no light, I am certain he knows it is there between us. But he does not take it. "There is no other way," I say.

The ewe fusses beneath me and begins to cry.

"Quickly, son. It is cruel to hesitate."

I feel the tip of the blade slide away, through my fingers, as he takes it from me. A mother does not need light to know when her son is quivering. I hope my son's hand will be firm enough for the task.

I squeeze the ewe between my legs and force her jaw open. "Steady," I tell Ham.

He grasps the ewe's tongue with one hand, and with the other, he slices it from her throat. I hear the cleanness of the cut. If Japheth were with us, he would be envious of Ham's skill.

The ewe thrashes beneath me. I press her jaw together to minimize the blood we will have to clean up. "I will keep hold of her. Do away with her tongue," I tell him.

Ham's footsteps move off toward the lion cage. There is scuffling that ends as quickly as it began, then the wet, satisfied sound of chewing.

I wrap Herai's tunic around the ewe, and Ham and I carry the struggling animal up to the second level. We do not take the ramp all the way to the deck until lightning has flashed and then left the world dark once again. We need as much time in the dark as possible. When Ham trips over his feet, I summon all of my strength to push him onward.

"Who goes there?" Japheth demands. I see the light of his lantern flickering through the rain. Ham rushes the animal to the side of the ark and throws her into the waves crashing below.

"It is done," I tell Japheth with what is left of my breath. "The ark is rid of evil."

Japheth's lantern moves toward us. "The lightning will show me if you have truly expelled the adulteress."

"Get Noah," I tell Ham.

Japheth and I lean against the wall of the deck. I say, "Hopefully, God will leave some righteous girl alive so that she may bear you sons."

He does not reply. Or maybe the rain cloaks his voice. But then he asks, "And what if He does not?"

Now it is my turn to be silent. If he is feeling remorse, I do not want to lessen it.

"Then I will take Ona for a wife," he says.

"You cannot take your brother's wife unless he . . ."

Lightning cuts open the veil of black over the sea. In the frothing water below, Herai's tunic with a body thrashing wildly inside it is visible for less than a breath. Long enough for Japheth to see it.

"Now the ark is *almost* rid of evil," he says.

It pains me to think of what an attractive child he was, strong, with big yellow-flecked eyes. Somehow he never noticed neighbors staring at him. He only noticed them adoring Shem. "Do you want your father to cast you out as Adam did Cain? God has commanded that your father and his *three* sons journey to the new world. He will not take only two."

When he does not respond, I am overtaken by two urges. I want to smack him, and I want to cradle him to me and ask forgiveness for whatever I have done to make him so hateful. I reach for him.

He knocks my hand away. "Keep your embraces. You have given your other sons all but the smallest crumb of your affection. That is fine, I will take what affection I want myself. I will have Ona."

"And will you provide for Shem's children when they are born?"

Again he does not answer. We are silent while we wait for Ham to return with Noah. When they approach, Japheth announces, "The adulteress is gone," as proudly as if it is he who has gotten rid of her. "One more sinner has been fed to the sea."

"Now God will bless us once again," Noah says. He sounds more hopeful than certain.

DAY 41

Usually, we squat and listen to the rain pounding the deck while we eat. But today there is a new sound coming from above.

"Do you hear that?" Ham asks.

"What?"

"Nothing."

"Boy," Noah says, "keep quiet if you have nothing to say."

"I hear *nothing* from above. The rain has stopped."

Shem opens the hatch. First water, then gray light, spills down upon us. Though it hurts my eyes to look at it, I cannot look away; I am afraid it will disappear if I do. I reach my hand into the daylight and try to grab it in my fist.

"Come on," Shem says, hesitating. For half a breath no one moves, and then Japheth hastens up the ramp to the deck. We follow, stumbling blindly into the light and then to the edge of the deck. We look at the sea, the one God has emptied of everything except us.

But the sea isn't empty at all. Rafts of half-dead bodies, with tiny morsels of life left inside them, float below.

How have they outlived the Nephilim? They could drink rainwater, but what did they eat?

"Hello," Shem calls to a woman who has lost most of her hair. She lies on a raft holding a blue, motionless baby to where her tunic has fallen away from her breast. "Come closer."

"Please, you must take my child."

It is not the child Shem wants, and the woman has no paddle or rudder with which to come closer. Our rope would reach only half the distance between us, and only with a strong wind behind it. And now there is no wind. When Shem leaves to look for more women on the other side of the ark, the woman begins to scream.

My eyes are adjusting to the gray pallor of the new world, and I notice that the birds have lost their color. As if they were bleached by the dullness of the light.

Noah is looking into the sea at the sinners. "They are not gone. *They are not gone.*" He snorts, happy that he is a preacher again. "Behold, children of the God of Adam!" he cries, throwing open his arms. "It is not too late for you. Proclaim your love for the Lord."

Japheth turns his angry gaze from the sea to Noah. His face is so flushed, it looks swollen. "The sinners have not been destroyed."

Without taking his eyes off the sea, Noah replies, "God pauses between the rains and the worst of the flooding—the *true* flood. He gives the sinners one last chance."

This chance looks quite small, unless we are going to throw down the rope.

Noah raises his voice so it rings out over the waters: "Repent!"

"Old man," Japheth addresses his father, "I must kill these abominations myself, since your God has forgotten them, along with us."

Noah cheerfully thwacks his staff against the deck near Japheth's feet. "God has not forgotten us." He raises his staff heavenward. "The rain stopped, as He promised it would."

A naked man raises an arm toward us from where he lies on a raft not much wider than he is. I look closer and see that it is a hatch cover. I also see that he is naked not only of any covering but also of the flesh that holds a man's skin off his bones. "Please help me," he calls up to us.

"How have you survived, brother?" Ham asks.

"I jumped from my ship."

"What ship is that?"

"The *God's Eye*. The captain would have eaten me if I had stayed on board. I would rather be devoured by the sea."

Noah leans out over the wall of the deck to peer more closely at the man and his raft. "Where did you get the wood?"

"He says he jumped from a ship," I tell Noah, "because he was going to be eaten. He must have taken the wood with him."

"You believe him?" Japheth says to me. "Look with your eyes. He is no meal."

"How long ago was it you jumped?" Noah asks.

"Long enough that I am colder than a man can survive for long."

"How big is the *God's Eye*? How many men, and what weapons have they?" Ham asks.

"Let me come aboard, and I will tell you everything you want to know and fight beside you when the *God's Eye* attacks. I was the fiercest sellsword for leagues in all directions. I have lived all the way until twenty-seven years, and I know I have many more years left with which to serve you." The man tries to stand but falls forward upon his raft. "I pledge myself to you."

"It is the God of Adam to whom you must pledge yourself."

If the man does as Noah commands, perhaps Noah will not stop me from taking him onto the ark.

"I pledge myself to your gods above all the others. I swear my allegiance to them."

Close enough. I go to retrieve the rope before Japheth can stop me. But when I reach for it, the ark is smacked by a wave. Then we are hurtling along as if we have a rudder and a place to go.

"Where are we going?" I cry. But Noah is not looking at where we are going. He is looking back. I do not know why God should wish to put us in one part of the sea instead of another. Is there any difference? The wave that pushes us is like a giant bull, charging ahead with a fly on its nose. We are the fly.

I search the sea for the man who pledged himself to Noah. He is a spot in the distance behind us, struggling to hold on to his raft in the havoc created by the wave that steers the ark. His struggle is brief.

I leave the rope on the deck floor and join my boys at the bow.

"The sinners are not dead yet, and the sea will not go still until it has them," Japheth says.

My stomach burns and rises toward my throat. I know he is right. The God of Adam kept me from throwing down the rope. I fear He has displayed them one last time before He drowns them, as a warning to us.

"After He has dealt with these sinners," Japheth continues, "the sea will return to its place north of the desert, and we will be back on our land."

"Then where is it we are going?" Ham asks.

"Yes, why would God put us back where He found us when the whole world is free for our use?" Zilpha says. I was so busy looking into the sea that I did not notice her.

"You would not understand no matter how carefully I explained it," Japheth replies.

"I am the daughter of a prophet. You, on the other hand . . ." She looks at Noah.

He is still gazing back at the sea where the sinners floated. Now no life is visible for as far we can see in all directions, yet the sea screams. It screams with the voices of those it has taken. A tear rolls down Noah's cheek.

I go to him, and put my lips against his cold, bony ear. "Husband, do not lose what is left of your command." But he hears only the cries of the drowned sinners.

Zilpha turns her gaze back to Japheth. "Your father thought God meant to give people a chance to repent. Mine would have known better."

Still, Noah says nothing, which causes me to hate him a little. I want to cry too, and to yell or break something. But I don't. We cannot give up what little order remains.

I take a step toward Zilpha. She is the only one I am not forced to look up at. "Kesh is dead. You would be an orphan but for Noah—a drowned one."

Japheth rarely laughs, but he does so now. Zilpha does not argue. She stares expressionlessly at me just long enough to make it seem my words have not affected her. Then she moves with much more haste than usual to the wall of the deck. She stands on her toes and tries to peer over. This causes Japheth to laugh even harder. Though Ham and Zilpha have said little and have never touched, she calls to him now, "Husband, can you help me?"

I hope my favorite son knows better than to do as she asks. She has insulted all of us by disrespecting Noah. "*Ham,*" I say forcefully. But he gets behind her, puts his hands on her little waist, and lifts her so she can gaze over the deck wall.

I feel as though someone has turned my weak stomach into a tight fist and set my skull on a cookfire.

Japheth laughs harder still. I think he is laughing at me as well now. "And you are worse than she is," I say. "You dare call Noah 'old man' in front of your mother and the God of all living creatures."

"Now that God has gotten rid of the prideful child's own father, Noah is *her* father too," Japheth says, "and her words were far worse than mine. Do not waste your nattering on *me.*"

It is only because of his injury that I do not slap him. "If you do not respect your father *and your mother,* you are a sinner, and you belong in the sea with the rest of your kind."

I have never spoken so sharply to him. His eyes bulge, and I think I have wounded him. But I will not take back my words or the feeling behind them. I turn away from him.

Behind us, where the sinners were, the God of Adam has turned the sea into a swirling blade. The remaining sinners are drawn under. Though they scream, surely they must also feel some relief.

MANOSH

*H*ave *mercy upon us.*

During the night, the wave broke apart, rushing away to either side of us. Now the sea rests. Is it digesting all it has consumed, or is God pausing while He decides what to do next?

Noah's crying roils my stomach. He is not crying out to God, he is just crying.

Dry up the fountains of my husband's eyes. Do not show us the fate of any more sinners. Please.

But God is choosy when He sifts through our prayers. Or perhaps the man who approaches through the gray light is not a sinner. Even hunched, with his back to us, he looks huge. He floats on bodies even larger than his. Bodies swollen with death gas.

As he comes closer, I see that he has tied planks to his arms with lengths of tunic. He is trying to row with both arms, but only the left plank moves with any force through the sea. I do not know what ties his right arm to his torso other than skin. It hangs lifelessly over the bodies of his raft, the plank dipping only a hand's length into the sea. His raft moves in curves as his left arm rudders and rows, rudders and rows.

When he is no more than thirty cubits away, he rows without ruddering and turns to face us.

I recognize him, though he looks older than his six hundred years. His wet tunic reveals both his strength and his mortality. The muscles in his left arm bulge like a mercenary's, but loose-hanging folds of flesh on his chest and neck are no longer hidden by his beard, which has been turned by the sea into one thin long rope that he has thrown over his shoulder.

His bare feet are pressing against the cradles of his cousins' necks. His back is bent. He is tired.

Still, he comes closer, in small arcs made by the strokes of his left arm. After each stroke, he leaves the plank in the sea to maintain his course toward us. It seems to me as though he comes more quickly than these efforts could bring him. As though the bodies beneath him are rowing as well.

They are faceup, the breadth of their shoulders making one side of the raft wider than the other. Their eyes are closed as if in concentration.

"Husband," Zilpha says, "please lift me higher. I want him to see me above all else."

"I see you, daughter of the great prophet." I know the prophet Manosh speaks of is not Noah.

"He would kill his own cousins in order to float upon them?" Japheth says of Manosh as if he were not close enough to hear.

"At least, dear Japheth," Ham replies, "they are not his *broth-ers*."

Without taking his eyes off the sea, Shem says, "Bodies do not float until they are already drowned for a day."

A miracle—my sons are speaking to each other, however harshly, and Noah has stopped crying. For a couple of breaths, despite the approaching raft of bodies, all is well.

Then Noah presses against the wall of the deck and leans out toward Manosh, as if this will keep his cousin from coming any closer. "You cannot come aboard," he says. "Only me, my sons, and our wives will voyage to the new world."

Zilpha writhes out of Ham's hands and runs awkwardly—veering slightly one way and then the other—toward the rope. I wonder if it is the first time she has ever run. Japheth easily arrives at the rope first. He waits until she grasps it to bring his foot down on it. She turns to Ham. "Husband."

It is unsettling to see my youngest son, the one who always knows to do the right thing, not know what the right thing is. He does not move.

"I cannot climb into the lumber I chopped from my own lands and dragged hundreds of leagues across the desert to bring you, cousin?" Manosh asks.

"Lands you stole—"

"What is the difference between stealing and conquering?"

"—and lumber that was not yours to give."

"Yet you took it."

"God told me I must."

Manosh continues rowing toward us. He is only about ten cubits away. "He told *me* I must see that my little cousin is well."

"She is sheltered, fed, and does little work."

"Good. She must save herself for bearing sons."

Zilpha lets go of the rope. "I am a prophetess, sons or no."

Manosh takes hold of two large hooks lying beside him. He flinches as he raises his injured right arm to show them to us. "Throw me the rope, or I will do what I need to in order to climb aboard."

Though Ham looks long at the rope, he does not take hold of it, and soon Manosh's hooks sound against the hull. He climbs. He has more strength than a young man. Perhaps even more than one of the Nephilim. I am certain that no man who can climb an ark with only one good arm will exist in the new world. God no longer trusts men enough to build them so powerful.

His hooks are puncturing the hull loudly enough that even Noah must hear. "The ark—" I begin. But I do not have to warn Noah that Manosh's hooks are damaging the hull.

"Send down the rope," Noah commands.

Ham moves toward the rope, but I stop him. Noah may send someone to see if the ark needs patching, and I do not want anyone to discover Herai. "Not you, Ham—*Shem* can throw the rope over. You go to the first level and patch."

"My great beast!" Zilpha says. She runs, slightly less awkwardly this time, to the hatch and disappears. Japheth hurries after her.

Manosh drags his body against the hull, struggling to bring his immense weight ever higher up the rope. The raft of his cousins does not linger below; it drifts away from the ark. Manosh cannot retreat.

Ham does not go to patch the ark. He and Shem watch Manosh in silence. I do not know what they will do when he reaches the wall of the deck.

The wind begins to blow. Soon it howls against the hull where Manosh climbs, so it seems as though it were coming from him. Whenever he looks up to work his hands higher up the rope, I stare into his open mouth as if I could will the air from his lungs. I back away from the wall as he nears the top.

Behind me, I hear footsteps approaching. I turn around. Japheth is coming across the deck holding one arm across Zilpha's chest, his knife at her throat. Zilpha does not struggle. The knife has been dulled by the blood and flesh upon it.

"This is one of the three girls who must bear all the children of the new world," I yell at Japheth. "Take your knife from her throat and let us hope you have not harmed her too greatly."

Ham takes a sword from Shem's belt.

"My knife is closer to her throat than your sword is to mine," Japheth says.

Ham hesitates, then sets the sword down. "The God you once feared will not look kindly upon you if you do not let go of my wife."

"You should have pretended to believe in Him earlier than this," Japheth replies. "Your timing is not very convincing."

I move to stand by Ham. I do not want any more harm to come to Zilpha, but I am more concerned for my son. I hope I am strong enough to stop him from doing something foolish.

Manosh hoists himself onto the deck wall. He swings his leg over, long toes pointed, searching for the floor. He breathes heavily through his mouth.

"Stop," Japheth says.

Manosh looks at my son, my least favorite son, the one I did not love as much as the others. The one I have let lose an ear. Manosh looks at him and goes still.

"Get back in the sea," Japheth says.

Zilpha gazes through Manosh as if she does not see him. He is a sight. He balances atop the deck wall, the loose flesh of his neck shaking as if the ark still tossed in the storm. He gasps for air. He must see what I see when I look at my son: a hunger for others' terror. A desperation for it that might make killing the daughter of a prophet the easiest way to become what he has always wanted to be: a feared man.

But I do not know if Japheth is willing to risk God's wrath by killing Zilpha. Manosh does not chance it. He lets go of the wall. There is a splash, and the sound belongs not so much to Manosh as to Zilpha.

Japheth lowers the knife, and Zilpha steps forward. As she goes to the wall, I see no cuts upon her.

"Husband," she commands.

Ham picks her up. The sea is rippling lightly, and she watches until it goes still.

"Thank you," she says.

Ham might assume she is speaking to him, but I know it is not Ham she is thanking. A great man was willing to die for his belief in her bloodline. How can we not believe a little ourselves?

THE POWER OF THE MARK II

When my family has returned into the ark, still I stay near the deck wall. I gaze at the water below, the water into which Manosh has disappeared along with Javan, her brutes, the people of Sorum, the traders I served goat stew and lentils, and everyone from the village where I was born. The flames of those who once called for me to be brought from my father's tent have been put out for good.

Can we truly be the last ones left? I turn in a circle, looking across the water, straining to see to the ends of the earth. It seems the ark is the only raft that has made it through the storm. My mark has brought me shame, humiliation, hatred, and, I realize, life. Each event that I had thought was a horrible consequence of being marked—the villagers calling for my blood and Noah coming to take me to the last town on earth I wanted to live in—was bringing me another step closer to salvation. Salvation hidden in a cloak of near-ruin.

The mark has saved me.

The mark has saved me.

And not only has it saved me, it has given me three boys who did not drown when all the other mothers' sons did. It has made me mother of all those who will come after me.

I reach up and tear the scarf from my head. I hold it over the sea, and then I am done holding it. It floats from my fingertips to the water below.

· · ·

The next time Noah sounds the horn two short and one long blast, I wait so that I will be the last one to walk into the gathering place. Then I walk carefully, head tilted to the right so they can all see my mark. If anyone says anything about it or looks too long, I will tell them, "This is why each one of you is here. It is our raft. All but Noah owes his life to this mark."

"Mother," Shem says without looking at me. He says it more to Noah than to me. My sons and Zilpha are waiting with their bowls in their hands, eager for Noah to notice that I am nearing so he will dole out rations. They do not even notice that I do not wear my head scarf.

Once Noah has given everyone a portion of lentils and dried lamb, we squat and stare over our bowls at one another. Shem's eyes come to rest upon the mark, but it is almost as if he does not see it. For a moment I wonder if somehow my head scarf floated up out of the water and fastened itself back over my brow.

Japheth does not dare look too long at it. He glances at it and then quickly away.

Noah does not notice. Ham smiles and then goes back to eating. Zilpha is the only one who speaks. "You have never needed to hide it from me."

Later, when I go to see Herai, she touches it. When she takes back her hand, her eyes remain upon my brow. It feels good to have someone gaze upon the mark with simple, innocent curiosity, then smile, as if thanking me for the chance to see something new.

But for all except Herai, the mark is not the true object of curiosity aboard the ark. Zilpha is.

CHAPTER 45

PROPHETESS

Even Noah is a little bit afraid of Zilpha. He squints his old eyes at her as if there is something he must figure out. Japheth pretends to be unaffected by Manosh's sacrifice, but he does not ever turn his back to Zilpha, though the flesh upon his knife was not hers. He killed the mammoth—both of them, really, since one of any beast is worthless to the new world.

My boys labor to get the grieving female on deck so that she will be easier to dispose of than the male, who had to be cut into pieces and thrown overboard. We had salt enough to save part of one flank. I do not know if I can bring myself to eat it.

With the female at the edge of the deck, quietly waiting to die, Japheth seems suddenly unsure.

"What stills your knife only now?" Noah says. He has given Japheth the task of stabbing the female's flanks so she moves away from him, over the deck wall. "Already, their blood, and the blood of all the generations of great mammoths who would have come after them, is upon you. You have taken one of God's creatures from the world."

I cannot watch, and I do not want to hear any sound that comes from this sad task. I go to the second level. But even from there I hear the breaking of the deck wall and a huge, horrible splash.

. . .

Zilpha often prays or appears to be praying. She sits with her little legs crossed, palms open on her knees, eyes closed, eyelashes fluttering. Once she caught me bending down in order to see if her eyes were really closed, and that answered my question. Or perhaps she heard me come near because of the creaking in my bones.

When she is on deck, Ham is always ready to lift her so she can gaze at the sea. He holds her there, at a respectful distance from himself, until his arms start to shake. I cannot understand what has happened to him.

Then one day, I realize: He has fallen in love with Zilpha. I would rather he had fallen into the sea. A place from which I could rescue him.

Now that Zilpha comes on deck sometimes, all the wings Japheth did not clip have started to flap again. Birds soar overhead and try to follow Zilpha back down the hatch when she leaves. Sometimes she sings to them. Her lips move, and though none of us can hear her, the birds start to chirp and caw.

I hope God can hear them. If He does, maybe He will remember us.

. . .

One day I notice: "The sky is coming closer."

"No, Mother," Zilpha says. "The sea is rising."

"But the rain has stopped."

"The rain has stopped, and now begins the flood."

Begins?

I go to the gathering place. "When will God be done with this madness?"

Noah does not open his eyes or get up from where he is kneeling. But he flinches.

"Is there no other way to destroy all life on earth?" I ask.

"Would you rather have nostrils filled with the smell of burning flesh?"

"I would rather the destruction were over."

"When it is over, it will be truly over. We will not bounce around upon the sea ever again."

"What will we do instead?"

"Tend our flocks—"

"How many of us will it take to tend a few litters of goats, a few of sheep—"

"They will flourish in the new world. When I pray, I feel the words flowing out of me once again, as though they are being pulled into God's ear."

Suddenly, I am laughing. "Do you notice, husband, how we pass hope back and forth between us so that we never have it at the same time?"

He opens his eyes partway. "Not only the herds but our children too will flourish."

I am glad for his words. I drop down beside him on his blankets. "I am tired."

"We must escort our children to the new world." His eyes do not open all the way anymore. His hands tremble. "Then all of our work will be done."

"You are tired too, husband."

"Between the day Shem was born and the first day of the rains, I aged a hundred years."

I do not know how this could be true, but I believe him. "I am sorry," I say, "that I did not notice."

"God does not age me so rapidly anymore. He will not let me go. Not until—"

"—our work is done."

.   .   .

"Mother," Zilpha says one day when I come back from Noah's sleeping blankets, "do not worry for him. God will keep him for at least three hundred more years."

"If so, He is crueler than I thought."

"He will not keep you so long."

It is strange to be so miserable and yet so deeply pained at the mention of my own death. *Just so long as He first bestows a name upon me.*

I walk past Zilpha up onto the deck. I will escort her to the new world. Then I do not wish to see her again.

CHAPTER 46

THE *GOD'S EYE*

No matter how big the world is, it is always too small for us and the things we fear. We are trapped between the sky, the ship in the distance, and the unknown. The unknown is the worst of these three. It looms larger as the ship nears.

Did Zilpha remember this ship when she predicted Noah's long life?

I no longer wonder what Noah will have us do if the people on board are friendly. The ship is not even a quarter so large as ours, but it has a sail of many hides sewn together. Some are the color of human flesh.

Japheth's eyes narrow. "It is closer than it was yesterday."

"And yesterday it was closer than the day before."

"By a hair's width, Mother," Ham says. "We will all die of old age before it arrives."

No more than a few days after Ham says this, my sons, Zilpha, and I are on deck when the wind roars out of the heavens. The sail of hides swells and begins to bring the ship toward us through the sea.

I have questions I do not ask aloud: *Whose side will God be on when our ships meet? Does He know yet? Are we supposed to fight or wait for Him to decide?* I do not need the answers to these questions. I will have no choice but to fight. I do not want to die without a name.

Zilpha cannot see over the deck wall. "Husband," she says.

As Ham picks her up to stare out at the sea, I seal my lips to keep from telling him to save his strength for the ship that is now only a hundred cubits away. He might scowl at my words and like me less.

"It comes toward us as if it is not touching the sea," Zilpha observes, "as if it is not pulled by the waters the way we are."

When the ship is not more than eighty cubits away, we see, drawn in blood upon the sail, an eye. No one mentions going below to alert Noah.

"So that is what God's eye looks like," Ham says. "I would have thought it would be bigger and not so red."

"Do not call that abomination God's eye," Japheth snaps. "And it must be shut for good before God will allow us into the new world."

"What he says is true," Zilpha says.

Japheth snorts and hurries below to get several creations from his collection. When he returns, he holds the weapons he has made over his head. "God is bringing the sinners' throats to these swords."

"Is that what these are?" Ham asks.

Japheth sets the weapons down, all except a sword, which he tries to hand Ham.

Ham looks at it but continues to hold Zilpha up to gaze at the sea and the ship that is now only sixty cubits away.

When did you become such a fool? Put the child down and take up your weapon.

"Enough, husband," Zilpha says.

Ham sets her down and takes the sword. Japheth watches as Ham turns it over in his hands. "What happened to your dagger?" he asks.

"I left it somewhere."

"Well, I mean to keep all of these." Next Japheth holds up a dagger he has made with a small backward hook near the base of the blade. "See," he says proudly, slicing his finger on the hook that faces him as the blade points to our enemies, "it will do as much damage coming out as it does going in."

"I will take that one," Shem says.

"No." Japheth licks the blood from his finger. "This one is mine." He has also brought a club into which he has whittled teeth. "Here is yours, Shem. Hold as tightly to this as you do to your mother's teat."

It is a cruel-looking weapon. I cannot gaze at the wooden spikes without imagining how they would strip the flesh from a man's face. I step forward and run my fingers lightly over the teeth. They are dull. I press harder. Still nothing.

"It is for our enemies' eyes, not their flesh," Japheth says, yanking it away from my hand. "Fear is more efficient than any blade."

Color flares in Shem's cheeks. "I thought you wanted to kill me yourself, brother."

"Do not risk all of our lives with your foolishness," I tell Japheth.

Japheth kicks the handle of a sword so that it spins toward Shem. Shem jumps back, then quickly reaches down to grasp it.

Now all of my sons hold weapons, and they wish to turn their backs to one another even less than they want to turn them to the other ship that is no more than fifty cubits in the distance. "You cannot fight each other and the rest of the world at the same time. You must choose. And quickly," I say.

Shem looks with great unease at the seared flesh where Japheth's ear used to be. His hand is tightly clenched around his new sword. "Do not worry," Japheth says. "We will not have our own battle until all of the others are done."

Still, Shem waits for Japheth to turn back to the other ship before he too takes his gaze off his brother and returns it to the sea.

Though we look with the full strength of our sight, we cannot see our enemy. The back of the ship is hidden by the sail, and the front of the ship is covered in the sail's shadow. All but the prow, which carries only gray light.

The ship comes within forty cubits, and still we cannot see the people aboard. Even Japheth steps back from the deck wall. If the ship does not slow down, it will crash into the ark's hull. After that, whoever is on board will not have far to climb to reach us. Especially if we start to sink.

"Brace yourselves," Japheth says. If a ship of cannibals were not hurtling toward us, I would be overjoyed that my middle son has shown some care for his brothers and me.

A man on the approaching ship moves out of the sail's shadow and stands upon the prow. I recognize him. His eye socket is covered with a cloth tied at a steep angle around his head. He holds a long sword in one hand, a club in the other. His legs are spread, his back is straight, and his head is held high.

"Demon woman, how ever have you been?"

Though Jank insults me, he has also shown me respect by addressing me instead of my sons. There is no one besides him on the prow to address, so I show him the same respect. "God does not mistake you for a great man because you yourself do."

Even from thirty cubits away, I can see that his smile is forced. "I do not claim to be great—only hungry."

I am certain he hungers for more than meat. He is fatter than he was before the flood, yet he tries to talk his way onto the ark—the very last human creation worthy of envy left in the world.

Behind him, men are yelling at one another as they labor to turn the sail a quarter of a rotation, so that it drops the wind. The shadow over the front of the ship narrows down to one lean line, and mercifully, the ship slows. There are rope ladders, planks, hooks, and axes scattered on the prow. They have prepared for this meeting. Four men come to stand with Jank, while two others remain with the sail's ropes. Jank is well fed, but the six men around him are skeletal. A few of them are naked. From twenty cubits away, I can count their ribs.

"Grandmother," Jank tries again, "you have a whole ark full of meat. All we ask is our share. Let us come aboard and take of your lamb and goat."

Men on either side of Jank shout in agreement as the *God's Eye* coasts closer: "Give it to us or we will take it." "Our share!"

"If you knew what your share was," I call to the hungry skeletons, "you would not starve with so much meat next to you." I look long at Jank.

They do not follow my gaze. They study my sons and me, and two of them look at my mark. But they do not seem afraid. At least not of us. What has kept them from ripping the fat off Jank? Nothing I want to imagine. As they near, I can see they are sallow-skinned and have not five teeth among them. There is not any amount of meat in the world that will satisfy them; their hunger has grown so large, it has entered their hearts.

A man whose scalp is a quilt of oozing sores opens his mouth to speak. Instead of sound, drops of blood fall from his lips. While perhaps this should be reassuring, as surely this man will not be as much of a threat as a healthy man, I would rather not see something so gruesome before the battle has even begun.

"There are seven of us and seven of them," Zilpha says. "Once we kill one of them, there will no longer be a lucky number of them, and the forces that watch over all things seven will no longer be able to see them."

I would love to tell her that she is wrong: There are actually eight of us. I would ask whether she is willing to jump overboard and make a lucky seven of us. But for Herai's sake, I keep my tongue still.

"There are seven of them coming to fight three men, a tired, creaky-kneed woman, and a little girl," I correct her. "But they are weak, and we are slightly less weak."

"Grandmother, your welcome leaves something to be desired," Jank calls up to me. "It is almost too late for you to graciously invite us on board. Soon we will make our way onto the ark, and you will wish you had not thought so little of us. The weak have not survived. Only the strong are left."

The prow of the *God's Eye* is not more than ten cubits from the ark's hull.

Japheth holds out wooden spears to his brothers. The tips are still hot from the sharpening stone. They each take one, leaving him with two. "Do not lose these," he says.

Jank squints up at me. "You are almost out of time, marked one."

"My mammoths would have given these raiders pause," Zilpha says.

And then the ark is rocked by the *God's Eye*.

I am slammed against the deck wall, and then backward onto my hindquarters. This time no one tells me to get below.

Metal hooks soar over the side of the ark and catch on the wall, except one that soars past it. I roll onto my belly The hook makes a different sound than the hooks that catch the wall—a sound like my knife used to make when I cut fresh goat meat. I do not want to know who the hook has fallen upon, and I do not want to know how badly he is injured. Would I sacrifice Japheth to know Shem is unharmed, Shem to know Ham is unharmed?

The knots keeping the sail of the *God's Eye* back give way, and the sail spins sideways, hitting the hull. It looms over me. I remember the heads on stakes so many years ago when Noah first brought me to his tent. These hides with a bloody eye upon them that menace me now are as gruesome as those heads, but I do not wish to turn back in the direction from which I came. Jank is the last person left in the world who calls me "demon woman." I am ready to be rid of him. I stand.

The trouble with starving men is that they are such small targets. My sons dislodge the old hooks from the ark, but this does little good. The men are easily able to boost one another onto the hull. From there they do not have far to climb. Though Japheth and Shem stab with all their might, they do not do so carefully enough to injure Jank's men. The men fall less than ten cubits, onto the deck of the God's Eye, and get back up. A few men are bleeding, but they do not seem to notice. These men must have endured far worse than spears. Something has taken their souls from their bodies.

Shem draws back his spear and aims it at a man climbing up the hull. The man's eyes take up most of his face. His pupils are too large for me to see what color his eyes are, and there is only red where his whites must once have been. It is like looking at black circles in little boats of blood.

I have kept my knife with me since Shem used it to cut off Japheth's ear. I unsheath it now. "Do not send this man back to the God's Eye," I tell Shem. "Hold the point of your spear to his head so that his hand can reach the top of the deck but he can go no farther."

Shem does as I have instructed. A set of bony fingers grasps the top of the deck wall. With his other hand, his left one, the man brings an ax soaring toward us. We jump back, and the man's arm hits hard against the edge of the deck wall. The impact jerks the ax from his grip and he withdraws his left arm. I raise my knife over my head and bring it down with the force of all the anguish that has built up over this long dark journey into the sea. I do not shudder when my knife cuts through sinew and the tiny bones of his right hand, staking the man to the ark.

The man reaches his free hand onto the hilt of the knife. I do not let go, and his fingers wrap around mine.

"*Shem*," I say.

The point of Shem's spear is no longer sharp. It is impossible that human flesh has dulled it so quickly. Yet there is no other explanation.

Shem stabs at the man's torso. It is like trying to drive one stick into another. Shem stabs him again, this time in the chest. Yet the man's hand remains tightly wrapped around mine.

Despite the fury in Japheth's thrusts, the other men have not given in to my sons' spears either. They are strong, instead of weak, with hunger. Unless the situation is even worse. *Perhaps they are already dead, and that is why they cannot be killed.*

The hand over mine squeezes harder. What little flesh remains to me does not cushion my bones from his.

"I do not want to lose the ability of my hand, Shem. Use your sword."

But Shem is using it already to fight another man who is hoisting himself over the deck wall.

I have only one weapon that the man whose hand is crushing mine does not have. I sink my teeth into the veins above his knuckles. His left hand releases mine. I try to pull my knife out of the ark, back through his right hand. I cannot leave it here. But I cannot dislodge it either.

Someone presses up against my back and uses a dagger on one side of my knife to stab at the man's hand. He slides back down onto the God's Eye.

"Grawdmwahfah," Herai says before turning to fight a man who has just come over the side of the deck wall. She has ripped holes for her neck and arms in the blanket I gave her when I took her tunic.

I do not see Zilpha or Ham. I pray my son will not lose his life defending Zilpha's.

The other person I do not see on deck is Jank. Some men lead their followers, but he is not one of them. He has waited safely below, but now climbs up the hull to the section of the deck I have been left to defend.

"Coming to fight an old woman?" I call down to him. "Your valor underwhelms me."

"God wants me to live, Grandmother, so this is the path He has put me on." I can see the green of his eye. It is bright even in the dull gray light. When his meaty fingers wrap around the top of the deck wall, I stab at his hand. He easily grabs my knife with his other hand and hurls it to the side. There is a small *clunk* as it hits the deck of the God's Eye.

Jank pulls himself over the wall, and his feet land hardly a finger's width from mine. I want to step back, but that will just bring

Jank closer to the hatch. If he advanced to the second level of the ark, he could release all of the animals, kill Noah, and kill Ona. Or leave Ona alive for his pleasure but beat upon her stomach until he kills my grandchildren. I look around for my sons. Shem and Japheth are battling the skeletons with Herai's help, and Ham and Zilpha still are not on deck.

Jank has a sword in his belt but does not unsheath it. Instead, he takes hold of my throat. With his other hand, he pulls the cloth tied around his head away from his black and red eye socket. If my breath had not already come to a halt because of his hand on my neck it would come to one now. "My father tried to take both of my eyes when I saw what another man did to him in battle. But I killed him before he could blind me." His hand loosens as he laughs. I see his sharpened canines and the space between them. "That you would think yourself capable of stopping me brings a certain joy into my heart, and I thank you for that."

Should I beg for my life to give my sons time to come to my aid? Or once I beg, will he finally have gotten what he wants and have no more need of me?

"I am the matriarch of the new world. The God of Adam will never forgive you if you take my life. The only life He would have you take is your own."

"Demon woman, do you really think He would want all the peoples of the new world to come from you?" His hand tightens around my throat.

"I know I am no demon and that no demon ever resided within me," I choke. "My sons are argument enough that I am a woman and no more. They are too imperfect, too mortal, for me to be anything but human."

He drags me toward him, lifts me off my feet, and turns me to the right, so that out of the corner of my eye, I can partly see Shem struggling with two of Jank's men. "Take a last look at your argu—"

I sink my leftmost teeth into the side of his face. He screams, and shoves me to the deck floor.

His scream reminds me of the boy he was when Noah and I first came upon him. He is still only a boy, except now he is a boy who cannot see. He thrashes his head about as if he can undo what has happened, then stumbles and falls backward. His head hits as hard as if it has fallen all the way from the sky.

I pretend to hold Jank's eye in my fist. I raise it up over my head. "This is all that remains of our enemy's sight," I cry loudly enough for Jank's men to hear.

It is as if I have taken their eyes as well. They begin to die beneath my children's blades.

· · ·

When the fighting is over, Herai and I stand Jank up. "Do not leave your work unfinished and my life in the hands of raiders," he begs me. "Take what is left."

"I am sorry, I cannot."

His hands grope for our weapons. But we have set them down, hopefully forever. We heave his fat, struggling bulk over the deck wall.

He falls onto the *God's Eye*, on top of his dying men. On top of him fall torches—first one and then another, thrown by my oldest sons. The flames crackle loudly and are soon joined by the sounds of boards breaking and then howling. I do not know which screams are from the flames and which are from the men.

The flames flare out into a huge sail. I step back from the deck wall. Those left on deck with me—Shem, Japheth, and Herai—step back as well. But the fire that touches the ark does not grasp it. When the wind catches the sail of flames and pushes Jank's ship back in the direction it came, no flames are left with the ark.

The ship leaves behind a smell more horrible than an animal sacrifice. But I cannot leave the deck; I cannot take my eyes from the blaze. With my children's help, I have rid the world of Jank. There is no one left in the world to call me "demon woman."

Burning pieces of Jank's ship rise into the air. They crackle, turn black, and disappear. Though I should not be able to feel the heat, I do. It burns hotter and hotter until the flames begin to reach for the sky. The smoke is like the long finger of Jank and his men coiling upward, beseeching: *Let us in*.

Shem, Japheth, Herai, and I move closer together. We watch the fire consume the ship until there is nothing left.

And then it is just us.

CHAPTER 47

THE SEA GOES STILL

Zilpha's perfect skin—baby-smooth, pale, untested by time or the slightest of facial expressions—was the skin I heard breaking apart when the battle first began. The hook hit the left side of her forehead, missed the hollow of her eye, and cut her cheek before slicing down her body and falling to the deck floor.

When I first come upon her after the battle, she is sheltered by her husband. Herai has come down before me, and she is standing completely naked over Ham. She has given her blanket to him, and he presses it against the gash from which Zilpha is bleeding to death. He presses too gently.

"Move." I put my palms flat against the blanket and press firmly. "Like this," I tell Ham and Herai. They put their hands on either side of mine. It is not enough. Blood wells up and soaks the blanket.

"Should we change the covering?" Ham asks.

"Do not move it, or we will lose her." Zilpha's eyes are closed, but I can feel her chest rising and falling jaggedly beneath my hands. "We will place another covering over this one. Get your father and brothers."

Herai extends one of her arms as far as she can along the bloody blanket while I pull my tunic over my head. I slide it onto the blood-ied blanket.

We wait.

Shem is the first to arrive. He kneels by Zilpha's head and places his hands upon my tunic so that his fingertips touch Herai's. But it is not enough. The blood continues to flow from the little body.

Noah is next. When I hear his staff hitting against the floor, I do not look up. I do not want to see his expression as his eyes fall upon Herai and then me. We are in danger of losing one daughter-in-law. He should be glad I did not throw Herai overboard. But I can no longer predict what he will do.

He gets down on his knees and places his hands where Shem has made a place for them.

Then Ham returns, alone. We all press our hands to Zilpha. Still, a small space—about two hands' width—remains uncovered. We try to cover this space with our flesh, to extend an arm, a thigh, a cheek against it. Her blood is hot against the side of my face. She is alive. But I do not know how much longer she can bleed like this before her heart dries up and stops beating.

Loud footsteps, angry heel-digging-into-the-floor footsteps, approach. Japheth drops down beside me. I lift my cheek, and he presses his hands down on Zilpha. As if this is what she's been waiting for—bleeding for—the coverings beneath us gather no more blood.

"Thank you, Mother," Ham says.

.   .   .

She sleeps. It is not the sleep of the dead. Her heart beats, and whenever I place my hand beneath her nose, I feel her warm breath. I check on her wound daily, and Ham feeds her lentil soup. Though she does not open her eyes, she is healing with remarkable speed.

.   .   .

"The sky feels farther and farther away," I tell Ham one morning when we are both on deck.

"The water is slowly setting us down."

Very slowly, which is quickly enough for me. This ark has taken the meat from my bones and surely years from my life. And yet I am afraid to get off it. I will not go back to being the obedient wife I was on land.

I am also afraid for Herai. Her belly has grown large, and her hands are always upon it. She stands away from Ham and me, holding it while she stares out into the sea. I think she wants to share her good news with her mother. It seems that the larger the life inside her grows, the more she misses Javan.

.   .   .

Noah shows no sign of being angry at me for not throwing Herai overboard. Perhaps whatever pride he had drowned along with the sinners. He squints at Herai's belly the same way she watches the sea: hoping someone will come from it.

Ona is so pregnant, she no longer looks it. She looks like something out of a tale that children tell to scare each other. A woman with a tumor that has taken over. I think Noah has given up on her ever giving birth and has fastened his faith upon Herai. It is for her that he has Japheth slaughter the first animal upon the ark. The time has come to feed the next generation.

Japheth slaughters the goat with apprehension that unsteadies his knife. He is afraid too. Of what, I do not know. I would have expected only anger from him. Noah has told him he will keep Herai as his wife and care for her child as if it were his and not Shem's.

And yet Noah thinks Japheth's fear is of God. "Son, do not worry," he tells him, "God had us take seven pairs of all the clean animals because He intended that we eat six of them."

.   .   .

One day, as I am going down the ramp from the deck, there is a great *clunk*. I crash to the floor of the second level.

When I stand, I am overcome by a strange sensation. It is in my entire body. I am not shifting from side to side. *I am not moving at all.* Nothing is. Not even my stomach. I had forgotten how it feels to be completely still.

For almost half a year, my hands have been poised to catch my weight against the wall or floor. Slowly, I let my fingers relax.

I turn back toward the ramp and go up to the deck.

Whatever we have hit must be large—much larger even than the ark and as dense as packed earth. Where is it that the God of Adam has brought us to through rain and darkness and floodwaters?

Ham is on deck, as is Herai. She holds her belly as if it would fall were she to let go.

"We have come to rest upon a mountain beneath the surface of the sea," Ham tells me.

"I do not see it."

"It is beneath us."

The wind is stronger than usual; my hair whips my face. "Well, I hope it stays there."

. . .

We spend our days taking care of the animals—feeding them, cleaning their cages, and sometimes trying to walk the tame ones now that we believe we will be on land again soon. But really, what we are doing is waiting. Waiting for the water to recede and show us the new world.

CHAPTER 48

TWO BIRDS AND A BRANCH

And he sent forth a raven, which went forth to and fro, until the

waters were dried up from off the earth. Also he sent forth a dove . . .

GENESIS 8:7–8

W e did not know we were surrounded by mountains until we saw them.

"I knew," Japheth says. "The water moves in clashing half cir-cles."

Actually, the water moves little in any direction except down, revealing a shade of green on the mountaintops that I have never seen. When the wind blows, the small amount of sea that still covers the grass stirs it like a stew. It is so rich, my eyes almost get stuck in it.

I wonder if this is a mirage or worse—if God has brought us to the edge of this paradise but will keep the waters from receding, so that it will forever be within sight but out of reach. I hope He is done punishing His creations. Despite my fear at leaving the ark, I must know what that lush grass feels like beneath my feet.

· · ·

One day Zilpha opens her eyes. "Send out a dove," she tells Noah.

Because she has told him to do so, he cannot. I guess not all of his pride drowned with the sinners, and this comes as a relief. He has not been broken by the sea.

"Doves cannot find their way home once they have journeyed a quarter of a league from their nests," he says. He calls to a scrawny raven instead. There has been no carrion for the creature to eat. As with many of the birds, the raven's feathers are dirty and frayed. They faded from black to gray within a few moons of our journey on the ark.

Still, when Noah launches him from a finger, the bird lifts into the air and flaps his wings upon the wind harder and harder until eventually he disappears.

"Bring us something of a tree, bird," Noah mutters.

After this, Noah spends much of his time on deck, squinting into the distance. The raven is an unclean animal, so we brought only one pair. If this raven does not return, there will be no more ravens.

. . .

Days pass, and still there is no sign of the raven. I think the creature has gone from this ark for good, and I do not blame him. If he did not find any trees, why would he fly back to us rather than drop his sad body into the sea?

God, please let us off this ark before we lose any more of Your creatures.

Like the ravens, the doves have turned gray. They were silent during the long darkness and even after it, until Zilpha got them to coo again. After she retired to the second level of the ark to recover from her wounds, the birds grew listless. But she has returned to the deck, so they have returned to their songs.

"This one," Zilpha says, pointing to a female with what looks like joy in her shiny black eyes.

"Her wings are not strong enough for this wind," Noah says.

"You did not think I was strong enough to withstand the wind either," Zilpha replies. With the scar on her face, she looks stronger, less delicate. I wonder if Noah can see this.

"The first dove to perch on my finger will go," Noah says. He holds his finger out, and the shiny-eyed dove lands only long enough to push off of it before flying out into the new world.

She is strong enough to return, then to go again. The second time she comes back with an olive branch in her beak. The third time she does not come back.

"Slaughter a ewe," Noah commands Japheth. "It will not be long now."

CHAPTER 49

THE NEW WORLD

It has been eighty days since the dove was sent out from the ark for the last time. When the dove did not return, we rejoiced—quietly at first, as if we did not quite believe that she had found a place to rest the sole of her foot, then with a great feast. The feast ended only today, when we finished the third-to-last ewe. We have eaten through all but two of each clean animal.

Our ribs are tucked safely inside our skins. Our eyes no longer take up half our faces. But God has not let us off the ark. "God commands that we wait until the water returns to the sea," Noah says.

Besides the occasional body floating below, the water is peaceful enough, but we can see that it is too high to stand in. Only the leaves on what must be the highest branches peek up out of the water. We wait while the earth drinks in a little more each day.

It is not easy. Almost all of the rainwater we collected during the storm is gone. My throat is so parched that the mass grave of the sea is starting to beckon me: *Drink, let me coat your throat and flow through you. Drink of me and be sated.*

Herai's baby entered the world crying and has not stopped very long since. He is a sturdy, clear-eyed child. His cries are not cries of sadness or distress. They are ambitious cries, as if he is testing the strength of his voice and its power over us. It does not take a lot of effort to imagine his cries being those of a boy going eagerly into battle. Herai has named him Javan.

The one sound loud enough for Noah to hear without my help is little Javan's crying. A milky film has gathered in Noah's eyes. I often find him squinting through it at the boy.

"He's a normal, healthy boy," I tell Noah.

Still, Noah listens intently to Javan's cries.

"He is not slow," I say.

"I pray you are right. He is all we have."

When he is not squinting down at little Javan, he is on deck. Each morning he asks the same question: "Tell me, wife, how far down the trees can you see?" I must lean close so he hears my answer. It is never the answer he wants.

· · ·

The sun has returned. Not just the brightness that came back after the rains but the *heat*. It has dried every ounce of the rains and the flood from my body. I would be happier to see it if I were not as parched as the desert.

Ham takes his sleeping blanket and goes to Japheth. "May I have a few of your wooden spears, brother? Just enough to stretch this hide for a couple of cubits in each direction." I often hear Ham asking Zilpha if she would like shade. She says she is no longer afraid of the sun, but I suppose Ham wishes to fashion a parasol for her in any case. "You can have my rations tonight and tomorrow."

"I would rather have my spears."

"What makes you think Father's God has left anyone for you to kill?"

Japheth answers by looking long at Ham.

"Enough," I say. "I will have your father give the most barren part of the new world to any son who stains the rest of my days with foolish malice."

After Japheth sulks away, Ham turns to me, as he does more and more. "Mother, we do not need all of the ark now, do we? Surely we can break off a small piece of the deck wall." The deck wall is already broken where the great she-beast rushed away into the sea. But we should not further dismember the ark when we do not know when—or if—God will allow us to come ashore.

"Patience. Water still hoards the ground. When it is gone, you can take the lumber from the animals' cages."

After watching Zilpha fight her way out of death's grasp, it is difficult to imagine her having any need of a parasol. But I say nothing of this to Ham. He wants to provide for Zilpha, and he does not yet have land and herds.

. . .

The water continues to recede until one day I go up on deck to discover that all God has left of the flood is one stream bubbling through the valley below us. Any fear about leaving the ark is forgotten. I want to drink from that stream.

I return to the second level, where I find Noah squinting down at his grandson. Herai has left little Javan crying on her sleeping blankets while she helps Ham clean dung from the animal cages. Noah senses me next to him.

"Tell me, wife, how far down the trees can you see?"

I put my lips near his ear. "*All* the way."

He turns to me. I do not wait for him to voice his question. "Below us is a valley with a clear running stream. It is surrounded by trees whose branches must be very strong to hold up their many fruits. The only thing missing from the valley is—"

"Us."

We let everyone else leave the ark first. Ham wants to stay and help us down the ladder, but I do not know what good that will do. "Stand below with your arms out," I tease him, "as that is the direction we will fall." He climbs to the bottom and stands there looking up at us. His brothers stand with him. Surely they are eager to explore the new world, yet there they are.

Noah insists I go first. My grip has grown weak, and my hips and knees do not bend easily. I was a younger woman when I climbed in.

I do not quite believe it when my foot touches the earth. I put a little weight on it, press down to make sure the ground is solid. Then I put the other foot down.

"Finally, we are home," I say.

Once Noah is on the ground beside me, I shoo away my sons and daughters-in-law. Ona is too unsteady with whatever is still growing inside her to refuse Shem's help. Noah and I wait for what feels like a very long time until they are far enough away. Then we lean against each other and walk slowly down into the valley. He is sturdy, and my eyes and ears are keen. Together it seems we are half dying and half in the prime of our lives.

Midway down the mountain, I stop. "Husband, lift your foot." He lifts first one foot and then the other so I can bend stiffly to free his gnarled feet from his sandals. Then I free my own. The grass is long and damp. It tickles. *It is wonderful.* Our sons are men now; they can take care of us. This land will be easy to prosper in. Our herds will grow very happy and fat while we relax in our tent.

"Our work is done, is it not, husband?"

"Almost."

I ask what is left, but he does not answer.

After drinking from the stream, we recline together on opposite sides of an apricot tree. Our sons are chasing the animals from the ark. When all the others have run or been chased from the ark, they unlatch the larger beasts' cages. Barking, howling, roaring, screaming, panting, and an earthshaking stampede echo through the valley. A little monkey flies from a nearby tree into a branch right above me, showering me with apricots. A pair of gazelles passes close enough that I feel a rush of air across my legs.

I am not afraid. God has brought me all this way; I am not going to die from falling apricots or a gazelle's hoof. I put one of the apricots in my mouth. It is the sweetest, softest one I have ever eaten. "Husband, we are in paradise."

He is silent, so I turn to him and say it again. When still he does not respond, I ask him if he is well.

"Yes. I was just hoping He would leave me a little sight with which to see it."

. . .

It is quieter at night with the animals dispersed through the valley. Though Ona's gasp is not loud, it wakes me. I get a lantern and hurry past the sleeping bodies of Zilpha, Herai, and little Javan.

I find her on all fours, with her legs spread apart. I gently touch her shoulder. "You are not alone, daughter." I do not think she hears me. What looks like a large mass of dark fur is trying to get out of her.

Now my heart beats not only from fear but also from hope. The fur is hair—black hair with little wisps of purple. *The last giant.* A nephil has managed to sneak past the all-seeing eye of God.

We will need to cut Ona open in order to save her and the giant. I get my knife and hold it over the fire we leave burning night and day.

My gentlest son is also the one with the steadiest hand. He does not want to hurt anyone, and this stills his knife. So I choose my words carefully when I wake him. "Your brother's wife is dying. Only you can save her."

I place the handle of the knife in Ham's hand. He curses and then stands.

Ona has not been able to lie on her back in many moons; the weight inside her is too great. She groans as I force her down on her side. But then I think of her heart and everything else that is inside her besides the child. In this position, it might spill out. "We must put her on her back."

Ham helps me lift and push her stomach so it is sitting on top of her. She gasps for air as the weight crushes down upon her.

"This will be quick," I promise.

Ham moves the blade deftly over Ona's belly, and her flesh falls open behind it. The bloody giant appears and rolls wetly off to one side. I see that he did not escape God's eye. To keep the giant from growing too powerful, God has given him a clubfoot.

But it is not God's eye that I am marveling at. I am remembering what my father told me about the Nephilim not being able to see well, and how that gave me hope that I might be loved by one of them. Now I see my father was wrong: If one of the Nephilim sought out Ona, the most beautiful girl I have ever seen, then surely they *can* see. And yet one fought the floodwaters to save me, despite the mark upon my brow.

"We will take care of Ona while you wash him," Ham says. I notice Herai and Zilpha have joined us, bringing blankets and a small amount of water with which to tend Ona. They stare in shock at the little giant.

The baby wears a matted tunic of blood and is as big as a six-year-old; I cannot carry him. I go to get some water. While I wash him, I gaze into his eyes. They are Ona's eyes, except they are not yet ringed with long black lashes. If she does not survive, I will try to live long enough to raise this child myself.

CHAPTER 50

SHAHAR

Ona does live. Though her body is slow to mend, and even sewn together, her skin does not fit her very tightly, she is full of joy. She sings to her child, Elam. She makes up songs about his father, a great giant who, she sings, must have been unlike any man she has ever known.

I did not see you that night, my love, but I see you now, see you in our son's strong arms and sweet face, and always in my dreams . . .

I do not acknowledge Shem's scowls while she sings. Or Japheth's. One of the comforts of getting older is that I can pretend I do not notice anything unpleasant until I do not need to pretend. My eyes and ears can hold only so much, and they are full of bright-colored birds and trees so fat with fruit that their branches threaten to break.

The raven has surprised us all by returning. The dove as well. Her feathers are as white as they were before the flood, as white as the occasional cloud that floats by in the sky. "We must make her a nest," Zilpha told Ham. The dove quickly filled it. Doves usually have only one or two hatchlings, but she has produced three. They coo day and night. If I were in mourning over something, their cooing might sound like a lament. But I am not in mourning. And so it seems to me that we are all quite happy. All except Noah.

Our sons have erected a sleeping tent for Noah and me, which Ham and Zilpha will share with us until she gets her woman's blood. But more often than not, Noah spends the night outside, under stars whose light is the last thing left in this world that he can see. His donkey has survived the journey to the new world and sometimes is with him.

One night I find Noah leaning against the trunk of the apricot tree, his donkey resting nearby.

"Husband," I say into his ear, "you must sleep."

"It is hard for me to sleep without the sounds of the sea or the sinners."

"If you listen, there are crickets, frogs, and doves singing, croaking, and cooing all night."

"Not loudly enough for me to hear them."

"I will rub your feet until you drift away."

"Can you rub away all I have done in order to bring us here?"

I pull back to look at him. He is slumped against the tree as though he might fall backward if it were to disappear. His eyelids are heavy. I do not know whether he speaks of how he did not stop Manosh's beast from trampling sinners, or how he had Japheth lure the slave woman off the ark to her death, or of how he refused Manosh a place upon the ark.

"You have only done what God has asked of you."

"Perhaps if I had not lost faith in the sinners, God would not have given up on them."

He does not want to be comforted. He keeps the sinners close to him with his sadness. There is nothing for him to do in the new world but mourn.

.   .   .

I see him early one morning on the peak of the smallest mountain. He stands tall, waving his arms out to either side, making his tunic billow in the wind. He seems more alive than he has been since crying out to the sinners one last time before God drowned them.

I hurry up to him as fast as I can, which is not very fast. Long before I reach the peak, he has dropped his arms to his sides and his head to his chest.

Panting, I come to stand beside him. His eyes are closed. "What is it?" I ask.

"I thought I had found a village of sinners who had survived. I heard their shouts, screams, and copper swords clashing. Women were laughing in the flesh tents. I saw their dark mass below me. I shouted at them as I used to, so loudly that I used up all the air in my lungs." He breathes as if catching the air before it can escape again. "Wife, do you know what I thought?"

"You are tired, good husband. You should rest."

"I thought, *This time I can save them*."

He opens his eyes and gazes to where he saw the sinners. The milky film in his eyes has stretched across the brown of both irises. "But the village was only a shadow cast by a cloud. The sun burned through it."

"Do not be sad, husband—"

"Yet if I look hard enough, I still see them there." His pupils shift slightly behind the white film.

I move to stand beside him. I squint until I see them too.

There is Javan, talking with her hired boys near one of her flesh tents. Outside other tents, whores are calling at passersby—cajoling, flattering, and insulting them. There is screaming, shouting, and laughter. Pain, elation, anticipation.

I take Noah's hand as best I can with the stiffness that has spread from my hips and knees to my whole body. Together we stand on the mountain peak and watch the sinners.

. . .

Often he is quiet, and I know he is thinking of them.

. . .

"Get!" Ham yells, and hurtles a rock into the sky. The vultures have been circling above me for many days now.

"Careful, son. There are only two."

"And only one of you."

I feel like a vine so twisted that it is being cut by its own thorns. "Walk me to Herai," I say. I am giving the next generation my blessing, and I have left Herai for last.

Herai is caring for the boys while Ona tends the cookfire. The birds' shadows loop around ours as Ham brings me to the Mothers' Tent. He lifts the door flap, and I walk in. Elam lies beside Herai on the blanket, pulling at one of her ears. The purple in his dark hair is shining in the sunlight coming through the tent window. If my fingers were still agile, I would tickle his belly, as I did my sons'.

"Daughter," I say, "I have come to give you my blessing. And ask you a question."

Her smile broadens. Little Javan is at her breast, but she offers me her arm anyway as I lower myself down beside her. "Mwahfah," she says.

I brush the bottom of Javan's tiny foot with my hand, which causes him to scrunch and unscrunch his toes. Herai marvels at this before returning her gaze to mine.

"There is something I have wondered for as long as I have known your mother."

Both of Herai's hands are holding her son. I press my palm as best I can to the back of one of them. "How did she get the X upon her forehead?"

Herai's smile falls away. She sets Javan down, and for once he does not cry. He looks into his mother's face, confused at being taken from her breast while he is still hungry. She does not pick him up again.

"Do not be troubled, daughter. I already know your mother

killed as many men as any mercenary. What could be worse?"

Herai's hands remain at her sides.

"Unburden your shame. I will not be around so much longer, and then you will have lost your chance."

"Mwee," she says.

I had never considered this. If Herai had not been slow, Javan never would have been exiled, and Herai would not be here now. Just as I would not be here if not for my mark.

"What a blessing we were born as we were," I say.

Herai looks puzzled. I am about to explain what I mean, but I fall asleep. I do this often now without meaning to. I dream of my father. He is not more than ten cubits away. I am a little girl again, and he holds his arms out to me.

Each time I dream, I get a couple of cubits closer.

When I wake, I am leaning against Herai. I think I have given her my blessing, but I cannot be sure. I straighten up, beckon her to place her head under my misshapen hand, and I bless her.

. . .

That night I wake suddenly and see that Noah is not beside me on his sleeping blankets.

There is a full moon, but I do not need its light to show me where he is. I go to the apricot tree and lower myself beside him. Though he says nothing, I am certain he knows I am here.

We sit silently in the moonlight until I thank him.

"For what?" he asks.

"My life and those of our children and grandchildren. If it were not for you, God would have started over."

He turns and squints at me for a few breaths. Then he reaches his hand out and touches my leg. He has never mastered the gentle touch, but it is nice to feel his skin against mine. "The mission the Lord sent me on is over and done, and now I do not know what to do with myself. You are one of the only comforts left to me. I will be sad when you are gone. I have been thinking of planting a vineyard so I can do something besides wait for the Lord to bring me from this world."

I am surprised that he will miss me, though it is true we have grown close in the new world. All I say is, "You are sad already."

"Not all the way. I have been thinking of a name for you."

A name. My heart beats harder. "Please, husband, do not hesitate. Tell me the name you would bestow upon me."

He is lost in thought. "Perhaps you were blessed not to have one before now. You did not have to fashion yourself to fit your name, like those of us who have had them our whole lives."

I did not think my blood was young enough to find its way to my cheeks, but suddenly my face is hot. "I did have names, they were just never my own. I was daughter, wife, then mother."

"You were. You were all of those things, my good wife."

I do not wish to taint the new world with old hurts. But I also do not wish to bite my tongue. "I needed something people could call me instead of 'demon woman,'" I say more harshly than I mean to.

We are silent, letting the night sift through my words. When it has taken the sharpness from them, Noah says, "God gives some a great burden to overcome. Only a righteous woman could have borne up under the weight of the mark that you have carried upon your brow for all the years of your life without complaint."

"I did not think you knew how heavily it weighed upon me."

"You have been tested, and the Lord has found you worthy."

It does not seem possible to me that the Lord was testing me or that He found me worthy. But neither does most of what has happened in the last year. Perhaps the God of Adam has been with me even when I did not know it.

"Of what am I worthy, husband?"

"Being the matriarch of all mankind. And now you need a name worthy of you. One by which you can be remembered."

I turn to look at his wrinkled face, which seems to be lined not only by age but by six hundred years' worth of sadness. Does he know of the vultures' shadows that loop around my feet when I walk in the sun? How they grow bigger, closer, so that I sometimes think I feel feathers against my cheeks?

His hand presses on my leg. "Tell me, what should we call you?"

The sun has begun to peek up over the mountaintops, and without taking his hand from my leg, Noah turns his head to drink in its light. And I know what my name should be. I have traveled all this way from my father's tent, and from one world to the next, in search of a name, and I could not have found one any sooner than this instant.

"You can see only light and darkness. Dawn is both, as well as a new beginning."

Noah considers for a breath, then snorts. "Yes. This is a new

dawn. Not for everyone"—the sinners are never far from his mind—
"but for you, for our children, and for theirs."

"So, then, what is my name?

"Shahar. It will come to mean dawn in the new world."

"Is that the name you thought of for me?"

"I wanted to call you Shifra, which will come to mean beauty
and brightness. Yet now I think that Shahar is your true God-given
name."

"God has spoken to you about it?"

"Well, no," he admits. "It is actually I who think it a fitting
name for you."

"That is good enough for me."

He is astonished when I kiss each of his hands and his forehead.

I laugh and rise, creaking, to my feet. Soon I will be reunited
with my father. But first I want to hear my sons and daughters call
me by my name. I hurry to bring them the good news.

I have a name. *I am Shahar.*

ACKNOWLEDGMENTS

Thank you to the following people who've helped me on this journey: all of my teachers at Talmud Torah Day School, especially Earl Schwartz; Rabbi Allen of Beth Jacob Congregation, who had his hands full preparing me for my Bat Mitzvah; Jerod Santek, Brian Malloy, and the rest of the Loft staff; family friends Rolla Breitman and Pete and Sue Stein; those personal friends whose encouragement has kept me going, Dawn Frederick, Diane Grace, Amber McKenzie, Margie Newman, Becky Novotny, Richard Nystrom, Tanya Pedersen-Barr, Karen Seashore, and Jessica Warren Rugani; my spiritual mentor, Lynn Nelvik-Levitt; the tireless members of my writing group, Sandy Steffenson and Richard Thompson; agent extraordinaire Carolyn Jenks, and all of the good people at the Jenks Agency who've worked on this project, especially assistant agent Jacob Seifert; my editor, Becky Nesbitt, along with the other lovely people at Howard Books; Scott Hamilton, without whom I couldn't have done it; my mother; my brother, who knows how hard, and also how rewarding it can be to chase a dream; and my father.